Immortal Grit

ALSO BY HALEY HEALEY

On Their Own Terms: True Stories of Trailblazing Women of Vancouver Island

Flourishing and Free: More Stories of Trailblazing Women of Vancouver Island

Immortal Grit

Haley Healey

This is a work of fiction. All names, characters, events, places, and incidents are products of the author's imagination or used fictitiously. Any resemblances to actual people, events, or places are purely coincidental.

www.haleyhealey.com

LIBRARY AND ARCHIVES CANADA CATALOGUING IN PUBLICATION

Healey, Haley

Immortal Grit / Haley Healey

ISBN 978-1-77782-810-3

Editor: Katie Heffring

Book design: Haley Healey

Cover design: Haley Healey

This book was written on the traditional, ancestral, and unceded territory of the Snuneymuxw First Nation. Although some characters of this book were settlers and newcomers to the area now called Vancouver Island, the author does not condone colonization or any of the shameful behaviours that accompanied it. The author fully and completely supports truth and reconciliation in all its forms and recognizes her own role in truth and reconciliation.

Printed and bound in Canada

For Steven. I'm ever grateful our paths crossed in that old red character house.

"The most beautiful thing we can experience is the mysterious.

It is the source of all true art and all science.

He to whom this emotion is stranger,

who can no longer pause to wonder and stand in rapt awe,

is as good as dead; his eyes are closed."

— Albert Einstein

Chapter 1

Brooke

September 1, 2017

Night closed in on me as I sat at the window seat in the living room. In the looming darkness, I grimly tapped away on my laptop, trying to finish an article for my university newspaper. Money from the article would pay for my food for the month. I was grateful for the government's Tuition Waiver Program, which paid for the tuition of students from the foster care system, but it didn't cover rent, food, or shampoo—and it certainly didn't make up for moving every few years and being raised by strangers. Luckily my jobs at Passages, the bookstore in downtown Doveport, and my job writing articles for the university newspaper helped cover my meager living expenses.

Earlier that day, I moved the six boxes holding the entirety of my worldly possessions into the house. Now, in the evening's dimness, the boxes sat unpacked by the front door. I tapped away, trying to extract the most exciting details from my handwritten notes on a new campus theatre onto the screen, when, out of the corner of my eye, I saw a flicker of light.

I looked over my laptop screen and saw it was the floor lamp standing beside the fireplace flickering. On and off and on and off, it went. I watched with trepidation but mostly tried to ignore it and stay focused on the words appearing on the screen. The lamp was from Derek and David, my last foster parents before I aged out of foster care and moved out on my own. They tried giving me more furniture, but I refused, feeling deeply unworthy of both their love and their house furnishings. The lamp had a thin bronze pole and an ivory lampshade sitting on top like a hat. It continued to turn off and on, illuminating the living room before making it dark again.

I had to finish this article that night, as it was due the next day. I tried to focus on the words and sentences, but my eyes were attracted to the flickering lamp. I looked out the window above the window seat instead —sometimes avoiding was easier than facing. In the day, I could see the street, a park, then train tracks, and finally the ocean. Now, in the darkness, all I saw was the road. In the falling rain, it resembled a black river. The rain made rivulets that looked like fish scales. I looked back to the lamp. The flickering had stopped.

I returned to typing, trying to make the campus theatre engaging. The tap, tap, tapping of my fingers on the keys was the only sound. Soon my gaze looked beyond the screen as an unsettling feeling distracted me. A shiver ran up my back. I pulled the hood on my sweatshirt over my head.

The house had been so cheerful earlier that day—tall ceilings, brick fireplace, and lines of daylight pouring through the window where I now sat. Now, the house was cavern-like—all angled shadows and dark corners. The fireplace, that in the day had looked classic and trendy, now reminded me of a large gaping mouth of a witch—bricks like teeth and blackness like a gullet.

I typed a few sentences when the lamp started flickering again. I let out an exasperated sign and walked toward the lamp. I yanked the cord from the outlet next to the fireplace, deciding it must be the faulty electrical wiring. *These old houses,* I thought. I would buy a new bulb tomorrow.

I walked back to the window, sat on the hard wooden seat, and began typing in the dark. I had to get this done. My other assignments were stacking up and my shifts at the bookstore ate away at the time I had to complete them. The familiar feeling of worry rooted in my stomach and throat as my mind went to the future. *Back to the present,* I thought. *Focus on the task at hand.*

Just as I had placed my fingers on the cold, smooth keys, my laptop screen glowed a brighter white. After a few moments, it returned to normal brightness. My heart beat faster. Another shiver ran down my back—this time from fear, not from cool air. I stared at the screen in shock as it flickered, alternating between normal brightness and a much brighter white. Something turned in my stomach, and my heart continued racing. The change in brightness was not my doing. The laptop was changing brightness all on its own. Goosebumps prickled my neck and ran down my back.

I thought there had to be a logical explanation and made a mental note to look up online if anyone else had a problem like this with this model of laptop. I ran my cursor to the bottom corner and clicked the power button to turn the laptop off. Maybe a reset would fix it?

I walked to the fireplace while I waited for the laptop to reboot. My books sat in a neat row on the mantle, spines lining up perfectly. I ran my hands over their smooth backs. They were the only things I unpacked. Like old friends, they came everywhere with me; constant companions in my life of frequent moves and inconsistent parent figures.

More fiction titles sat on the coffee table, stacked like beach pebbles on top of one another. Just looking at them made me feel better. To me, they were portals I could escape to when my life became chaotic or stressful, when the assignments felt like they would never end, or when the unsettled and worried feeling in my stomach settled in like a dark cloud that refused to blow away.

But now I had to finish this article. It was nearly eleven, and I still had paragraphs to go. My laptop was back on. I typed my password under Brooke Daniels and continued typing.

Two sentences later, a thick and rich scent invaded my nose. The smell was smooth—earthy, soft, and warm with a hint of spice. It took me a moment to name the smell—sandalwood. Rich and earthy, it might have been soothing if it hadn't come from an unknown source. Not knowing its origin was becoming deeply unsettling. I lived alone, and the windows were closed.

I walked a few feet away, toward the entranceway to the house. No smell. I walked back to window seat and the smell was instantly noticeable: thick and sweet. But what was causing it? There were no vents nearby. No other suites in the house. There was no logical explanation for the scent hanging heavily in the air. The jittery feeling in my stomach changed to full-on fear. *What was going on in this house?*

Finally living on my own should have been happy and exciting, but something was wrong—something strange lurked in this old yellow character house that was my new home. I had no roommates but felt like someone was nearby. A skin-prickling feeling crept up my body, the one you get when you feel you're being watched and when you look around and realize that you are.

I finally concluded that someone or something was trying to get my attention.

I looked around. Nothing in the house appeared different. The living room was dim, except for my laptop screen, and the kitchen beyond the living room was a cavern of darkness, as it had been moments before. Cobwebs hung in the upper corners of the living room like the beard of an ogre: white, filthy, and tangled. The hardwood floors, that in the daylight had looked like floors from a country living magazine, now looked tired and derelict. Scratches striated every board like maimed skin that was once smooth.

Questions ran wildly through my mind. I tried inhaling deep breaths and exhaling even deeper ones. Was the lamp flickering, the laptop brightness, and the smell connected? What was trying to get my attention? Did whatever it was want to hurt me in some way?

Perhaps I was imagining things. Maybe the transition from living in a bustling house of five roommates to living on my own in an old character house in the oldest part of town was getting to me. It was hard to tell what was real and what was not. The feeling of fear that I hadn't let penetrate my being for several years now was quickly coming back. Like a ship filling with water, anxiety rose in my body.

You're overthinking it, I thought to myself. *Overthinking is your go-to when you're scared.*

But I wasn't overthinking this. The feelings I was feeling were real and I couldn't shake them. I couldn't quantify the strange sensation in my gut, but it was solidly there. I knew from my twenty-three years of life that my gut was never wrong—and this time, it was telling me there was something strange and sinister about the house I had just rented.

I looked out the window. Rain fell even harder, making a hammering sound on the roof. Dark drops pelted the window where I sat. An eagle glided over the street and landed in the treetop of giant evergreen tree in the park. The smell was still strong; it fuelled my fear.

I closed my laptop, walked to my bedroom, and closed the door. I would finish the article in the morning. Once worry overcame me, concentration was impossible.

I crawled into my bed and closed the lace curtains above it. The cute, classic curtains now fell solidly on the old and creepy side. White paint peeled from the ancient windowpanes, falling off like scabs from ancient skin.

Once I lay down, fear flicked like a light switch to anger—anger at whatever was in the house, at the anxiety that had so much control over me, and at the person who had spurred me to get my own place for my fourth and last year of university. I breathed in deeply through my nose, trying to dissipate the anger and soothe myself.

All I wanted was somewhere safe, somewhere peaceful. More than anything, I wanted somewhere to finish my last year of university so I could get that degree that would launch me to a job.

So I did what I always did when I got mad: I tried to stop the angry thoughts from circling in my mind like a furious hamster on a rapidly spinning wheel by acting toward my immediate goal, which was finishing university. I reached over to my bedside table and grabbed the novel I was reading for a Canadian literature course. I rolled to my back, opened the book, and began reading.

But a page into the book, and I couldn't retain the words I was reading. Red-hot anger had turned to dull tiredness. I couldn't overcome the unshakable feeling that I wasn't alone in the house and that someone or something was desperately trying to make its presence known. I closed the book, turned the light off, and tried to let sleep overcome me. Thoughts drifted around my mind while I tried to find sleep. Somewhere in those thoughts, I finally accepted it: I wasn't the only being inhabiting my new house.

Chapter 2

Hannah

May 3, 1887

I was stirring a wooden spoon around a pot of chowder on the iron cookstove when a thundering boom jolted me. The house shook violently like somebody had lit a barrel of fireworks directly outside its walls. My bone china teacups, carefully transported when I moved from England, rattled against their matching saucers on the shelf. The pots, pans, spoons, and lantern hanging behind the iron cookstove clattered against one another. Before fully taking in the first boom, a second one sounded, nearly as loud as the first. After that, the eerie wail of a siren echoed up our street.

Three pairs of frightened wide eyes stared at me from the wooden kitchen table. My three children—Emerson, ten, Tristan, eight, and little five-year-old Alice—were awaiting dinner when the boom erupted outside.

Emerson was the first to speak. "Mother, what was that sound?"

"Something that doesn't affect us, children. Might have come from the port or the coal mine, but nothing for us to concern ourselves with. Dinner is ready." I didn't want the children to sense my concern over the booms and the siren. I had to keep an air of control and confidence for their sake.

Alice was next. "Mother, that sound outside now is like a person screaming."

She was right about the shrillness of the siren. It wailed like a screaming baby as I dipped the spoon into the pot and poured steaming liquid, with chunks of clams and potatoes, into four bowls.

"Yes, but it's still dinner time. Almost six o'clock on the nose. We'll eat as we normally do, and then I'll investigate the sounds."

I took a seat on a wooden chair at the head of the table with my own bowl of steaming chowder. We brought spoons to our mouths and filled our bellies. On a normal day, I would have asked the children about their days, they would tell me stories of school friends, and there would be laughter. But today, we ate in silence, with the ear-splitting siren an unwelcome visitor at our dinner table.

I tried to hide my concern as I spooned mouthfuls of soup into my mouth. Though I kept my worry concealed from the children, I couldn't stop wondering what caused the booms and why the siren sounded. It couldn't be good. It had been the unmistakable sound of an explosion—what had caused it?

Dinner first, I thought. *Then I will investigate.*

By the time our bowls were empty, the siren had stopped and the street was quiet again, save for the birds chirping in the park. The newfound quiet was unnerving after the perpetual siren wail. Tristan and Alice went to their bedroom, while Emerson stayed behind, dutifully insisting that he help me clean up, as he did after every meal.

I scrubbed the bowls while Emerson dried and put them back on the kitchen shelf. With my hands in the warm water, I looked around our house and tried to stop my mind from wondering what had been the cause of the deafening booms. Evening sunlight streamed into the kitchen window, and the fireplace stood strong and comforting. Though far from where I had grown up, this house felt more like home than anywhere I had lived.

Richard and I had moved here five years ago from southern Ontario and, before that, from the seaside town of Bude, in southern England. We had been classmates at school, and when I was eighteen and he twenty, we walked down the aisle of a stone church on a high cliff overlooking the sea. My veil was a tidal wave of delicate lace flowing behind me. A handful of orange lilies overflowed in my arms.

As we stepped out of the church and descended its steps to the lawn, the wind grabbed a layer of my veil and pulled it straight up toward the heavens, toward whoever was looking down on us. Overnight, I changed from Hannah May to Hannah Hatherly. We were untouchable in our happiness. I smiled to myself as I moved the cloth over the bowl and handed it to Emerson.

After the wedding, Richard and I became restless in Bude. Canada was a new land that seemed bursting with prosperity, newness, vast land, and thick forests. We couldn't resist the lure of an adventure. Much to the shock of our family and friends, within a fortnight of deciding to move to Canada, we packed our belongings into steamer trunks and boarded a ship. Bowmanville, Ontario, was where we first settled. Richard opened a leather shop, and we had three children.

After several years, we became restless once again and moved west, chasing the abundant work opportunities. During this journey, we were much more heavily burdened. We had pounds more of material belongings and three children in tow when we boarded a steam train. We rode the train west across Canada until we reached the ocean. Then we got on a barge and rode over the sea until we reached an island. The settlement was called Doveport and sat on the island's eastern shore.

Doveport was our final stop and our new home. Like Bude, it was a seaside city but with far fewer inhabitants than anywhere in England. It's land and sea had been home to Snuneymuxw First Nation peoples long before anyone from Europe came. Where the Doveport River emptied into the ocean, these people lived in big wooden houses and dug clams from the sand, ate fish, and paddled long wooden canoes over the sea. Canoes truly were the superior transportation vessel in a coastal town. Long wooden dugout canoes gracefully floated over the water, oblivious to the weight of their loads, while horse and buggies contended with thick forests and battered roads with deep holes. Buggies were painfully slow when heavily loaded.

Doveport's streets fanned outward like a wheel. The hub of the wheel held the port, the mine, and a Hudson Bay Company fort. The city was a different world than Bude—wilder in every way possible. Bude was overflowing with people and buildings, while Doveport was rugged and mostly towering trees and rocky shorelines. Bude's buildings lined up neatly, side by side, while Doveport's buildings were wooden ones put seemingly wherever people pleased. Bude had a stifled feeling; in Doveport, it felt like anything could happen.

Richard got a well-paying job with the Doveport Coal Company. Coal was like black gold, dense lines of the stuff running under the wooden boardwalks and fenced houses. The Doveport Coal Company employed most of the men in the town. Most days, Richard was at the coal mine for ten hours or more.

When he got home, he barely took off his shoes and blackened clothes before he was reading a story with Emerson, pushing trains around the floor with Tristan, and tucking Alice's covers around her before she fell asleep. Then he would come downstairs and ask about what I did that day. He listened as I told him the pleasures and annoyances of keeping the household running, keeping the children from breaking their bones, and concocting various meals to feed the hungry mouths. I didn't think that years into our marriage I would still get a warm and excited feeling when I heard the door open and heard Richard taking off his shoes after returning from coal mine late in the day. But I did.

As I scrubbed the last bit of potato from the pot and handed it to Emerson, I wondered if the boom had come from the mine. I had a sinking suspicion that it might have. The siren was concerning and couldn't be anything good.

I lifted the bowl of dirty dish water and took it out the back door. Careful not to spill on my long dress, I poured it down the sink hole behind the house. Outside, the air was cool and fresh. The sweet smell of a blooming wisteria tree drifted toward me. I drank in a deep breath of the sweet scent and admired its cascading mauve blossoms. Clusters in the shape of grapes, but instead of grapes, they were purple flowers. I couldn't shake the dark, sinking feeling from the uncertainty of the boom noise and siren. Deep in my belly, I knew something bad happened.

I didn't know then, but the cause of the thumping boom would change the direction of my life forever. It would become divided into two parts: life before the boom and life after the boom. I didn't know this then, but that tremor would be a moment of turning for me. Nothing would be the same after that day.

Chapter 3

Brooke

September 8, 2017

My best friend, Jade, and I were squeezed into a single bathroom stall of our favourite pub and pool hall, Hawthorne's. The stall reeked of pee and bulk pink hand soap.

"I've almost scraped away the first word," Jade said, out of breath from scratching the wooden stall door with her house key.

Jade and I met in our first year of university. Now, we were in fourth year, Jade finishing recreation and myself English. We studied at Harbourview University, a village of buildings clustered among lush ferns and tall cedar trees up on Mount Alfred in Doveport. Jade was a go-getting workhorse with the ability to talk anyone into or out of anything. She was the kind of person who had ten things on the go that included organizing a family reunion, working two jobs, and training for a half marathon.

Her black hair fell over face and she swept it away from her furrowed eyebrows as she scraped black letters off the stall door. The words "Brooke Daniels is an orphan slut" were written in large black sharpie letters.

"Why would she stoop to this? Isn't it enough to bash my name and post nasty things about me online?" I asked as I worked with my own house key on the last word.

"She won't stop at anything. You need to confront her and stand up to her," Jade said. Jade didn't focus on the negative of a situation but instead on its solutions.

"I can't. It would only get worse if I stood up to her."

The thought of standing up to Beverly made my heart speed up and my throat tighten. So did reading the words on the stall. Vile words next to my own name.

Together, we worked to scrape the black sharpie from the wooden door. It was painstakingly slow work, and we stopped every so often to let the blood rush back to our hands.

"Her nasty ways are only going to continue if you don't do something about it. If it was me, I would walk right up to her and tell her to stop."

"I can't do that. I won't do that," I said. I avoided conflict at all costs. It was one of the things that paralyzed me with anxiety.

"Do you want me to? I'll talk to her for you. She can't keep doing this. I would report it to someone at the university, too. These are acts on the continuum of aggression and would be considered harassment." Jade's arms moved back and forth as she started scraping the letter *D*.

"Definitely not. That will just make her madder and she'd retaliate more," I said. I had almost finished getting the last and final word off the door as I wondered how one woman could call another woman that vile word.

"Well, you're going to have to stand up to her one day, or it's never going to stop."

I knew she was right but didn't say anything. I couldn't stand up to her. I would rather tolerate harassment than create conflict, especially against Beverly. The scratching of both our metal keys on wood sounded between us.

Earlier that evening, Jade and I had played pool and discussed our last year of university, about what we were looking forward to and dreading. I had successfully managed to begin enjoying myself and had ripped my mind from Beverly Robinson and her exclusion, hatred, and increasingly aggressive behaviour toward me until I went to the bathroom.

With all these worries safely compartmentalized to go over later, I entered a stall, and while hovering on the toilet, read the graffiti on its door with a detached curiosity. Then I noticed my name. And some awful words beside it. They had been written in big bold capitals with a black sharpie. *"Brooke Daniels is an orphan slut."* My world slowed down as shock overcame me. The feeling was the same as when I had been told I was moving to yet another foster home—the disbelief and wishing it wasn't true, but knowing it was.

"What's wrong? What happened?" Jade had asked when I returned to our pool table blinking back tears.

"Beverly wrote something horrible about me in black sharpie in the bathroom." A tear escaped, and I quickly wiped it with the back of my hand.

"What did it say?" Jade asked.

"Doesn't matter. I don't want to talk about it. Whose shot? I just want to forget about it."

Jade's face registered no emotion as she started walking to the washroom.

"We're not forgetting about this. Show me."

≈

Later that night and once every letter of graffiti was scraped off, Jade and I left Hawthorne's and walked until we reached the yellow house. I looked at its peeling paint, then turned away from the house to look at Jade. She returned my gaze but with creased eyebrows.

"Promise me you'll consider reporting what happened tonight?" Jade said.

"I'll think about it," I said. We both knew I wouldn't.

Jade gave me a look of concern, then turned and walked into the darkness down the street that led to her house.

I started up the front steps, sifting through the events of the night: the sinking feeling in my stomach as I saw my name in black sharpie and the sound of keys scraping on wood. I thought of how this yellow house had become my home after I decided living with Beverly was dangerous and that I needed to live alone.

The yellow house was the third place I viewed. The first time I saw it, thick fog hung like smoke in the air, shrouding everything like a grey wash of paint. The yellow house stood tall and sturdy, its canary yellow cheerfully contrasting the greyness of the day. The miner cottages were content being unmemorable and nearly identical, but the yellow house wanted the opposite. Its yellow colour and intricate lattice work made it stand out. Show off. It stood directly in front of me: 701 Winfield Crescent.

Intricate Victorian gables, bay windows jutting out, an old brick chimney sticking up toward the fog, and a wraparound porch with white railings—what could be more charming and romantic than a wraparound front porch with white railings? It was straight out of some happy fiction novel. It was grand.

A man in jeans, a forest-green fleece sweater, and brown hair flecked with grey appeared from behind the house.

"Hi, I'm Brian. I own the house," he said as he reached out his hand and flashed a white-toothed smile.

"I'm Brooke," I said, trying to get a good grip on his hand, doing my best to give a firm handshake.

"Let's go in and take a look."

I followed Brian up the white steps to the front balcony that looked out to the ocean. Two wooden chairs sat on the balcony, with a small wooden table between them. I indulged a fantasy thought of drinking my morning tea there. Brian opened the solid wooden door and we stepped into the house. Somehow, it felt more like home than any other house I had lived in. It smelled like a health food store, like cinnamon and other spices.

A bench and mirror greeted us as we entered the house. Hooks on the wall stored hats, coats, and a picnic basket. Curtains swung from the windows. The interior was a comforting detour from new apartments and their sleek lines, white everything, and trendy modern building materials.

"The house is more than a hundred years old—one of the oldest in Doveport. This part of the city was bustling back in the day, the hub of coal mining, which ultimately formed the city. This house started as a single-family dwelling owned by a mine employee, then a labour union man, and, after that, countless other people over the years."

Brian opened the bathroom door. A clawfoot tub dominated the space, with shower curtains hanging up above it to make it a shower. The wooden board stretched across the tub made me think of candles and a book. This place had more charm than any others I had viewed. It was paradise compared to the dank basement hovel that smelled like a dirty dishcloth and the one-bedroom place with suspect smears of rusty dark red on the wall. No place came anywhere close to this one. It rang with character and charm.

The kitchen was a galley style, like a galley of a ship, cramped and tiny. But enough room for me. The ceilings in the bedroom were high, giving it a palatial feel. An imposing brick fireplace in the living room was unusable according to Brian but gave the living room the feel of a log cabin high up in the mountains. The backyard sealed the deal; like a private park, it had thick green grass and a tree with climbing green vines. I had to rent this house.

"Lately, it's been hard to keep people. But it's got good bones," Brian said.

Now, I wished I had asked why he had difficulty keeping tenants. But in that moment, I had one goal—and that was to secure the house. Things would surely get better if I lived there. In the yellow house, I would stop waiting for anyone's approval and ditch the anxiety once and for all. In the yellow house, I would give myself permission to be who I truly was, and rise above Beverly's aggression. In the yellow house, I would thrive.

"Thank you for showing me the place. It's beautiful. I look forward to hearing from you."

"I'll let you know by next week," Brian told me.

After the viewing, I returned to the house I shared with Beverly and three other classmates to find my laptop open on my desk. I always left my laptop closed. Moving homes so much as a kid made me strange with my belongings. Perhaps it had to do with control; my own things were the only parts of my life I could govern. I soon forgot about the laptop being open, as I hoped as hard as I could that I would be the one chosen to rent the yellow house.

A week later, I got a phone call from Brian offering me the house, saying he thought I was genuine, tidy, and reliable. The house was mine. Well, not mine in an ownership way, but mine to rent. I was thrilled. At first, arriving at 701 Winfield Crescent had felt like arriving home.

Now, as I turned my key in the door and stepped inside, it had felt more hostile than welcoming. I dropped my leather satchel and locked the door behind me. A wave of unease and tiredness flooded over me. Reliving the past year in my head that night had exhausted me. Then I remembered the strange events from last week. I let out a deep breath and glanced around the dim space that was my new home.

It appeared the same as when I had left earlier that evening, but I wondered when the next strange event would happen. When the unknown presence, an intruder encroaching on my rented space, would make itself known again. Perhaps likening whatever it was to an intruder was a bit much. I was working on ridding myself of a victim mentality. I could change how I felt about the house if I changed the way I thought about it. Besides, perhaps the presence wasn't an intruder after all. Perhaps they had been in this house for a long, long time. The house was over a hundred years old, after all. I turned on the light and headed to my bedroom.

My heart sank as an unsettling notion donned on me: perhaps I was the intruder in the yellow house.

Chapter 4

Hannah

May 3, 1887

I untied the apron from my waist and hung it behind the stove. I paced back and forth, formulating a plan. I had to find out what made the thundering booms. I thought about waiting until morning or until Richard returned from work, but that was too long. I had to know sooner.

I didn't like asking things of others; I would rather abandon a recipe than ask a neighbour for an egg or a cup of flour. I could handle any matter on my own; I didn't need anybody.

But I couldn't go without knowing. And to know, I had to ask. *That's it,* I thought. *Eva Ling*. My friend and neighbour was someone I wouldn't dread asking. Surely, Eva would know. I would go to my Eva's house to investigate. She always knew Doveport happenings, whether it was a steamer arriving late or a downtown saloon brawl.

I walked down the hall to the children's room and peered in. They were all in there—Tristan with an open book, Alice and Emerson pushing a train around the floor.

"Emerson, mind the others while I go to Eva Ling's. I won't be gone long."

I stepped out the front door and pushed the wooden door closed. I locked it, pulled it to be sure it was locked, and hoisted my dress as I stepped down the porch steps and onto the side of the street. I strode down our street, toward Eva's. It was 1887 and there were no telephones yet. Had there been a receiver and buttons on the wall, my investigation would have been a simple phone call to Eva. Instead, I walked down the street to find out the source of the booms and siren.

Eva Ling's house was seven doors down the street. She was a no-nonsense woman, and I had met her when we first moved to Doveport. She lived with her husband and two children in a small miner cottage.

Spring in Doveport was my favourite time of year. That would later change, but at the time, I feasted my eyes on the bright yellow forsythias, tulips, and dense green grass. My long dress brushed over cherry blossoms that gathered on the ground in cotton candy pink piles. *Colour after winter grey,* I thought. Winter had so much grey: grey skies, grey evergreens in front of faded grey mountains, grey ocean, and tired grey streets. Days strung together in a jumble of grey rain and grey clouds hanging low over the city. I never noticed how dark winter was until spring arrived, with daffodils reaching their yellow faces toward the warming sun and daylight that endured until nearly nighttime. It was still light out when I arrived at Eva's. The heavy feeling of worry prevented me from enjoying the soft pastel shades of blue, pink, and purple that adorned the evening sky like a watercolour canvas.

Eva sat on her front porch when I arrived. I opened the gate and stepped into her yard. After closing the gate and before speaking to Eva, I crouched and ran my hand over the downy black fur of her cat, from its head to its tail.

Eva was staring off across the street with a strange expression. It made me worry that something was very wrong. Eva was never on her front porch. And she was never sitting still.

Our husbands worked together in the mines, and though they did the same job, my husband made three times more than hers. My husband was called by his name, Richard Hatherly, while her husband was referred to as a number because he was Chinese. Nobody talked about this.

People of Doveport seemed to accept this unjust reality as it was. In their minds, it was just the way things were. But I often thought of it and how vastly unjust and discriminatory it was—what made one man's time worth more than another's while doing the same job? Mine work was dusty, dangerous, and back-breaking. Every man should be compensated the same.

Eva and I met at a horse race on Baker Street, the street up the hill from Winfield. It was July 1—named Dominion day, as it was the first day Canada became part of the Dominion. Horse races were a Doveport tradition on Dominion Day. Baker Street was a sea of people, crowded together to watch horses and riders fight for first place.

It was my first Dominion Day, and I would learn it was a noisy and boisterous tradition. People were like wild animals suddenly released. I suppose they were newly released in a way, let go from their houses after a wet winter and cool spring. Crowds of people leaned in further to see the horses better, so much so that race officials, wearing suspenders and bowler hats, came over shouting and pushing the crowds back. Louder crowds gathered on the top porch of the Dew Drop Hotel, with mugs of frothy beer and boisterous shouts. People overflowed from the balcony onto a proper rooftop to watch.

From where I stood on the street, one horse caught my eye. It was golden—the colour of tea once the perfect amount of milk has been added. It held its head higher than the other horses warming up and threw its head back unapologetically. At the starting line, its eyes grew wild and nostrils flared. Then it sprang forward when the starter's flag dropped. With each stride, firm muscles rippling underneath its golden coat, the golden horse's gait became bolder and more confident; its mane, caught by the wind, blew upwards and out like a lion's. It wanted to run. We watched its rider's arms flap wildly in the air, and then the pair passed us, the horse's tail flying out behind it, hooves kicking up a trail of dust in its wake. It was thrilling to see the road taken over by the muscles, hooves, and wild manes of horses, replacing docile horses pulling buggies.

"I would place my bet on the cream-coloured horse," a woman beside me said.

I was startled to hear someone speak to me, as at the time, I knew nobody in Doveport.

"It does have some spirit, doesn't it?" I commented back.

We began talking and discovered we lived on the same street. I craved female friendship. Though my conversations and relationship with Richard was deeply fulfilling, I was eager for the connection that exists only between women. While we talked, our children looked curiously at each other and then began interacting in the strange and uninhibited way that children do. A few minutes later, the golden horse crossed the finish line before all the others.

After the Dominion Day horse race, Eva Ling and I became fast friends and loyal confidants. We met in late afternoons when chores could be put off and before dinner was imminent. Our conversations were sometimes serious, other times frivolous, and always over cups of tea the same colour as the horse from the first day we met. I once noticed a neighbour woman with a pointed nose giving me a sideways glance and nasty eyes as she walked past us talking on the street. I only ever noticed those looks when I spoke to Eva.

From eavesdropped snippets of neighbourhood talk, I gleaned that the culture of this town was that people from England didn't speak to people from China, and people from China didn't mingle with people from England.

I mulled this over in my head, finding no logic to it. I wasn't in England anymore, and I would do what I pleased. Let them talk. Let them stare. I'll speak to whomever I please and I'll be friends with whomever I please. My parents back in England taught me to be kind to everyone and give everyone a chance. I cared more about a person's character than their looks or what country they were born.

Now, as I walked toward her, Eva Ling stared blankly ahead and seemed to barely notice me.

"Good evening, Eva," I called.

She continued staring off across the street, clearly lost in her thoughts.

She finally noticed me and looked up, not saying anything.

"Eva, what caused that boom noise?"

I had never seen Eva this distraught. She was usually even keeled, like a boat at sea with plentiful ballast. But now, her face broke and her shoulders sank into the chair. Tears ran down her cheeks, and she let out a few sobs. My heart sank as I braced for what she was going to say.

"Eva, what is it? What happened" I tried again, at this point needing to know. I had learned that when getting horrible news, it was always better to know than not know. Without the truth, your mind makes up horrible stories.

"Hannah, have you not heard?" she said, sobs subsiding a bit and resorting back to gazing with a blank expression ahead.

"Not heard what? Goodness, Eva. Go on, tell me." My voice came out sharper than I intended. A queasy feeling worked its way into my throat. Whatever she was going to tell me was ominous if it had brought unflinching Eva to tears. After what seemed like hours, she let it out. The force of her words and the future effects of them hit me as if someone had struck me with a stove stoker in the stomach.

"There was a horrible accident in the number one mine—an explosion. The miners are trapped in the mine shaft below the sea. They can't get them out."

Chapter 5

Brooke

September 15, 2017

Questions about the yellow house darted around my head while my eyes stared at the front of the university lecture hall. The professor, who was wearing grey pants and a grey sweater, droned on about modernism and literature without any enthusiasm, facial expressions, or movement. I tried desperately to focus on the professor's words—something about eating peaches and walking on the beach—but thoughts of my new house invaded my head. Concentration was impossible.

I had to find out what was going on in the yellow house. I hoped it would be a place of refuge, a place to drink cups of tea after school, type papers, and study for exams, a place free of roommates and devoid of stress. Instead, the house had become a stressor of its own. Each time I was at home, I felt constantly vigilant and on high alert, waiting for something strange to happen. When I wasn't at home, I felt a sense of dread and concern any time I thought about the house. It was that familiar feeling of there being something wrong, even though everything appeared to be fine.

I had many questions about the yellow house, the obvious being who or what was responsible for the strange instances? Other questions were more complex. Was it a spirit? And if it was a spirit, why did it remain earthbound after its death? What in its life remained unfinished?

I tried to push these questions from my head and focus on the lecture. I carefully wrote words in my notebook that would hopefully help me study come exam time. When I noticed myself letting worried thoughts circle through my mind like a Ferris wheel of worry, I tried to ground myself in the present and focus on the task at hand. So, now, I looked down and tried hard to focus on my hand moving over the page. I took a few deep breaths through my nose, hoping they would bring some calm.

My head was down and my hand was quickly taking down notes when an apple core hit my notebook, leaving sticky brown apple chunks on the page. It then landed on the floor at my feet. I swung my head around and looked behind me. Three rows back sat Beverly Robinson, tapping away on her phone. She then showed something on it to another girl in our program. I turned forward and heard laughing.

My face flushed red and became hot. I first felt embarrassed and looked around to see if anyone else had noticed. Other students were either watching the professor or looking down at their own phones. It didn't look like anyone had noticed. A small rush of relief flooded over me.

But then anger started to well up inside me. My entire body felt hot and I unzipped my hoodie. I thought about walking out, but I was too nervous. Whenever I felt nervous, action was difficult. Plus, I didn't want everyone watching me. I would escape as soon as I could after the lecture.

I also thought it would let Beverly win if I left, so I resolved to stay. I checked the time on my phone. Fifteen minutes left. I could do this. I pushed the apple core away from my foot until it was under the chair of the row in front of me.

Concentration was difficult for those fifteen minutes. Beverly hated me, and she was doing things to make it known to me and everyone. I wished I didn't care, but I did. I wished I didn't care that I was rejected from Beverly's friend group, but I did. I missed the potluck dinner parties, arriving to a party together, and congregating in a circle before lectures. Now, I felt like they had reeled me in, only to let me go when I did something that displeased their leader. I couldn't turn around again to face Beverly, but I almost felt her eyes boring into the back of my head.

I met Beverly in my first year at residence. She had the trendiest wardrobe, the newest phone, and was on the cutting edge of anything new and popular. Her parents had an enormous house in Ellington, the huge city across the ocean strait from Doveport. She had a swimming pool, and both her parents worked in banks. Everyone wanted to be Beverly Robinson's friend. She had wanted to be my friend. I wasn't good at making friends after so many years of moving and avoiding friendships, but Beverly made it feel easy. She pulled me into the friend group she created. For the first time in my life, I had a friend group and I was invited to parties. People came by my dorm room to talk to me. People took an interest in books on my shelf and in my life before Harbourview. In my second year, Beverly invited me to live in a house with her and a few friends. Of course, I said yes.

Then, in May of my third year, Beverly's boyfriend, Chatham, suddenly broke up with her and had no intention of getting back with her. She was devastated, and we were devastated for her. I realized that having all the money in the world and two biological parents doesn't protect you from bad things.

Beverly retreated to her parents' house in Ellington and sat by the pool for a few weeks. When she returned, she cried, and cried, and cried. I did my best to comfort her, wrapping my arms around her whenever her tears started. I cooked dinners for us while listening to her talk about Chatham and alternate between hating him and missing him. I made her favourites: coconut curry with lentils, thick bean chili with chunks of cheese, and homemade focaccia pizzas topped with spinach and tomatoes. Never being in love before, I didn't know how to heal a broken heart, but I figured food and a listening ear were a start. I had liked cooking for others, anyway, and enjoyed using the recipe book I got from a high school foods class.

Then, in June, something awful happened—Chatham took a liking to me. He started talking to me on campus and asked me if I had some cute boyfriend somewhere. I told him I didn't but would not date him. Beverly was the obvious reason, but I also didn't like Chatham. It was easy to turn him away; he made bland conversation, wore skinny jeans, and smoked cigarettes. I didn't know what my type was, but it was not him.

For some reason, Chatham didn't give up pursuing me. My disinterest fuelled his affection for me. He left comments on all my Instagram photos. He brought me chocolate and candy at work, and one night at a party, he approached me and put his arm around me. Just as I was pulling sideways out of his grasp, Beverly entered the room. Our eyes locked, and she looked at me in a way I will never forget: her eyes widened and filled with fire.

That was it. Life as I knew it ended. Suddenly, I was the enemy. Beverly had someone to hate and someone to blame for Chatham leaving her. Her blame was without logic, but I was a convenient scapegoat. She came after me with a vengeance, doing whatever she could to ruin me socially, academically, and emotionally.

Beverly was not the person you wanted to be your enemy. She had a powerful energy over people and was the kind of person everyone adored. Like a magnet, people were drawn to her and wanted to be close to her. Even I had fallen head over heels.

Beverly was unyielding in her anger toward me. She swiftly started rumours—the biggest being that I was the reason her and Chatham up. She stopped inviting me places. She wrote me threatening text messages and put nasty but passive-aggressive comments on Instagram. Comments that could be interpreted in different ways but were meant to hurt.

Our friends took her side. My former friends stopped talking to me, calling me, and ignored me at the house we shared. They knew I turned down Chatham—everyone knew I turned down Chatham—but nobody would stand up to Beverly. Everyone saw Beverly tarnishing my reputation but took her side for fear of her turning on them. Nobody wanted to be on Beverly's bad side.

I had always been a worried person, perhaps from the instability of moving homes all the time and the lack of consistently caring adults in my life. But then, my worry bubbled up inside me and spilled over into all areas of my life. I turned my phone off most of the time. I stopped signing into Instagram. I stopped going out, only leaving the house for groceries, work, and university. I wouldn't have grocery money if I didn't work. I took the bus to a different grocery store far from the university, a store I was sure I wouldn't see Beverly in, and then, I stopped attending classes.

Isolation wrapped its cold black wings around me. I felt abandoned and utterly alone. All the underlying feelings I had of abandonment and being unlovable from my years in the foster care system came back.

Never in all my years of school had I conflicted with anyone; people had liked me.

My life became a bad dream, and every morning, I woke up hoping I would wake up from it. The bad dream became dangerous late one night in August. I was walking home from work at Passages Bookshop when a black truck in the oncoming lane swerved off the road and onto the sidewalk, heading straight toward me. Adrenaline shot through me and I ran onto a nearby lawn, tripping on its rock garden border and falling into the dirt. The truck swerved back onto the road, and I heard female laughter coming from it. I saw Beverly's face in the driver's side. I stood up, brushed dirt off, and felt my face go red. A strange combination of fear and humiliation swept over me as I stepped back onto the sidewalk.

I didn't go home that night but walked to Jade's. On my phone, I searched the rental listings and decided to live on my own. Jade assured me it was relational aggression and I needed to protect myself. I was not one for swift action, but the night with the truck had scared me. Living under the same roof as Beverly, I was genuinely becoming worried for my safety. Jade also convinced me to start attending classes again.

The sound of people packing up their things and leaving the lecture hall pulled me back from my thoughts. The lecture had ended while I had been day dreaming. Beverly walked past me, gave me the up and down elevator glare, and started whispering and laughing with those around her. My heart beat faster, and I felt the gnawing start of a stomachache.

I stuffed my notebook in my leather satchel but waited until most people left the hall before leaving the lecture hall. I stepped outside into the rain and breathed in the fresh rain smell. I walked home, trying to focus on the colours of the lawns and the trees, forcing my thoughts back to the present moment whenever they drifted to Beverly or the house.

≈

I opened the door to the yellow house and stepped inside. I draped my raincoat on a hook, walked to the kitchen, and placed my leather satchel on the floor. But the calmness that used to envelop me when I entered this home was replaced with a feeling of uncertainty. Again, no matter how hard I tried, I couldn't shake the feeling of being inside with something strange and potentially dangerous. I set up my laptop at the kitchen table and began typing an assignment. I would keep going with my courses. I couldn't let the events of the day derail me from finishing my fourth and last year.

I tapped away on my keys and had just finished a paragraph when something stopped me. An unmistakable change in temperature had settled over the kitchen. It was more than your body cooling off when you go from moving to sedentary. No, this was a drastic feeling of cold settling over me. The air was frigid where it had been mild moments before. I shivered and felt my heart start beating faster. I walked to my room to get another sweater. The air in there was five or seven degrees warmer. After pulling a moss green sweater over my head, I went back to the kitchen. I filled the kettle, turned it on, and waited for it to boil. Maybe a hot drink would help, and if the temperature didn't dissipate from there, I would type the assignment in my bedroom.

While I waited, I plugged my phone in the same outlet as the kettle. Next to the outlet, a small knob caught my eye, one that I had never noticed. I pulled it and discovered a small cupboard. My mood lifted with the surprise. *What a strange little storage space. What could it have been for?* This house got stranger by the day. The cupboard looked like a miniature medicine cabinet, and I soon discovered a small piece of lined paper, much like the kind I took notes on. I pulled it out and unfolded it. A note was written on the paper, which read: *"I hope you are brave and not superstitious. This house is full secrets."*

My heart started beating hard in my chest. I startled when the kettle began whistling. I rushed over to it and turned it off. Then I stared at the note and realized I was holding my breath. I let it out. So, the other renters had things happen to them, too. It wasn't just me. Maybe that was the reason for the strange comment from Brian when I moved in. The cheap rent was too good to be true. I should have known there was a catch.

I poured hot water over a triangular teabag of black tea, stirred it around, and extracted the bag with a spoon. After a splash of milk, I went to the kitchen table and put down the mug. It sent off a vertical line of steam, like smoke coming from a tiny cabin in a winter forest. The temperature in the room had not warmed.

Too distracted to work on the assignment and too scared to be in the kitchen, I went to my bedroom and closed the door. I sipped milky mouthfuls of my tea and looked outside. It was still raining. In thinking back on my life, I knew overthinking was the start of bad things for me. I needed to act on the house problem, so I went through my options. I couldn't move because I had signed a lease for six months. I would have to endure the strange happenings or find a way to rid the house of whatever it was.

Perhaps I should ask someone for help. I went through my short list of supporters. I didn't want to bring it up to Derek and Daniel. They were firm non-believers in ghosts. I didn't want to bother Ms. Ellis, my former school counsellor, about it. She might believe in ghosts, but she was so busy. Plus, I didn't want to bother her with this when I would probably need to call her about my returning anxiety sometime soon. Better to save my phone calls for her for when they're most needed. Jade would understand the issue but would be frustrated by the lack of a practical explanation. She had no patience for things unless they had a firm solution.

I kept going through people in my life and thought of work, where I would be tomorrow for a shift. With that, my boss at Passages Bookshop came into my mind: Edgard Frost. Of course! How had I not thought of him before? Edgard was the ideal person to ask about strange happenings in a house. He wouldn't laugh and might even be intrigued. After all, he owned a metaphysical bookshop with a vast selection of books on the subject.

I felt mildly better after having a plan, but I still felt disappointed. Just as I was nearly done university, things were so hard. Last year, I thought was finally doing well for myself. After a lifetime of instability, I was finally getting my life in order. I had zipped up the chaos of my early life and had gained hope. Now, it felt like the zipper was going to break under pressure. Beverly and the house were becoming too much. I tried typing my assignment but could only focus on what I would say to Edgard at work tomorrow.

≈

The day was a slow at Passages Bookshop. Not only did the bookstore sell books on the metaphysical, the unexplained, and the whimsy, but it also sold crystals, gems, and incense—all to the most outlandish characters of Doveport. Standing alone on the corner of two streets, it was a tall three-story building hugged by green ivy. On grey days, the twinkle lights strung about the windows, making it look like a mirage in a desert. A black sign on the sidewalk said "Bookshop Open"—always warm and cozy refuge from the rain.

Rosemary and other herbs grew in planters and pots that lined the shop, creating a barrier between stone and sidewalk. Inside, books were stacked, piled, or filed in shelves. Jagged purple amethyst crystals were scattered among the books, sage sticks sat in woven baskets, and sea green jade pendants of shimmering abalone shells hung from silver stands. Passages was a dreamscape, a break from my everyday life and the ongoing nonsense with Beverly. Not today, though. Today, I felt drained and anxious about what to do next.

Edgard wasn't in yet. He wasn't like any boss I had had before. Though consistent in mood and action—things you wanted in a boss—he was inconsistent in coming into the shop. Sometimes, I wouldn't see him for weeks. Other times, he would be in every shift, helping me serve customers, talking on the phone, or working in his crowded office doing inventory, ordering books, or speaking to some crystal seller about a new shipment of amethysts. He was a good boss—friendly, fair, and often bought jelly-filled, sugar-topped doughnuts from the Finnish bakery a few doors down. Today, he wasn't here.

Rain fell in sheets outside the shop and puddles grew as the day dragged on. Several people came in, shook off the rain like dogs, and looked around, but mostly, it was dead quiet. From experience and counselling, I knew that keeping myself busy was a way to stop any unwanted thoughts, so I dusted the crystals, did some inventory, swept, posted on our social media pages, and looked around. Being surrounded by books on the supernatural didn't help. I knew that if I gave into any worried thoughts, they would pull me into them and wrap around me like a strangler fig around a tree; they would drag me down until I became irritable and upset. But these mindless tasks did nothing to quell the familiar unsettling feeling of anxiety nagging at me. My desire to know what was in my house possessed me.

And it creeped me out.

Getting tired of letting my imagination take over, I decided a way to feel less anxious might be to find out more. Of course, what better place to find out about strange events in old houses than a bookshop? Time to do some research.

I headed to our metaphysical aisle. I scanned the titles and finally pulled one out that caught my eye: *Eerie Encounters with the Other Side*. I flipped through it, skimming until I came to a paragraphs of interest: *"The activities of a ghost could be arbitrary and for their own entertainment. Other times, actions are a repetition of past events, or a ghost might be trying to get the attention of the living—trying to ask them, warn them, or teach them about something or tell them what they want. Spirits often stay earthbound if something in their life was left undone."*

Something was trying to get my attention; that much I was sure of. What I didn't know was what it was. Did it want to hurt me? Did it want me gone? Perhaps its actions were meant as a warning, meant to scare me away. I wondered if it had done this to other tenants of 701 Winfield Crescent. Did Brian know? Surely the owner of a house would know if it was inhabited by a spirit or otherworldly being.

The bell at the bookshop door caused me to jump and my heart to leap into my chest. I stood up straighter and returned to the present. I slid *Eerie Encounters with the Other Side* back into its shelf and walked to the front of the shop.

There, I found Edgard lowering and collapsing a black umbrella. His curly grey hair more unruly than usual from the wet.

"Greetings, dearie!" he started with.

After filling him in on the day at the shop, I tried to ask him about what was going on in the yellow house. I started a sentence, only to stop. Eventually, he went into the office and closed the door.

I helped a few customers find presents for loved ones and went back to the till. I tried to imagine what it would be like to have aunts, uncles, and grandparents who bought gifts for your birthday and other special occasions. A feeling of mild warmth started in my chest but quickly left when I remembered that I was about to ask my boss about a ghost in my house.

How would I start? I could begin by telling him the straight facts, or I could come at it subtly to see if he was going to laugh at me. Maybe I would wait for another day. Another customer came in and I greeted them.

Without saying anything to Edgard, my shift felt like it came to an end faster than it normally did. Moments before I left the store, I had a momentary burst of courage brought on by the urgency that once I left, I was going back to the yellow house. That, and I had nobody else to ask about this situation. Finally, I spoke.

"Edgard, have you ever had the feeling you're living with a spirit of some kind?" I braced for him to laugh or look at me strangely, maybe suggest I was stressed and needed time off. Or tell me I was fired. Surely, a boss couldn't fire someone that easily, though. I needed to stop thinking of the worst-case scenario.

Edgard was neutral as he replied, "What ever do you mean by that?" His voice rose more than it usually did. He looked straight at me and cocked his head ever so slightly sideways.

I stuttered as I tried to get started. “Well, there are some strange things going on in my house, and I’m weirded out.” It took all I had to get this out. It felt somehow even harder than recounting my foster care experiences when sorting through them in counselling.

“What sorts of things?” Edgard asked, still not giving anything away with his expression.

I recounted to him the light flickering, the laptop screen, the sandalwood smell, the note, and the cold spots in the house.

This time, Edgard’s eyes widened, glistened even. His mouth turned into an upturned smile. “Ah, your house has a malevolent spirit dweller, my dear. A departed soul.”

“Do you think? What is it? Do you think the landlord knows? Do you think it makes itself known to everyone?” Questions streamed out of me like water released from a dam.

Edgard continued, speaking slowly. “A spirit will manipulate electrical and electronic circuitry. Classic. But an olfactory one, that’s more unique.”

“What do you mean, ‘more unique’?” I decided to proceed with one question at a time from now on. Getting information from Edgard was always tricky. His conversations meandered on his own terms, and when it was a topic that excited him, there was no keeping him on track. Any effort to lead the conversation in an expected, logical direction was pointless.

“Hmmm, seems like whatever it is has had ample practise in interacting with the physical world.”

“So, they’ve been around a long time?”

“It would appear so.”

"What should I do?" I wanted all my questions answered. I felt some hope he may help me. It fuelled me to keep going.

Edgard stared out the window of the shop, into the falling raindrops. "Hmm, well, that all depends how confrontational you wish to be. You could try something minor and step it up if that doesn't get you desired results."

"What's a minor step I could start with?" This felt like a treasure hunt, where I had dig for any small nugget of information.

"You could start by asking what it wants and leaving it an offering of some kind."

"An offering?"

"Yes, an offering. A goodwill gesture, if you will. It could be food or a physical object that means something to you."

The buzzing ring of the phone broke our conversation. Edward picked it up and began explaining our selection of books on shamanism.

I busied myself wiping down the counter with a cloth. By the time, Edgard finished on the phone, our conversation had lost steam. The moment had passed. The antique clock on the wall showed my shift was over.

"Thanks, Edgard," I said.

"You're most welcome. Oh, one more thing," he said as he scuffled into his office. I heard him shuffling books, shifting of papers, and then a crash—the unmistakable sound pile of books falling to the floor. More rummaging, this time on the floor, and then Edgard was back with me, beside the shop door.

He handed me a dusty book with a dark red cover—*Eerie Encounters with the Other Side*—the same book I had been consulting with earlier today. Did he know that?

"Take this, to help with your voyage."

"Ugh, thanks," I said. "See you next week."

"Good luck and Godspeed," he said.

The door jingled as I opened it, and I left the cozy room filled with books and crystals to step outside into cold, sideways rain.

≈

When I pushed open the heavy wooden door to the yellow house, my anxiety returned. Walking usually helped the unsettling feeling of dread. Step by step, I pulled myself into the present moment, the problems moving momentarily to the back of my brain while I focused on what I saw, felt, and smelled. I slid off my shoes and put down my bag. I took out the dusty book Edgard had given me and went to the kitchen to put on some tea. I opened the book and started reading.

The book contained sections about spirits in all forms and gave a detailed history of spirits through the ages. Of course, Edgard had this in his own personal book collection. But I was still no closer to finding out what or who was in this yellow house.

I was deeply engrossed in the difference between spirits of the dead, deities, and demons and halfway through my mug of tea when a vibration jarred me back to the kitchen table.

I nearly jumped out of my chair; my heart started pounding. My phone was buzzing from the kitchen counter. Caller ID told me it was Jade.

"Hello."

"Brooke! Haven't heard from you since you moved in. How's the new place? Haven't fallen through a rotten floorboard yet?"

"Ha-ha, no. Been busy trying to work and write articles and keep up with school. Bit weird living alone and some strange things about the house, but it's fine." I immediately regretted telling her about the house.

"What kind of strange things?"

"Just some cold spots and weird things with the lights." I downplayed it. I didn't want to get into it.

"Well, I did warn you that the house has been there since forever and is in the oldest part of the city. Want to come to Hawthorne's and play a game of pool?"

Part of me wanted to, but part of me was wrapped in anxiety and didn't want to see other people. "I'm tired, actually. But let's get together soon."

"Are you sure, Brooke? Getting out of the house is a good thing, especially when you live alone. It will be fun."

I nearly said yes, knowing she was right and going out would probably make me feel better, but I couldn't make myself say yes. "Next time I'll come. I promise."

"All right, well, take care of yourself tonight. See you at school this week."

After hanging up, I put the phone on the table and continued reading a Buddhist tradition of leaving offerings out to appease hungry ghosts. I decided to give it a try. What did I have to lose?

I opened my fridge. Not much, as I usually got groceries on Sundays, which was the next day. I grabbed a clementine and some cheese. After cutting a slice of cheese off the block, I arranged the food on a small china plate with blue flowers and went to the front door.

I opened it and was just about to place the plate on the doormat when I heard voices. Women. Laughing and talking over one another. A moment later, I saw the source of the noises: three women walking down the street, clucking and scuttling along like hens. I stood up from my crouched position, hoping to make it look like I was going onto my porch for a late-night snack. They passed without noticing me. I hoped no other neighbours were out to see me as I bent over and placed the plate on the front porch. I hoped this offering would appease the hungry spirit.

Maybe, just maybe, something material and of this world would fulfill its greedy spiritly wants and it would leave me and the yellow house alone. I took one last glance at the plate on the bristly doormat and went back into the yellow house. The heavy smell of sandalwood hung in the air.

I sighed and hoped. I went into my bedroom, firmly closed the door, and read with my light on until my eyelids were heavy. Then I fell into a restless sleep.

Chapter 6

Hannah

May 7, 1887

I stood rigid and still while Eva's words set in. I felt dizzy. My head spun, and time slowed down. I looked at Eva, who stared out at the ocean. Her words hung between us, suspended like a foul stench. This moment would be etched in my mind for life—the moment my life became divided between time before the mine accident and time afterwards, the horrific event that changed so many of our lives from that evening onwards.

I felt strange, like I had left my body completely. I was numb. The words sunk in further. Richard was trapped underground in a mine-shaft explosion, and there was nothing I could do to save him.

Eva had no more information. I had a sudden urge to return home and ensure the children were safe. I also wanted to run to the entrance of mine number one and try to put out the fire myself, but the children needed me.

Eva told me to come by anytime, even that night if I wanted, and that she was here for me. I didn't have much to say to that. That level of intimacy in a friendship wasn't my way. I would manage this situation on my own. Somehow. We said solemn goodbyes, and I left her garden through the same white gate I came in. It clicked behind me. The black cat crouched on the fence, eyes scowling at me as I started back down the street.

The light was no longer soft and gentle. The air seemed hot now, suffocating even. The cherry blossoms now smelled smothering and acrid. I hoisted my long dress so it no longer caressed the wilting blossoms when I walked. My mind tried to register the information; I refused to think the worst but admitted in my mind that this was bad.

This morning had started as a regular day, with Richard's easy smile and kiss on my lips. He had walked out the door like he had every week day since we moved to Doveport. I couldn't fathom this was happening. Why had I not stopped him from walking out the door?

More immediately, what would I tell the children?

When I got home, none of the children asked about their father. It was common for Richard to return home after they were asleep.

I conducted the children's bedtime routine in a daze, desperately trying to focus on not showing that something was wrong. I needed to wait until I knew he was all right before telling them anything. I needed to process the news for myself before relaying it to them. Once Emerson and Tristan were breathing deeply and Alice was making clicking noises of sleep, I padded downstairs.

I walked into our room, took off my dress, and brushed my hair. I shivered. The fireplace was cold, but I didn't have the energy to light it. I wanted to talk to someone, but I didn't want to expose my thoughts. I thought about walking to Eva's like she offered and letting the tears flow out of my eyes. Tell her how scared I was and let her comfort me. Sit in the ambiguity with someone else who was feeling the same raw fear and sweeping uncertainty that I was.

Instead, I collapsed into bed, curled up, and let the tears flow from my eyes to my temples to my pillow. Sleep didn't come, even for a moment.

≈

The next morning, I hauled myself out of bed. I stared at myself in the mirror as I dressed and saw dark bags and blotchy skin. I felt utterly drained. I took to the kitchen and filled up two pots: one for oatmeal and one for tea. The children weren't up yet. A loud knock at the door interrupted my frantic thoughts about the events of yesterday.

A man I had never seen stood at the door wearing boots, pants, and suspenders.

"May I help you?" I asked, staring at him straight on.

"Morning, ma'am. I'm with the Doveport Coal Company. I have some information about the events of yesterday."

"Well, go on then." I realized I sounded a bit rude, as people in Canada almost always talked about niceties before getting to the real conversation, but I was too tired to try at pleasantries. On the outside, I may have looked pulled together; on the inside, I was panicked for answers.

"May I come in?" the man asked.

"The children are sleeping, and I would rather them not hear. Let's stand on the porch."

The man looked slightly annoyed but obliged. I then found out many things. The information he granted me became increasingly grim as he went on speaking. Time slowed like it had the night before when he told me the crux of the information.

"Men worked through the night to put out the fire. They weren't able to get the men out."

I found out one hundred and seventy men were killed in the mine—one hundred and five were Caucasian men and sixty-five were Chinese men. I found out that the first thumping boom was a massive explosion, and the second blast was the coal dust igniting. The cause of the fire was found to be improperly laid explosives.

I found out that only seven men survived the explosion. But worst of all, I found out Richard was not one of them.

It was an underground death of massive proportions. Some men died instantly; others were trapped for some time and eventually died from asphyxiation or from poison gases. Some bodies were never found. Some were found together, like two brothers who were found kneeling, arms around each other with coats over their heads, trying to shield themselves from the fire and loss of oxygen.

"Your husband is at the funeral home being readied for a funeral."

And just like that, I was a widow.

≈

The next day was a blur. My life had become one long nightmare that I couldn't wake from. I was one of forty-seven new widows in Doveport. My children were three of one hundred forty-seven fatherless children. Telling them was the worst thing I had ever done. I tried to be honest but straightforward, not showing emotion. Everyone in Doveport had lost someone—father, brother, husband, son, or uncle. Nobody was spared at least one loss.

Two days later, I woke up and rolled over in a dreamy morning haze to look at Richard. He wasn't there. When the past few days came back to me—the explosion in the mine, the man coming to the door, Richard being dead and never coming back—a sinking feeling came over me. This was my new life.

I got out of bed, dressed quickly, and went outside for water. I found if I concentrated on tasks at hand, the emptiness in my stomach hurt less. I arrived back in the kitchen with the dripping bucket and set it down. The stove was cold. Usually, Richard would have started the fire while I was dressing and fetching water. If he had been here, the flames would be licking at the stove by the time I brought water in. Instead, I kneeled over and began arranging small sticks in the fireplace. The sticks wouldn't light. When I finally had a small flame, a draft swept down, extinguishing it.

The children made their way downstairs and waited at the table for breakfast. Tristan fidgeted while Emerson and Alice argued.

I restarted building up the sticks. Twenty minutes later, I had the fire going and water on for oatmeal. I hurried the children, but the morning routine was late. They fussed and dallied. We finally left the house, now a full forty minutes late. We arrived at school to the school mistress's biting stare. Could she not have some empathy after the unprecedented events?

I arrived back to the house to begin the daytime chores. Chores I used to do while idly daydreaming about Richard and the children or planning routes for a leisurely walk when I next got the chance. While taking several trips to carry wood inside from the woodshed, I bargained in my head—I would have given up anything to have Richard back. I would have given up coming to Canada. I would have given up all the fine china I owned. I would have even given up the house, a place I loved more than anywhere I had ever lived.

When I moved the broom over the floor in a daze, I went over the day of Richard's death in my head, wishing I had told him to call in sick that day and wondering why I hadn't had a premonition to stop him from walking out the door that morning.

Everything I did that day made me think of Richard. I thought of him as I measured flour into a big wooden bowl for bread. I thought of the patience required of making bread and the patience Richard had been full of. I lacked patience, but Richard made up for that. He took his time with everything. In everything he did, he was calculated and careful. I was brash and hasty with everything, darting around the house quickly. Even now, as I stirred the bread ingredients too aggressively, flour escaped the bowl and landed on the wooden counter. Richard had time for anyone and anything. Whether it was adjusting the damper on the fireplace, helping Emerson with math, or tucking Alice and Tristan into bed, Richard took the utmost care and time. Before he died, his patience would bother me. Now I missed it desperately. Richard had lived like he had all the time in the world. The horrible irony and unjustness of it made my head hurt and my body ache. I rubbed a tear from my cheek, leaving a line of flour.

It wasn't fair or right. But nothing seemed right now. The Doveport Coal Company was blaming the mine explosion on the Chinese workers. The same men they didn't have the respect to call by name, only number. The same men they paid a third of what the other men made. Thinking of the unjustness of it all, I felt my face get hot. I punched the bread with my palms, taking my anger out on the stringy dough.

I started on laundry: getting water, soaking clothes, rubbing the clothes, more water, rinsing the clothes. I felt something wet on my cheeks. It was tears. I had began crying without realizing it. I tried to stop, but it was like a dam had opened; I had spent so much time hiding my tears from the children. Tears now flowed down my face as my hands worked in the water: water and emotion, emotion and water. I hung the clothes and went back to the kitchen. I glanced at the clock; I was late to pick up the children. I ran out of the house, half running, half walking to the children's school.

I looked out to the ocean as I walked and at its rocky shorelines. They were solid, like Richard had been, steadfast and stoic to the waves and whatever the ocean did that day, shifting from one thing to the next. I was several minutes late to pick up the children and again caught a cold stare from the school mistress.

I hurried the children home, glad for them to have a day of normalcy. No doubt some of their classmates had lost fathers in the explosion. It was a slight comfort that they weren't alone in their misery.

We stepped in the door, and I cursed myself for letting the stove go out. I started another fire and reached for some kindling. The kindling box was empty. I went outside to get some, and there were none there either. Large unsplit pieces looked at me as if mocking me. Yet another chore Richard had done. All these things he had done that I hadn't noticed. All the questions from the children that were now my burden. Richard had done so much for our house and children—all without me noticing. I sometimes had felt as though Richard spent more time than me with his feet up. Now, I felt a terrible dark pit in my stomach when I remembered feeling mad at him for that.

I picked up the axe. I loosened my dress at the back, looked behind me to make sure the children weren't there, and brought the axe down on a large piece of wood. The axe bounced off the wood. I did it again. This time, it went in an inch. I took a moment to catch my breath and got angry. I needed to make a fire and I wouldn't let this stop me. I brought the axe up over my head and brought it down, using the full weight of my body this time. It went in further than before. I repeated this technique a few more times until I was through the wood and repeated the whole process until I had enough wood to make dinner. Double the work without another person here.

We ate two hours later than we usually did. It was dark. The children went up to bed, and I asked Emerson to help them get ready while I cleaned up. Guilt racked at me for not helping them with their bedtime routine like usual. When I went up to check on them, sounds of deep breathing told me they were asleep.

I went into our bedroom and closed the door. Separate from the practical things Richard did, I missed his presence. The secure, warm feeling of knowing there was someone else in the house if something went wrong. He would boil water for a bath for me. No bath tonight. I was shattered tired. I missed the way he checked the house and locked the doors at night. After this thought, I realized I hadn't checked the door, so I walked the house as Richard did, checking doors and adding some last wood to the fire.

Back in our room, I fell into bed. An ache started between my shoulder blades, in muscles I didn't know existed. I hadn't slept well in days, thinking of the empty spot in the bed where Richard should be but wasn't and frantically planning for the next day. This night, however, I was exhausted from the chores, the wood splitting, and the constant heaviness of grief—a grief that held my heart in a dark shadow. I wanted a break from what my life now was.

Eventually, I fell hard into a deep sleep.

Chapter 7

Brooke

September 16, 2017

I awoke in the early morning hours. Outside was dark, and I was groggy with sleep. It took me a moment to realize that a sound must have woken me. I lay in my bed, my heart beating against my chest. Then I heard the sound—scratching coming from the front porch. Through a morning haze, it took me a few moments to remember the day before. Then I recalled everything: the yellow house, the strange sounds and smells, and my offering left on the porch.

Now something was on the porch. Maybe the spirit was taking the offering. Maybe it was Beverly. I didn't want to investigate, but I knew I wouldn't sleep unless I did. I pulled on some grey sweatpants and a baggy t-shirt and swung my legs out of bed. Then I crept out of my room and tiptoed through the living room, past the fireplace and toward the solid-wood front door.

I unlocked the door and grabbed its cold handle. I was about to turn the handle when I stopped, removing my hand from the door. Suddenly, I didn't want to know what was outside; it seemed safer not to know. I wasn't ready to come face-to-face with whatever was outside. I wasn't ready to know what was going on with the house, or confront Beverly if it was her outside. Maybe I could get used to the sounds and smells and never know for sure what was causing them. The tapping and scratching on the other side of the door became more agitated; if only there was a peephole in the door, but there wasn't. I had to open the door to see what it was.

All at once, curiosity outweighed fear and I pulled the door open. What I found behind it was not at all what I expected. My breath caught as I saw the source of the noise: black wings, white head, and yellow talons. It swiftly left the porch upon seeing me with a hop, hop, hop and then a swoop into the air. A bald eagle was helping itself to the offering —not a spirit, but a bird of prey having a snack. My heart rushed in my chest as I watched the eagle ascend across the street, up, up, and into a tree in the park between the yellow house and the rail yard. It had taken the remaining clementine with it, clever thing that it was. I took a few deep breaths, trying to normalize my breathing.

I stooped over and picked up the plate. Then I stepped into the yellow house, closed the door, and went back to bed. I tried to sleep but couldn't. I was somehow simultaneously wired and tired, making sleep impossible. I thought I heard scratching a few more times, but it had only been the house shifting around. After tossing and turning, I gave up on sleep. My mind was racing with thoughts, and I had school assignments to do.

When I got out of bed, I peeped out my bedroom door. Not seeing anything, I went to the kitchen and turned on the kettle. I turned on my laptop to write a paper. The air in the kitchen was getting colder by the day, and like an army penetrating a kingdom, this coolness had begun infiltrating the rest of the house. I made a tea to keep warm and tried to type, but my thoughts went to whatever was in the house and the issue with Beverly, which was increasing by the day.

The apple throwing had shaken me up. That was the first time her behaviour had crossed the line to a physical nature. Until then, her harassment had been distanced—either verbal or online. Even the incident with her swerving in her truck didn't physically touch me. The apple thrown at me in the lecture hall was a concerning escalation. If it had been high school, I could have told somebody, but this was university. There was nobody to tell.

I typed away, trying to work as quickly as possible while still producing good work. Soon, I got into a rhythm and drank several cups of tea. The paper was coming along, and I was even enjoying myself. Not having roommates upped my productivity and made me calm in many ways. I was more than halfway done the paper when a knock came from the front door, startling me. I clicked save on my paper and went to the front door, again wishing for a peep hole. Then I opened the door.

It was Jade. Thank goodness. Her younger sister, Florence. was with her. Florence was five and was Jade's youngest sibling. She often got roped in to looking after her, so Florence was often Jade's shadow on the weekend.

"Hi, stranger!" said Jade.

"Oh, hi," I said, perhaps seeming less enthusiastic than I usually did. "Come on in."

She and Florence stepped inside.

"You sound worried on the phone last night, so we wanted to invite you on an ocean walk." Jade's smile was so bright. Sometimes I wished happiness really was contagious and I could borrow some from her.

"I would love to, but really have to do this paper," I said. I was feeling scattered and unsettled, worrying about the house and Beverly.

"Oh, come on. It will be good to get out of here for a bit. Place looks good, though," she said, looking around. Florence stared into the living room with a strange look on her face. She didn't move her gaze from the window seat.

"I really have to get this paper done. I'm on a roll," I explained, starting to talk quicker and feel hotter. "There have been some weird things happening."

"Come on, Brooke. I promise you'll feel better if you come out. And I want to hear what's been going on." She looked at me with a warm smile and was so cheerful that I started to feel a bit better.

"All right. I'll come for a short walk."

"Excellent!"

Before Florence stepped outside, I noticed she looked back at the window seat one more time. I slid on some shoes and followed them onto the porch.

As usual, Jade was right. I felt immediately better being outside the house. The air was cool and energy-giving; my thoughts were clearer. I felt in the moment and not in my head.

I followed Jade on a path through the rail yard that led to a secret beach. The area was so industrial that nobody walked down there.

Florence ran in front of us, and Jade said, "Tell me what's really going on with you, Brooke. I can tell something is wrong. I'm here to help."

I filled Jade in about the house and about the apple core.

"You've got to do something about it, Brooke," she said, with a furrowed brow. "It's really not going to stop until you do."

"I don't want to talk to her. I just want to finish this year and be done with her."

"I can't believe she threw something at you in a lecture. That's crossing a line."

"Yeah. I can't decide what is worse: Beverly or this house stuff."

"Strange for sure. You could try burning some sage and telling it to go away. I saw it on a show once. I do have some sage."

"Hmmm, okay, maybe I'll try that. My offering didn't go so well."

"Right, well let me know when you want me to sage it with you."

After some time on the beach, we walked back to return in front of the yellow house. My thoughts were more organized, and I felt slightly happier than before.

"Jade, I did need that. Thanks," I conceded. I felt better about going back to the house. I had a plan: salt and sage.

It was then that Florence piped in for the first time the entire walk, and what she said made all the relaxion of the walk dissolve.

"Who was the lady in the big dress in your house? I saw her by the window when we came inside to get you before the walk."

Chapter 8

Hannah

May 10, 1887

It was seven days after the mine disaster. I was making dinner while reading the *Doveport Newspaper*. It had published a list of men confirmed dead in the mine disaster. It also said where they were from: England, Scotland, Wales, Ireland, China, the United States, Holland, and eastern Canada. The Chinese miners were listed as numbers, not names. This angered me. What made their lives less valuable than other men? The injustice made my face red and my head spin. I skimmed the names and places until I saw one that made a pit in my stomach—Richard Hatherly. Tears welled in my eyes. A loud knock at the front door caused me to jolt and spill the tea down the front of my dress. I grabbed a tea towel and dabbed the spots. Not too eager to see who was there, I gave the dinner pot a quick stir before walking to the door. Who was knocking at dinnertime?

I pulled the heavy wooden door open and found myself face-to-face with a man wearing black pants and a black vest with a button missing from the bottom. He had grey stubble on his chin and tired eyes.

"May I help you?" I asked, looking him straight in the eyes.

He spoke quickly, "Good day, ma'am. I'm from the Doveport Coal Company. Our sincerest condolences about your husband. I am here to deliver some messages."

I crossed my arms. I had been battling feelings of resentment toward the company and their safety, or lack thereof. "Well, no message will bring my husband back." My pain was raw. I was constantly on the edge of anger since the accident. It was not this man's fault, but I was upset.

The man alternated from looking at me to looking at the paper he held in his hand. "Yes, ma'am, you're right. I don't mean to bother, but some writings were found on the miners' shovels. There was one on a shovel from your husband. They said some of the men had quite a bit of time down there . . . enough time to write a goodbye message. The message that was on your late husband's shovel has been written on a paper in this envelope if you want it. I'm so sorry for your loss." He spoke quickly and looked down at his feet as he reached forward and handed me the envelop.

I felt bad for my biting comment earlier and uncrossed my arms. "Oh, thank you," I said quietly. Tears stung my eyes. I breathed in deeply and tried to force the tears back. Instead, one escaped and rolled down my cheek. I quickly brushed it away with the backside of my hand.

"But there is one more matter: this house. Since your husband is no longer an employee of the Doveport Coal Company, the house will have to be returned to the company."

Sadness turned to anger as I pieced together my thoughts and formulated a response. "How is this possible? My husband is deceased from an accident. What options do I have other than handing the house over? I would like to stay here."

"One of your sons can work for the company. With him as an employee, your family would be entitled to stay."

"That is not an option. What are the other options?"

"Well, you can apply to pay an inflated amount to continue leasing the house. Most families find it too costly and don't take that option."

"Well, that's the option I will take. I will be in contact about the application."

"Good evening, ma'am," the man said as he turned and started down the front steps.

"Good evening," I replied and slowly closed the door.

Red hot anger burned within me. The injustices at this mine ran as deep and thick as the veins of black coal they extracted from the ground. Now the house was an added problem.

I then remembered the note from Richard's writing on the shovel. Inside the envelop was a cream-coloured paper folded to the size of my palm. I couldn't take my eyes off it, the message he wrote in his last hours.

I washed the plates from dinner, the entire time wondering what the note said. My heart hurt thinking about how he must have felt those last hours. Once the children were bathed, stories read, and cozily in bed, I took the note to our room, my room, rather.

I stood in front of the mirror and looked at the woman staring back: dark hair, with its usual wave plus some frizz, eyes sunken from tiredness, and a dress with a high neck. I looked exactly as I was—a woman grieving.

I climbed into bed but didn't unfolded the paper. I was worried to read it. Perhaps there were gruesome details of his death. Perhaps he wrote details of the disaster. Death. Panic. The resolve that they would die underground. But mostly, I was putting off reading it because I couldn't bear to think of him in his last moments, knowing what would happen to him but not what would happen to me and the children. Richard would have remained dignified—I knew it.

I wanted to save the note, to savour it, like a last piece of chocolate or a final sip of tea. I knew it was the last message I would get from him. I wished it could last.

I looked at the paper for a moment, then placed it on the table beside my bed. I began reading a book but was unable to focus on the words. All I could think about was the note I could see out of the corner of my eye.

Finally, curiosity overtook me. I unfolded the paper and let myself look at the writing. I knew it wasn't Richard's writing and that someone had transcribed it from the shovel, but it was easy to imagine that it was Richard who had written the letters that turned to words.

At last, I allowed myself to read the words:

I love you H. Raise our children bravely. R.

I rolled onto my side and curled my knees to my chest. My eyes flowed with tears. It was a slow flow, and my breathing came in small gasps. I couldn't wake the children. I read the note three more times and folded it back up. I wiped my eyes with the back of my hand and took a full breath.

I will, Richard, I thought. *I promise I'll raise our children bravely. I don't know how, yet, but I will.*

I stayed on my side and unconsciously wrapped my arms around myself. I lay awake for hours before finding sleep. The words from the note floated around in my head and I began planning how to bravely raise them, thinking about how I would pay the inflated lease for the house. That night I resolved something: I would not remarry. Other women could do as they pleased; I would not think worse of them. But for me, there would be nobody else. I would find some way to make this work. I would commit myself to Richard's words. I owed it to him, to the children.

But mostly, my decision not to marry again was made because it was what I wanted.

≈

Three days later, I woke in a haze. I rolled over expecting to see a mop of dark hair and the peaceful, morning-asleep face of Richard and then I remembered.

It came back to me like a punch to my gut.

The mine accident. The note. My vow not to remarry. It had been three full days since the note was delivered.

The children didn't have school, but they needed breakfast. I dressed and trudged into the kitchen. Sun poured into the kitchen window and lifted my spirit ever so slightly. As I went from morning task to morning task, I went over the note word for word and tried making sense of it.

Richard's words could bring me down or they could uplift me, I thought. I realized it was my choice. I tried to think of the blessings of the day. It was sunny. It was a weekend. We were free for a day. Today, we would do something different. What would Richard suggest? It came to me and my heart lifted: a surprise for the children. I started stirring the oatmeal with happiness.

When I heard the feet come down the stairs, I was suddenly excited to see them.

"We're going to the beach today," I announced.

Three sets of eyebrows went up, and Alice let out a small squeal.

"We haven't gone to the beach yet this year," Emerson said.

"That's right, we have not. But we're going to go today after breakfast. It will be good to get out of the house and spend the day in the spring air and sunshine and play in the sand and waves."

They seemed surprised but didn't protest. The note from Richard had slightly revived my energy; perhaps the children sensed it. When the last pot was scrubbed, bags were packed, and the picnic basket filled with bread, cheese, and sausages, we left the house. I closed the door behind us.

We walked down our street for several minutes before turning onto a path through an overgrown meadow. Walking along the path, I watched Alice, Tristan, and Emerson trod on ahead of me and my thoughts wandered to the land that existed before the town did.

Eventually the path, we walked changed from dirt to sand, then ended all together and left us on a beach. Alice ran, spun, and threw her hands onto the sand, feet in the air and feet back on the ground. Sand flew all around her, and her hair flew in all directions. Emerson carried the picnic basket, and Tristan and I were the last to arrive at our usual spot.

I threw down the blanket I had carried under my arm. Alice waded in the ocean, and Tristan threw rocks out to sea. Spring sun warmed my skin. The wind played with my hair. But something was nagging at me, other than the ever-present darkness of grief.

I felt solid in my decision not to remarry, but there was one major problem: How would I make money? Either of the boys working in the mine was not an option, so paying the inflated lease was the only way to keep the house. I had not considered this when I vowed not to remarry. All that had mattered was the promise to Richard.

The note had spurred me to think of the children and to do my best for them despite not having Richard. I had to give them the best lives possible. As I saw it, I had two options: live off the twelve dollar a month pension or remarry. Remarrying wasn't an option and the pension was not near enough to feed four children and myself.

The issue of putting food on the table, paying for the house, and buying clothing for the children began to weigh heavily. I was rubbish at sewing, and I didn't know the first thing about fixing houses.

The small pension from the mine company would not be enough. Some women were already talking about remarrying. For the first time, I realized why. Most of the widows had three or more children to feed and clothe. They lived in houses owned by the company. Keeping a house meant remarrying.

I watched Alice wade knee-deep and admired the sparkle off the water in the brilliant sunshine. It really was a beautiful day. I felt guilty as I thought of the chores waiting to be done at home. This was important—I couldn't remember the last day the children and I had done something fun. This was raising them bravely.

I pondered ways to make money. I could make bread and sell it. But someone else was doing that. I could work at a laundry. I could look after other children, but everyone looked after their own children. Women didn't have many options. I felt defeated, and I hadn't even begun.

I tried to push it out of my mind and enjoy the sun and sea. I tried to enjoy the sand under my body and savour the children's squeals and the focused look of concentration on Emerson's face as he turned pages of his book. But I couldn't stop wondering how I was going to pay for the house and expenses with only one income. It was like a puzzle with several pieces missing, frustrating and senseless.

Eventually, the sun became a duller orange and the wind made goosepimples appear on my arms. A hungry gurgling noise came from my stomach.

"Time to go home!" I shouted.

We walked in a neat line along the path until we were back on our dusty street. We climbed the white steps of the house, somehow both tired and rejuvenated.

That night, grief tortured my mind and ravaged my body. Ways to make money turned over in my head. Sleep was impossible now. With Richard, sleep had come easily to me. After his death, I rolled around in my bed until the early hours of the morning. Other nights, I found sleep first, only to wake up in the depths of darkness and night, unable to find it again. Sometimes, I would lie there trying; other times, I would give up and sit by the window and look out to the street. The quiet spooked me, and the people walking by in the darkness of night unsettled me. I woke up with bags under my eyes and, by midday, felt too tired to do anything.

The foggy, tired feeling reminded me of the years the children were babies and how sleep had been a luxury I had taken for granted. In the day, I was now a flimsy shell of the woman I was before the accident. I went through the motions of making food, cleaning clothes, getting the children out the door to school, and arranging Richard's details. Before, I would visit with friends, go walking for myself, read books, and take pride in rearranging furniture in the house to keep things fresh and exciting. Now, all my energy was taken in keeping the household running so everyone had clean clothes and none of the children went hungry. Before the mine accident, I was swimming breaststroke effortlessly; now, I was struggling even to tread water.

As I saw it, I had two choices: live off the insurance or figure out some way to make some real money. It seemed like living off the insurance would allow grief to enter me, whereas the second choice left me feeling a bit excited and hopeful. Keeping the house was necessary —option two it was then.

I had not dreamed of this happening. Coming to Canada was our shared dream. The house had been our shared dream. None of this should have happened. There was no such thing as fair, and wishing it away wouldn't put food on the table or allow me to pay for the house. I would do the best I could with this situation. I would persevere.

I wanted to feel better. I wanted to forget about the past weeks. How would I continue another day? I crawled into bed and tried to let sleep overtake me so I could escape for a few hours.

Chapter 9

Brooke

September 16, 2017

I didn't know what to say to Jade's sister Florence, so I looked blankly at her. She seemed unbothered and genuinely curious about the figure she had seen in the house. It seemed like Jade hadn't even noticed. She looked down at her phone tapping away at her screen with an amused smile on her face at whatever she was typing.

"What woman?" Jade asked, not looking up from her phone.

"There was a lady in a big black dress. She had curly hair and was by the window," Florence replied with a detached indifference, like she was specifying her preferred flavour of ice cream. She wasn't the least bit scared or worried.

"What are you talking about? Where was this lady?" Jade looked up from her phone, put it in her back pocket, and looked down the street.

"In Brooke's living room, by the front window. She looked right at me."

"Nonsense," Jade said. "Stop making up stories. Let's go home."

The shiver that had tingled down my spine was still there as I watched them walk away. Jade took her usual giant strides; Florence at her side, nearly running to keep up. I immediately wished I had asked Florence more about what she saw. I briefly thought about calling them to come back but didn't. I stood, paralyzed with fear. Inaction was my usual way to face fear or negativity. Avoidance. If I didn't engage, I didn't have to cope. Now, I was wishing I had demanded answers of her. Any information would be helpful in figuring out what was in the house, why it was there, what it wanted, and most importantly, how to get rid of it.

I watched them until they turned off my street. I didn't want to go into the house, but that paper needed writing and my stomach was empty. I knew that my tortuous thoughts would be worse if I didn't eat.

I walked up the steps, pushed the door open, and looked inside—nothing out of place and no strange smell. I closed the door and took off my shoes, then locked it and walked to the kitchen.

I put some leftover curry in a small pot on the stove and turned on the burner. I put on the kettle and looked around while it boiled. The house was vastly different than when I had viewed it. At first, it felt like a place where I would finish papers and reach my goals. Now, it felt untrustworthy and illogically, as if a place where bad things could happen.

My book collection, in a neat row on the fireplace and piled on the coffee table, gave me a small feeling of home. The water boiled and I poured it over a tea bag in a mug. I stirred the tea bag around until the liquid in the cup was a satisfying brown colour, then splashed milk into it until it was cream coloured. Lines of steam shot straight into the air.

I sat at the kitchen table and wrote the paper I had started that morning between bites of curry and mouthfuls of tea, eventually making satisfying progress. At least this paper was going well, if nothing else in my life right now.

As soon as that thought left my head, the screen froze. The letters I was typing stopped. I was pressing the keys, but no letters showed on the screen, just that infuriating loading icon circling and circling. No amount of mouse clicking or pressure on the keys helped.

This had never happened before. The spinning circle continued, and I suddenly felt very cold. I brought my shoulders up to my ears and crossed my legs. What was going on? The temperature outside could not have changed this drastically. An icy haze set over me. I shivered, but I was too scared to go to my bedroom to get a sweater.

Was this the spirit making its presence known again? What was it trying to tell me?

I had secretly hoped that the offering had worked before the eagle got it, but clearly it hadn't. Whatever the thing in the house was, it was still trying to tell me something.

I had to try something else. As I thought of what to do, I sat shivering but stubborn, unwilling to move. The laptop screen was still frozen. I decided I had to get out of there. I picked up my phone and crept through the kitchen and out the back door. It was disconcertingly warmer outside as I crossed the yard, sat on the bench, and let out a small sigh. My shoulders dropped. I looked at the house which, although a bright yellow, now looked much darker than before I lived there. I wished I had never moved. Even living with Beverly might have been better than this.

But that was no longer an option, so I had to find out what was going on. Maybe the rabbit hole that was the Internet had some suggestions for me to try, some ways to get whatever it was to leave the house and leave me alone for good.

Using my phone, I googled "spirit in house." Many articles popped up. I scrolled through them, skimming a few. Nearly all of them mentioned unexplained temperature changes and technological glitches.

They also mentioned strange smells and weird sounds. Everything that was going on in my house. I touched the top search bar and this time typed "ways to get rid of a spirit."

All suggested sage and salt. I pictured the long wands of green dried-up sage in Passages. It looked more like regular grass from a field in the fall, but every article said that that was the best way to rid a house of spirits. I made a mental note to get some salt; I had lots of that. It couldn't hurt to try both. I was becoming desperate.

The advice from one article stood out. It suggested talking to the spirit and telling it to go away. The thought of doing that terrified me, but it too was worth a try. I read the entire article, rehearsing what I could say. I would try it when I went back into the house. I had to do something.

I needed a break from thinking about whatever was in the house, so I opened Instagram and idly started scrolling through the never-ending colourful photos that made up its world. I scrolled through photos of lattes and leggings, beaches, and sunsets. Happy families, people with parents and grandparents; blissful backyards, and cozy restaurant patios. I thought of my drafty and cold house, of my non-existent parents, and that I had never been on a beach holiday. I cringed when I saw a photo of all the girls in my program gathered on a patio. Beverly was in the centre, with her glowing, bronzed skin and long blonde hair.

I scrolled on, trying to put it out of my head. I stopped scrolling when a photo caught my eye. The photo was of me, in first year, very drunk, very underdressed, and leaning over a toilet. I was the epitome of foolishness—immature and unrefined. She linked an article I had recently written for the university newspaper about American writer Jack Kerouac on his advice to writers. The article had been better received than I expected, and I was still getting emails about how much people enjoyed it, how it inspired them to write more bravely and how it inspired their writing style. Now here it was with a photo of me beside it and a caption reading: *"Why write like Kerouac when you can drink like him too?"* It wasn't written in my article, but Jack Kerouac had died of liver cirrhosis in 1969. But her comment wasn't a bash to Kerouac; it was a bash to me.

There were ten likes already, but not as many as her other posts of her sparkly and successful life: a turquoise pool, shopping on a busy city street, and one of her on a sea plane over to Doveport. Every photo documented her perfect, airbrushed life.

Why this and why now? On top of everything else, it was the last thing I needed. Embarrassment, betrayal, and loneliness hit me simultaneously. I couldn't call Jade because she would just tell me to stand up to Beverly, which was impossible. Jade didn't understand being with fear and unable to act. She was a straight shooter and would tell anyone where to go if they crossed her boundaries.

There was nobody to report it to, no school counsellor or principal, nobody who would investigate and have my back. I was on my own.

I slumped back on the bench as it started getting dark. I usually liked this time of day—when daytime was closing and the calm of night taking its place. But today, the fading daylight felt sinister and hostile. I felt cold and exposed—literally out here in the yard and figuratively online with the comments next to my published article.

Anger eventually surpassed embarrassment. I had paid rent for this house, and I would go in there and tell whatever it was to go away. I strode to the back door and threw it open. I stepped into the kitchen.

"I don't know who or what you are. I understand this is your house. I appreciate you letting me live here. All respect to you, but I would appreciate that you stop making yourself known. I'm just trying to get through my last year of university. All I want is to graduate and to have this girl in my program leave me alone. So, yeah. Stop with the cold and the strange happenings."

I had planned to use a strong tone and an even stronger message, but my voice came out scared, the message more of a plea than a demand.

Nothing happened. Not a sound in the house.

I put my bowl in the sink, closed my laptop, and crept to my room, closing the door. I got into bed and tried to find sleep.

Chapter 10

Hannah

September 4, 1887

Months after getting the note, I awoke to the deep, gurgling croak of a raven outside the bedroom window. My eyes started stinging a bit as I watched it; I still couldn't escape my grief, but I didn't give tears a chance. Instead, I sat bolt upright. I would get on with the tasks of my day. I refused to give in to the rampaging thoughts in my head.

I dressed, pulled back my hair, and threw some water on my face from the bowl. Then I walked with purpose to the kitchen.

Our morning routine was different now, but we had adapted. First, I would make a fire in the stove. When I was nearly done, Emerson, Tristan, and Alice would come down the stairs, usually in a noisy, chattering line. Emerson would grab the water pail and walk outside, returning a couple of minutes later with a full bucket, water lapping over the sides. Tristan would bring in a handful of wood and lay it beside me, while Alice would place bowls and cutlery onto the wooden table. I would then start a fire. After several minutes, once the flames were eating the wood and flashing around in the stove, I boiled water on the stove and readied oatmeal and tea.

I now awoke half hour earlier to make up for the fire and other additional chores that were now mine. I refused to get discouraged and was trying to get on with life the best I could. The children and I hadn't asked for the dark turn of our life back in May, but we were working with the circumstances. Life was far from perfect, but we were managing. We spooned oatmeal into our mouths over talk of school, which was to start the next day.

"I'm keen to see Walter and William," Emerson said. He was sitting straight, and though school until the next day, he was already wearing his trousers and jumper that made up their school uniform.

"I would rather make sandcastles at the beach and play in the yard than do maths and do all that writing work," said Alice, as she ran her fingers around the inside of her oatmeal bowl and licked them clean.

"Tristan, what about you?" I prompted the middle child. Tristan was hesitant to express himself, and I was trying to encourage him to talk more. He had always been more withdrawn than the others—more likely to have his nose in a book—but since his father died, he seemed even quieter.

He looked out the kitchen window into the back garden for a moment and then spoke, "I like summer, but I also enjoy the playing at school and the exercise classes and when we get to kick around a ball and run outside. I like the stories in books that we get to read and then talk about."

"Very good, Tristan. You speak well," I said and noticed his back straighten ever so slightly.

Alice pulled a face and piped in again, "Ugh, the stories. The maths makes my head hurt and the writing makes my hands hurt."

"Well, no matter your feelings about it, it's back to school for everyone tomorrow, and that's that. Might as well make the most of it.

School is the best thing you can be doing for yourself and your future. I'm very proud of all of you and your various strengths. It will be a good year."

After bowls were cleared from the table, washed, and set to dry, I wiped my hands on my apron and looked out to the back garden. The wisteria tree had retreated to green vines, long devoid of the purple flowers that adorned it in spring.

I filtered through the past months: the first horrible weeks of funeral arrangements, the shock, and raw grieving. The next weeks of muddling through running the house on my own, and the final weeks of summer as I forced myself to get out of bed and create some semblance of normalcy for the children: beach picnics, walks by the river, street parades, and other community events.

My thoughts landed on the present as a finch landed in the back garden next to the wisteria and hopped around pecking at something on the ground. This morning, I felt different than I had in months. I felt a lightness I hadn't felt since before Richard died. The morning had gone smoothly. The kitchen was clean and tidy. The windows were open and let in fresh outside air. The lace blinds swayed a bit with the gentle breeze.

The pain of losing Richard felt less raw. My thoughts were clearer and flowed in and out of my head rather than entering my head angrily, causing my attention to settle over them and brew over them for minutes, sometimes hours at a time. The grief decreased each day. Sometimes, it flared up, like a cut almost healed only to be reopened. The grief hadn't gotten smaller, but my strength had grown bigger around it.

≈

Later that morning, after lunch, while the children were in their rooms playing with trains and books, I stood by the bay window and looked at the ocean and grey sky. It was a rare overcast summer day. Without notice, the clouds blocked out the bright sun. It was one of those days where it was warm but overcast and everyone stayed inside, tired and subdued from the greyness—a day far from the early days of spring where we were desperate to be outside. There was no urgency to be outdoors. We had savoured plenty of sunny summer days and were content to be indoors.

I decided to clean and declutter. I could finally look at Richard's things without tears welling up under my eyes and without going over various scenarios for how I could have prevented the entire tragedy. I finally felt brave and sturdy enough to go through Richard's things. It had to be done sometime, might as well do it now when I had summoned my strength.

I strode into my bedroom off the living room with both trepidation and determination. I hoisted my dress, lowered myself onto my knees, and looked under the bed: Richard's storage space. I pulled out a few trousers he had never worn and I had bothered him to get rid of. I thought he had until now. My lips turned into a small smile.

I pulled out a box and opened it: model trains and various train parts. I put them aside to give to the children when time was right. I pulled out a few more boxes of clothes and sorted them into two piles: keep and give away. Under the bed was nearly clear now, but there was a box still back there, at the wall and surrounded by rabbit-sized dust bunnies. I could see the box but couldn't reach it.

I reached around my back and loosened my dress. Then I placed my hands flat on the floor, lowered myself onto my stomach, and wiggled under the bed toward the box. I reached forward and touched the box but, in touching it, sent it further away from me. I twisted myself so my ear was on the ground and inched myself forward using my toes. I finally reached the box with the tips of my fingers. I pulled it toward me, wiggling back, pull, wiggle, pull. I sat up, my dress coated in dust-bunnies. I knelt back and opened the lid.

Inside was something I hadn't seen in years. Material things are strange for that reason. There could be something you saw many times years ago, didn't have a thought of for years, and then remember clearly when you see it. Inside the wooden box sat a camera. It was a rectangular wooden box of dark brown mahogany colour with the slightest reddish tinge. There was brass trim against the wood and the folded bellows in the middle were made of black cloth. Its lens was also brass also and had many small screws on it.

It was Richard's camera when we had first moved to Canada. He had always loved new and unusual gadgets, especially technological ones, and had dreamt of trying his hand at photography. But he never got a chance. The move to Canada sucked every bit of time and money. The hours he spent with the children and working at the mine. He had no time for photography. I hadn't known he had kept the camera, but it had been under the bed this whole time. Finding it felt a bit like Christmas—when you are surprised and happy at the same time, when you think you don't like material things but then getting something material excites you.

It shamed met to admit that my first thought was to sell the camera. I started thinking of potential buyers and whether I should sell it myself or give it to one of the shops to sell. I was muddling numbers through my head as I pulled it from the box and turned it over in my hands. It was in perfect condition. Typical Richard to take utmost care of it. It was fine wood, and the box had stopped any dust from getting in. I looked through it and felt oddly comforted thinking Richard had been the last one to do so.

I thought of the shop keeper near downtown Doveport, who had wares from faucets to watches and horse saddles to children's shoes spilling out of his shop on the boardwalk. The inside of his shop housed many fine things like this. Surely, he would buy it from me with few questions. But I couldn't picture myself walking in there, leaving the camera, and walking out with a stack of paper notes. This had belonged to Richard and was a meaningful connection I still had to him. But the children needed new shoes and our pantry items like flour, oatmeal, and rice were running very low. We needed money.

I thought about the bigger city of Ellington and the photographic studio we had seen when we passed through before coming to Doveport. It was crowded with people—a line up curving outside the shop like a river. People wanted their photos taken. They talked about it here in Doveport, but I hadn't seen anyone taking photographs. Doveport was still living in the world of paintings.

Then a thought came to me. Perhaps I didn't need to sell the camera for money. Perhaps I could use the camera to make money to keep the house. In doing so, I would be able to hang onto this small part of Richard—and maybe, just maybe, accomplish something great.

Chapter 11

Brooke

September 23, 2017

The following Saturday morning, I awoke to the sound of trains on tracks across the street, metal hitting metal, and the sound of a man yelling. I turned over and picked up my phone: Nine o'clock. I put it down and rolled over onto my other side.

Though it had been a week, the comment Beverly made on my Kerouac article came back to me, with nearly as much humiliation and anger as when I first saw it. I couldn't believe she did that. I hadn't talked to anyone about it. I didn't want to explain it to Jade, Derek, or David. I wanted to sort it out myself before sharing it with anyone else. That was just the way I worked. I had gone through the week holding it in. But like a hot coal, holding it only hurt me and did nothing to remedy the situation.

I got out of bed and went into the kitchen. Sun streamed through the window, but I was still hesitant about the house. I was now constantly on edge and waiting for something to happen. Outside was a sunny day, which could be the last day like this until winter came in with a rainy vengeance. I made tea and toast and did not touch my phone while I sipped and nibbled. I tried to focus on the creamy taste of the tea and the crunch and peanut butter crispiness of the toast.

I decided to try forgetting Beverly's comments below my Kerouac article. I also decided to try forgetting about the house. I vowed to enjoy myself. It was the weekend, and I didn't have to work. I was determined to have a good day. I chewed my last bite of toast and picked up my phone. I scrolled through Instagram to see what was going on. A farmers' market. What a perfect way to spend the day. It looked like the girls from the program were going, too. I could try one last time to insert myself back into the friend group. Since Beverly decided she was done with me, the girls had ignored me, but I felt like I should try one more time. I would go to the farmers' market and then go for a walk at the estuary. I got dressed in some jeans and a moss-green sweater, grabbed my leather satchel and a water bottle, and left the house. I texted Jade to see if she would come. Then, I started to walk.

≈

I arrived at the harbour park that held the farmers' market. The sun felt like it was summer, grass yellow after scorching hot days on end. Tents outlined the park in a colourful circle. Vendors, wearing sun hats and aprons, stood behind tables that held yellow and orange squash, colourful beaded treasures, or sweet-smelling pies and cookies. Tall masts of sailboats and sleek lines of yachts formed a serene nautical background.

My phone pinged in my purse, and I pulled it out.

"Can't make the farmer's market today. Have to help my Dad with firewood."

I took a big breath and sent Jade a quick reply. I would do it alone then. I would approach the girls and see if there was any chance of being part of their group again.

I scanned the grassy area in the middle of the park. Amid the families, couples, and individuals milling about, I picked out the group of girls from my program. Beverly wasn't there. Most weekends, she went back to Ellington to stay at her parents' house. A sea plane delivered her to her life of convertibles, backyard swimming pools, restaurant patios, and two parents—the absolute opposite of my life.

This was it: my chance to talk to the girls from the program and see if entering the group again was possible. One more kick at the can. If they didn't change their tune here, I would let it go. To be fair, I hadn't communicated with them since the apple incident. I gathered my courage and walked up to their circle. My stomach hurt and my heart raced.

They were sitting in a circle on a blanket and chatted incessantly. One was eating a stalk of kale. This close gathering and kale eating made me think of a group of bunnies that often congregated together on the grass on campus at Harbourview.

"Hey," I said as I walked up to the circle.

"Oh, hi," said one of the girls, Shannon. She just barely opened the circle, only enough to not be completely rude, but not enough for me to squeeze in and find a space on the blanket. I sat down just outside their circle. No one made a move to open the circle; this was not a good start. I was starting to feel anxious and I felt a dull stomachache. Everyone but Shannon looked down at their phones.

"Any good finds at the market?" I asked, trying to push the anxiety out of my head and stomach.

"Just some veggies and a book by a local author," Shannon replied shortly. Then even she put her head back down to her phone.

I got the distinct feeling I was unwanted here. I decided to get right to the point. “Hey, so I know I haven’t been around a lot, but I wanted to tell you that I never did anything with Chatham. I didn’t even like him. I know Beverly isn’t happy with me, but I still want to be a part of the group. I didn’t think the comment on my article was fair. Any support would be encouraged.” I felt my throat tighten as I finished. There it was. I did it.

Six pairs of confused eyes looked up at me like I was a two-headed monster.

“I would really rather not talk about Beverly behind her back,” Shannon said.

“I wasn’t hoping to do that. Not at all. I just wanted to set a few things straight and let you all know the truth. I never had any interest in Chatham.”

“Well, I still would rather not talk about Beverly without her here. I’m really not into that.”

The others nodded their heads in unison.

And just like that I knew this was a terrible mistake. My stomach sank. How did I ever think they would include me back into their group? They would not break their alliance to Beverly. Even if they thought the comment on my article was wrong, they weren’t going to admit it, let alone do anything about it. They were safe together, safe in numbers in their unjust treatment toward me.

“Okay, well, I just wanted to let you know and see if you saw the article.” I stood up, slung my purse around my shoulder, and tightened my ponytail.

Their eyes glanced on me, their eyebrows up; I could almost feel them judging me. A few mumbled murmurs goodbye and then eyes back on phones.

I walked out of the farmers' market, not even stopping when a customer from the bookshop waved at me from across the market. I had to get out of there. I felt rejected and stupid for putting myself out there.

Rejection like this hurt me more than most people because it brought up all kinds of complicated feelings, feelings about not having parents. University had been the most normal my life had ever been. Shortly after being born, I was put up for adoption, but no one adopted me, so I was put into the system. My mom moved and I have no idea who my dad was. I went from foster home to foster home, from social worker to social worker. Nothing in my life was constant, and I had no sense of who I was, where I came from, or where I was going.

Elementary school passed as a string of avoidance—hours of avoidance turned to days of avoidance, which turned to months of avoidance, and eventually years of avoidance. I was avoiding people, school, and taking responsibility for anything in my life.

I didn't bother making friends because what was the point? Nobody in my life stayed for long, so I made no effort at connection or friendships. Books became my friends, my escape, my world. I read books all day long, at home, at recess, and in class. I read instead of listening or participating in class. Books were my mechanism of disappearance and I was addicted—addicted to the stories that were far from my life, to the narrative, and to worlds far away and vastly different from my world where I didn't belong.

I handed nothing in. I failed tests. I sat outside the principal's office. I followed the main rules and guidelines of behaviour at school and in class, though, but only raised my hand to ask if I had to go to the washroom. I did try once: the time they made me do tests to see if I had learning problems. The tests showed I was above most people in my grade. Teacher after teacher tried convincing me to try. My academic capability drove teachers and principles mad. My defiance was passive and secretive. Like a knight wielding their last dull sword, I was wielding the only power I had. I would not do what was asked of me. I was committed to remaining in the world of books.

Now, as I left the park and walked along the waterfront toward the estuary, the sting of rejection felt much the same as when I was six years old and was told I was moving foster homes again. It hurt. I was glad I had planned to go to the estuary. Being in nature was the best way I knew to heal myself from the hurt of rejection and loneliness—that and walking. I would walk to the estuary despite it being several kilometres away. Hopefully moving my legs combined with time in the forest would soothe the pain of rejection.

I gazed out to the glassy calm ocean as I walked along the harbour. I looked at the colossal yachts and fantasized about living on a yacht instead of in the yellow house. I walked past a boat holding four healthy-looking, tanned, and leathery older adults with white hair. They sipped red wine from oversized wine glasses and nibbled cheese and grapes from a wooden board. For a second, I felt a lightness of what it would be like to be retired and sailing from port to port by boat. The thought gave me a momentary break from the pain of rejection from earlier.

An hour and a half later, I entered the trail to the estuary. The trail was lined with tropical-looking sword ferns and felt worlds away from the city. The massive ferns and enormous cedar trees looked like a tropical forest from the dinosaur days. Eventually the forest opened to a clearing where the Doveport River met the Pacific Ocean—one of my favourite places.

The best part of the estuary was that it was different every visit. Depending on the tide, it was sometimes a clear, freshwater river where you could swim and see down to the pebbled bottom. Other times, the tide was incoming, bringing with it brackish water and gifts from the sea: seaweed, crabs, and salty and opaque ocean water.

It was too cold to swim today, but I fondly remembered many summer days spent reading and swimming there. Today, I needed to walk, to process what was happening in the house and to my social life, and to get over losing friends and being rejected. There was nothing fair about it. I knew I had to accept it. I should have been good at acceptance, having been bounced from home to home and not getting to meet my parents no matter how much I wanted to, but some part of me thought that maybe at some point, life would become fair. I knew I should get over that, but hope was always there.

I walked along the trail that paralleled the river. I grounded myself in the present moment by looking at the river, focusing only on my footsteps, and breaths in and out. The path passed an expansive field that used to hold five big houses of the Salish Peoples. The field was still burned once a year to keep the forest from filling it in. It had a special feel to it. I passed the field and continued along the trail.

Eventually I reached my favourite place in Doveport: a cathedral-like cedar forest next to the river. I often came and sat here, sifting through my thoughts and reflecting on school, day dreaming of the day I would graduate and get a job. I sat with my back against a cedar tree, hoping to borrow some of its strength, and then I heard a strange clicking noise on the other side of my forest cathedral.

Had the spirit followed me? No. Please say it didn't. I couldn't cope with it infiltrating my special place at the estuary; it would be utterly violating. Perhaps my mind was making it up. I took a deep breath and looked around me, hoping I had made it up.

Another clicking sound, louder this time. It was certainly coming from the other side of the grove of cedar trees. It came from a place that was dark and full of bushes. The same welling of fear that had been a familiar feeling since I moved to the house filled my chest now. I had hoped for a break from the fear, but here it was.

What was making the sound? I hoped deeper than I had hoped in a long time that it wasn't the spirit. I decided to investigate; I had to know. I stood up and walked across the cedar clearing toward the strange sound. A strange whooshing and sound of dirt scraping came this time, with no clicking noise. I kept walking toward it. I could hear it, but it was around a massive cedar tree. When I was at the giant cedar tree, I peeked around it.

On the ground on the other side of the cedar tree was something enormous—an eagle, lying on its side, beating one wing against the ground, the other wing bent at a strange angle. I was amazed at its size. I knew eagles were big, but to see one this close was amazing. Its wingspan was nearly my height.

I was scared it would hurt me until I noticed an irregularity on the wing that was strangely still: a round hole, and a whole lot of blood that stained the dirt on the ground.

A bullet wound.

Someone had shot this beautiful bird.

My heart broke for it. How could someone shoot something so beautiful? Something that wouldn't do any harm to a human?

Fear changed to anger. I would help this animal. I would do my best to make up for the actions of a bad human.

I took off my hoodie and pulled from my leather satchel a picnic blanket I had brought for the farmers' market. I inched toward the eagle, looking with admiration but fear at the sharpness of its talons and beak. In a moment of bravery, I threw the blanket over the bird. Its movement stopped. I stepped closer and threw my jacket over the blanket.

It was then that I heard a sound behind me. I whirled around.

An enormous white dog with long fur stood beside a tiny woman. She had grey hair and cobalt blue eyes.

"Oh, dear," she said, looking at the poor creature under the blanket.

"It's been shot and I don't have a car," I explained.

"I do. Do you want me to take it somewhere? You can come along too if you want, dear."

"Yes, that would be great. I think there's a rescue centre for birds just outside of town."

"Okay, but you'll have to carry it."

"Do you think its claws will get me?"

"It might. But it seems more subdued under the blanket."

I inched closer to the blanketed bird, which now was now motionless and quiet. I felt bad for the poor creature, wishing I could communicate to it my good intentions.

My heart beat quickly as I got within a foot of it and saw the dark pool of blood on the dirt. In one swift motion, I put my arm over the blanket and scooped it into my arms. It was heavy, and I walked with it as quickly as I could, the woman and dog following behind.

We arrived at the woman's car—a tiny white hatch back—and she opened the back. I put the blanketed bird down and closed it. A dog gate in the back of the car ensured the eagle was constrained to the back of the car if it panicked. The dog sat in the middle seats, and I got in the passenger seat. We headed down the highway, an unlikely foursome—two humans, one dog, and an eagle—travelling down the highway in a tiny car.

When we got to the Doveport Wildlife Rescue Centre, a woman in khakis used a big net to get the eagle out of the back of the car and into the rescue centre building.

"No promises he'll make it, but we'll do our best," she told us. She took down my number and said she would call if there was good news. I grabbed one of their cards from the counter. The woman with white hair drove me home. I walked up the steps and into the yellow house.

≈

Later that night, hot water fell over my shoulders and I crawled into bed with a fiction book not for school. The day had drained me physically and emotionally. What had I expected from those girls? Really, I should have known Beverly is a more valuable friendship than I. Beverly had a big car, a house with a guest room filled with pillows and little shampoos, and a swimming pool out the back. I had a house that was drafty and haunted.

Then I thought of the eagle with the hole in its wing. I couldn't stop thinking about its eyes and how vulnerable it looked unable to move or fly. How scared it had seemed when I saw it last at the animal rescue centre. I asked myself repeatedly: How could someone shoot such a beautiful bird? What makes someone do something that evil? Human beings were horrible. I recognized this as black-and-white thinking—a thinking trap and not good. I began to try to prevent myself from falling into a spiral of anxiety or sadness, but in that moment I lacked the energy to examine the incident in a more balanced way.

As I read my book, an idea came that made me feel immediately better. Tomorrow, I would take a break from school and do my coursework from home. I would put a few days distance between me and those girls. I was too humiliated to face them. *I would only miss one day of class,* I told myself. *Just one*. I would go back as soon as this had blown over and the rejection felt less raw. I pulled the heavy covers over me and settled onto the pillows. The thought of not going back to school made me feel calmer and uplifted. *Just one day,* I said again to myself.

Chapter 12

Hannah

September 29, 1887

It was a Thursday morning in late September, and the children were at school. I moved the broom over the floor in the entranceway and caught a glimpse of myself in the mirror. My face was angular; my upper arms had tones of definition where before they were soft. My shoulders were stronger. I felt strong in body, but weak in mind. September brought routine, each day like the last. Days stretched out alongside one another; weeks passed quickly.

There was comfort in structured days compared to the openness of summer. The days had rhythm. Mornings were spent in a flurry of readying the children for school, daytime chores, and keeping the house going, then dinner in the evening and books and baths at night. I got used to staying on top of my usual chores, as well as Richard's: hauling pails of water, chopping wood, making kindling, and keeping the fire going at all hours when the weather got cool. But the rhythm of routine didn't stop my grief. I missed Richard every day, every moment. We all missed his absence from the house and our lives.

I carried a basket of dirty clothes out to the back garden. I filled up a bucket with water and began the washing that took hours each week. I began with Alice's dress. I submerged it and moved it up and down over the washboard. I scrubbed hard at the green lines that were all over it, evidence of constantly playing in the grass. When it was done, I submerged Tristan's grey shirt, which had lead stains from pencil marks on paper. When I got to Emerson's trousers, my heart sank. They were nearly thread bare, and I could picture how they hung on his ankles. He desperately needed new ones. I was smart at mending the children's clothing, but sometimes mending wasn't enough. There reached a time when an article of clothing was no longer usable. Many of our clothes were at that point. My dresses were tired and out of fashion, but that didn't matter. I had to find a way to buy the children clothes.

Every bit of the pension went to oats, flour, sugar, and milk and the house. But we still owed more. There was simply nothing extra for clothing. I tried to enjoy the bird song and not fret over paper money and coins and the holes in the clothing I worked around and tried not to widen. I tried to enjoy my hands in the warm water and my feet in the cool grass. When each piece of clothing had been moved over the washboard and washed, I hung them so the sun could do the drying.

I walked inside the house, thinking of the ways I had devised to make money. For several weeks, I had been thinking more seriously about using the camera to make money. At first, it had seemed frivolous and fanciful, but the more I thought about it, the more it seemed possible. A portrait studio was an obvious way I could make money from the camera, but the thought of making a portrait studio from nothing made my head spin and stomach queasy. Besides, who would look after the children after school and what if it didn't work out after I had poured money into it? Did other women have this trouble of deciding how to make money? I pushed thoughts of other peoples' lives out of my mind and moved on to my next task.

Household chores were in no short supply. I was happy to have something to keep my hands and mind occupied. I decided to make some pies from the apples in the yard. Perhaps I could sell or barter with several of the pies. Trouble was, we were clean out of butter and milk. I couldn't believe how much food we consumed. I exhaled and grabbed my hat and gloves. I left the house, closing the wooden door behind me.

The sun shone, but the wind robbed the sun of any heat it had created. I walked briskly up the hill to Tong's General Store. I arrived out the front of the building and stepped onto the porch. In the big windows, among the stacked cans and humdrum food items, something lovely caught my eye.

A hat. The most beautiful hat I had ever seen.

Wide turned-back brim and black velvet, it was elaborately decorated with a dark purple ribbon, black rooster feather, and a few ostrich plumes. It was magnificent.

I pushed the white door and a bell tinkled as I entered the store. When my eyes adjusted to the dim light after the bright sunshine outside, I saw the hat even clearer. I couldn't resist and picked it up. The velvet was cool and soft in my hands, and the feathers were fanciful. Just looking at them made me happy. I turned over the small rectangular paper tag: $15. My brow furrowed. I carefully placed the hat back on its stand and put my hands at my side. I walked past stacked flour bags, stacked cans, and headed toward the butter. I picked up a cool stick and a small glass bottle of milk. A pair of men's shoes caught my eye. I thought of the holes in Albert's shoes and grabbed them. My child would not have holes in his shoes.

I took one last look at the hat, went to the wooden counter, and placed down my items.

"Morning, Hannah."

"Mr. Tong," I said, but nothing more. I was in no mood for conversation.

"Comes to one dollar, seventy-five cents," he said.

I rummaged in my change purse and pulled out the coins. There were not enough. I was short twenty-two cents. How could this be? I was sure I had enough. I always wrote down my expenses carefully in my little red notebook at home. Then I remembered that we needed to buy wood, and so we were off three dollars. We would be very short until the next pension check arrived in the mail. My cheeks got hot and red.

"I'll put back the butter," I said tersely. I would have to make it with no butter. Another pension cheque would come in five days, and I would get butter then. It was more important for the children to have milk with their porridge in the morning. Only if there was leftover milk would I put it in my tea.

"I can put it on credit if you want, Hannah." Mr. Tong looked at me with caring eyes, further crinkling the lines surrounding them.

"No, thank you. That won't be necessary. I have simply left my coins at home." It was a lie, but I felt hardened and suddenly angry at my situation. Never in my life had I been short money at the store. I was mortified. I grabbed the shoes and the milk and left, the bell dinging behind me.

When I returned from the general store, I lay down on my bed and cried. I cried for Richard, cried for the unfairness of life, cried for missing England, cried for the children who didn't have a father, and a cried for being short coins at the general store. When no more tears would come, I got up and looked at the dark mark my tears had left on the pillow. Then I stood up straight, threw some water on my face from the basin on the dresser, and fixed my hair.

I would get on with my day. Nothing was bringing Richard back, and it was up to me to lead this family. I made myself a cup of tea without milk and sat by the front window. I looked out to the ocean while I sipped the hot liquid.

I had to act soon. I was done with living tightly. I would not live like this. I've never had a great deal of money in my life, but I never had this little either. It was a constant, heavy burden of lack. I longingly thought back to the time where days or weeks passed and I didn't think about money because we had enough. Days where I didn't scribble numbers in my red notebook, trying to stretch out a small amount.

I thought of the actions needed to open a photographic parlour. My head spun thinking about it. My spinning head beat the angry, stalled feeling of being helpless. I needed some way of making money myself. I would not remarry, I would not give up the house, and I would not deprive my children of a good life. The thought of starting a photographic studio, although scary, also excited me. Perhaps if I did something exciting for money it would feel less like a job.

In that moment, I made up my mind: I would have my own photographic studio.

I took out my red notebook and a quill pen. I sat by the window and made a list of steps that needed to be done. Learning to use the camera was the first on the list. I went into the kitchen and my mind started planning next steps while my hands chopped apples into bite-sized chunks for the pie.

≈

Several hours after I decided I would open a photographic studio, the wooden front door opened. I heard shoes coming off, bags being dropped, and voices talking over one other. Emerson, Tristan, and Alice were home from school.

"Hello, darlings!" I yelled from the kitchen. "I made apple pies and I thought we could eat them on a picnic blanket in the sunshine."

"Yum!" Alice was the first one to the kitchen. She grabbed the picnic blanket and ran outside. Emerson and Tristan trailed behind her.

"It's like we're at the beach again, but we're at home," Alice said, with pie filling on her cheeks and nose somehow, crumbs gathering where her dress covered her crossed legs.

"Yes, a home picnic. How was school?" I asked.

"Good, Mother. It is good to be back and summer feels a long way away," Tristan answered.

"I wish it was still summer. Kids are making fun of the holes in my shoes," said Emerson, a sad look on his face.

"I bought you new shoes today, Emerson. Pay those children no mind. They are rude and poorly raised. Keep your head held high and keep showing kindness to all folks. That will get you far," I said while feeling enraged at those unkind children. I swiftly changed the subject. "I have something to show you all and I need your help." I pulled the box camera from its box that sat behind me.

"Ohhh! What is it, Mother?" Alice said as she crawled over. Pie crumbs dumped from her dress onto the picnic blanket.

"It's a box camera. I am learning how to use it, and I need subjects to practise on."

"Me, Mother! I can sit very still!" Alice ran over to the wisteria tree and stood with her hands clasped in front of her.

Tristan's eyes opened wide and he inched closer to me. He looked carefully at the camera and said, "Is that the lens?" He pointed but did not touching the brass circular hole.

"Yes, dear."

"Father showed me it once, but I did not know we still had it," Tristan said thoughtfully.

"Yes, it belonged to your father. I'm going to learn to use it and have a photographic parlour." I sounded more confident than I felt.

I walked with the camera toward Alice at the wisteria tree. I held the box camera in front of me and opened the shutter of the lens, trying to project the image on the ground glass. But the image of Alice was dim and nearly impossible to see. I pulled the ground glass back and opened it wider to try to focus better. Once it slid into place, I closed the shutter. Then I started the process again. Focusing the image was impossibly tedious. The movements had to be minute or the image went too focused or too unfocused. It was made harder by my moving subjects.

This was only the first small step toward my photographic studio, and it was a battle. This was going to be hard. I took a deep breath and opened the shutter of the lens once again.

I didn't know how I was going to do it, but somehow, I would keep going. I thought of the butter I had to forego this week and looked harder at the image. I tried not to think of all the steps ahead and tried to solely focus on keeping the camera still and capturing the image of Alice and the wisteria vines clearly on the plate.

I clicked the shutter closed and began the process all over again.

Chapter 13

Brooke

October 31, 2017

Libraries were my favourite places. I loved their walls of books and stairways leading to more walls of books. I love all the books: books stacked, books on display, books on posters, books on rolling carts. More books than I could read in a lifetime, and I could take home whichever ones caught my eye. As a kid, and even now, I usually left with a backpack full of books and a delicious feeling of anticipation.

I loved that libraries were one of the last places in society where you could exist without having to hand over money. Maybe my love of libraries also stemmed from a happy, childhood memory with a foster family, one of eating those light brown teddy bear cookies while sitting with a group of children and listening to a librarian read books during some library program.

It was the afternoon of Halloween, and I stepped into the Doveport Public Library. The Doveport Library was grand, all glass windows and smooth lines. Enormous ceilings gave it a palatial feel. I headed straight up the twirling staircase toward the fiction section. I wandered through the aisles leisurely, pulling out titles that caught my eye.

Browsing the shelves of the fiction section was like being in a giant bookstore, where any of the books could be mine for free. I picked three books and tucked them carefully under my arm. The thought of going home was as unappealing as finishing a boring book. I didn't want to deal with the constant feeling of being on edge.

On a whim, I sat in one of the black leather armchairs and cracked open one of the books. I had nearly forgotten the outside world and that I was in the library at all when a warm, deep voice brought me to the present. At first, I thought they were speaking to someone else, but when I looked up, he was looking at me. He repeated his remark.

"What are you reading?"

I don't normally speak to other library patrons and must have looked slightly confused. I tried not to let my eyes visibly widen when I looked at who was speaking to me.

He was a guy, about my age, in a button up shirt and green khaki pants. He had an open smile and stubble.

"A new historical fiction," I said, feeling my face go red.

"I love fiction. I study accounting at Harbourview University, but fiction is a different world. A welcome break from numbers. Who's your favourite author?"

"Ugh, I like a lot of different writers. Classics and some contemporary authors." I didn't want to get into detail. I felt my cheeks reddening and getting hotter.

"Variety is good. There's an author reading by a local Doveport author at Harbourview next week. Would you want to check it out with me?"

His smile was wide, his teeth white and straight. Dimples indented his cheeks slightly. His eyes were blue—an unusual colour for his dark brown hair. It was as if I was in a movie and this movie-star gorgeous guy was asking me out. At first, it was all very exciting and then several images interrupted the moment.

Beverly swerving on the road toward me flashed through my mind. The apple hitting me in the lecture. The loss of my group of friends and the graffiti on the bathroom door. I felt overwhelmed and sick.

"I can't. I have to go, actually." I stood up, closed my book, and started toward the twirled staircase. I stopped at the top and turned around when I heard him speaking. He seemed immediately concerned, but he didn't persist, not like they do in the movies.

"I'm sorry if I was too forward. I didn't mean to upset you. You're unique, is all. And it's cool to find someone into books other than university ones. Here's my number in case you change your mind." He quickly scribbled something on a receipt and hesitantly stepped toward me. I reached out and took the receipt from his hand. His fingers were very warm as they brushed slightly against mine.

"Ok, ah, thanks" I said, and descended the staircase.

At the bottom, I took a furtive glance back up the stairs. He was gone. My stomach sank. I had missed an opportunity. With the empty feeling of having missed out on something very valuable, I pushed open the heavy library doors and stepped outside. The feeling of missing out reminded me of being indoors on a sunny summer day. I walked down Doveport's tree-lined main street toward the yellow house.

≈

I turned the key in the wooden door and entered the house. I dropped my leather satchel and went into the kitchen. I sat at the kitchen table with my elbows on the table and my head cradled in my hands. I couldn't stop thinking of the library guy's blue eyes and dark brown hair, his earnest questions and genuine interest in me, and that he was in the library getting books too. What had I done by refusing to get to know him? I had never had a boyfriend but wasn't opposed to meeting someone. That had been the perfect opportunity and I had blown it.

Beverly's behaviour was getting to me. Beverly and the strange yellow house were bringing up issues from my childhood. They were affecting my life.

I turned on my laptop and opened my school email account. Eleven emails: five from the advisor and the rest from professors about my attendance to lectures or about outstanding assignments.

The one day I promised myself off school after the day at the farmers' market had turned into two days. Then two days turned into going to school once a week. I told myself it was temporary. That nobody would miss me and that I was caught up in my assignments. I would work from home and get back to school soon. But after a few weeks, I felt disconnected from classes. When I did show up to a class, I was behind and didn't follow what was going on. So, I started attending even less. It was a vicious cycle. A bad pattern. I knew this but couldn't fix it.

I knew avoiding school was a Band-Aid solution to anxiety—something that covered it up but didn't fix the root cause of it. It was not good for my mindset. Anxiety controlled me and was stopping me from living my life. I knew avoiding class was harmful and would get worse, but I didn't know how to fix it.

I tried to remember back to what Ms. Ellis, my high school counsellor, used to tell me about coping with anxiety. What would she have told me to do? Start small. I remembered her soft voice telling me to start small while I sat in the soft chair in her bright office filled with plants.

I tried my best to think of ways to start small, but my mind drifted to Ms. Ellis, high school and how I ended up at university.

Despite reading books instead of doing school work, I was eventually pushed to high school. I arrived the first day with a book, ready to do my usual routine, and I did. I read books during class time. I read books during lunch beneath a window in the hallway of an upper floor. I read books while waiting for the bus and while on the bus. While most students were in the worlds inside their phone, I was living in the worlds inside my books. High school teachers seemed to care less than elementary ones. They only tried to get me to do work and get out of my book for a few days before they told me they were letting the principal and counsellor know and were emailing home. After that, they mostly left me alone.

In Grade 9, a young lady with straight, shoulder-length chestnut hair appeared at my math class door. All the students looked over at her expectantly, waiting for her to call a name.

"Brooke, there's someone here to talk with you. Please go with them," the teacher said.

I looked up from *The Chrysalids*, closed it, and took it with me as I walked to the door and stepped into the hallway with this new woman.

"John Wyndham—solid," she said. Her brown eyes had crinkles on the sides of them, but she was still younger than most teachers.

I was taken aback. I was secretly surprised that she knew the author I was reading and didn't rush into an interrogation of my lack of completing and submitting schoolwork. Still, she couldn't be trusted, and I wouldn't open up to her. I didn't need help from well-meaning educators and helping professional types.

"I'm Ms. Ellis, the new school counsellor here. I was wondering if you could help me put some scholarship posters up around the school. Thought it would be helpful to have help from someone who knows their way around."

"Sure," I said flatly.

I was fully aware this was an obvious ploy to talk with me, but I would follow along harmlessly in the spirit of missing math. I wasn't going to tell her anything or let her think she was helping me in any way, though. *Let's see what this one has to say,* I thought to myself, not expecting anything and continuing with my passive disobedience.

We walked down the hall toward the bulletin boards in the front foyer of the school. I knew the main reason she had come to my math class. After school one day, the week before, I had lit a small fire by the rocky creek that rushed behind the school, lined with cedar trees. I was back after being suspended, and she had been tasked to "check in" with me. I was used to people coming and trying to help me.

I nearly forgot my plan to ignore her when she didn't ask me how I was and how things were going for me lately and instead said, "Have you heard of Wyndham's book *Web*? It's lesser-known science fiction and very cool . . . if you don't mind spiders hunting in packs and like Wyndham's style, that is. I enjoyed it, but books are a personal thing."

I nearly replied with interest but caught myself. Instead, I quickly reined in my interest and remembered that most people who came into my life left it just as quickly and that deep down I wasn't worthy of being loved. After all, even my parents didn't want to keep me. Why would anyone else want to love me?

"Huh. Haven't heard of it," I replied, not looking over at her.

When we reached the front foyer bulletin board, she said, "Here's some tape."

Ms. Ellis came to see me once a week, and we talked in her office, which had one wall of windows and every spare space held a plant. Plants cascaded off her desk and the side table. Plants with big red flowers with yellow middles. It was like being in a jungle and it calmed me down somehow. It was a welcomed change from the sterile, institutional feel of the rest of the school. The chairs were soft and I could lean back on them.

She didn't force me to change but, over many conversations, helped me see that by reading in class and refusing to do any work, I wasn't succeeding in taking revenge on anyone. The only person I was hurting was myself and my chances of further education. I was narrowing my options for the future.

So, I tried something new at school. I started doing work and handing it in; I started putting a genuine effort into what I was doing. At first, I was self-conscious to be trying in school. I felt raw and exposed in my vulnerability, like if I failed classes now, I might as well stop coming to school because now I was genuinely trying.

But I didn't fail; actually, the opposite happened. Papers and tests appeared on my desk with passing grades and comments like, "Excellent work," "Great insight," and "Well done on this." Weeks after I got passing grades, I started getting much higher than passing grades. By the second semester of Grade 9, my lowest mark was 89%.

One day in Grade 12, Ms. Ellis asked me if I was applying to university. I told her no and that there was no point. She didn't ask again, but one night, I looked up Harbourview University's entrance requirement and thought I might as well try. If I got in, I didn't have to go. I applied for a few programs, including a bachelor of arts in English. Ms. Ellis offered to help me apply for the Tuition Waiver grant for children of the foster care system.

One afternoon, I clicked the big blue "submit" button on the application page. Outside the window, an eagle surfed the wind, like a skier carving turns down a mountain. Maybe it was a good omen.

A few weeks after applying to Harbourview University, I showed up at Ms. Ellis's door holding an email on my phone. She looked up and stopped typing on her keyboard.

"I got in," I told her.

A broad grin covered her face. "Well done. That was all you." Ms. Ellis always made it seem like you had done all the work, even if she had helped you realize it was possible, like a hockey player setting up a play and giving all the credit to the forward who had scored the goal. Before meeting Ms. Ellis, I was drifting down a river going wherever the current took me. I was passive in every way. Ms. Ellis showed me I could to steer my own boat, and she showed me that what I did made a difference. So, I made some decisions and learned to steer. Turned out, taking charge of my life made it better and made me feel better. I still had deep-seated abandonment issues and felt unworthy of good things because I had no parents, but learning to steer was a big step to things getting much better for me.

"Thanks for encouraging me to apply," I said, remembering how I had talked to her just to humour her.

"That was all you," she repeated, as if she had never meant anything more in her life.

To my surprise and delight, I was going to university.

Now, I sat in my house thinking of all the university classes I missed. How could I start small now? It was Halloween. Maybe I could see Jade. I wasn't ready to face anyone from school, but Jade I could face. So, I texted her, and we made plans to meet at Hawthorne's later that night. I felt a bit better. I had taken a small step to fight the avoidance. A small step.

≈

"Why not have a séance?" Jade asked. We were at Hawthorne's, at our favourite pool table by the window looking out to the street. Every square inch of the wooden windowsill was covered with names, quotes, and dates, either engraved or written in sharpie.

That night, through the window, we could see the moon hanging above the street, poking out from a hole in the clouds. We were too old to trick-or-treat, but too young to grant candy, and neither of us liked house parties. That left us together at Hawthorne's playing pool and discussing how to spend Halloween night.

"I doubt it would work," I replied. I sipped a beer and knocked a yellow solid into a corner pocket. I shot at a solid red and scratched.

"Worth a try. Can't hurt. It would be fun." Jade knocked a blue stripe into the corner pocket and took a big swill of beer.

I lined up my shot and took it before answering, "What if it makes it worse?"

"Doubt it would. Might find out more about whatever it is. Someone once told me Halloween and the fall is the most likely time for paranormal activity. Something about the earth being closest to the land of the spirits."

"Oh, great. More activity in the house. Not that I need any more action there. I'm constantly on high alert as is."

"Let's give it a try. You have candles?"

"Yeah," I said, unconvinced.

Jade sunk the black ball into the side pocked.

We skulled our beer, sank the last balls, and walked out into Halloween night in Doveport. I dreaded the séance we were about to embark on.

≈

The moon rippled on the black ocean surface as we walked home. Bathed in moonlight, the yellow house looked sinister, older than it ever had, a true character house. The chimneys gave it an old-timey look, and the storm shutters further aged it.

I turned my key and pushed the door open. I flicked on a light, and we dropped our purses. Jade pulled two beer out of her backpack. The hiss and then cracking sound of the cans opening broke the silence.

She handed me one and I took a sip. It was bubbly and smooth. I took another one.

"We need candles," Jade said, not missing a beat. "Spirits like heat and light. And it's got to be a soft light like candles."

"Yeah, okay," I said, and took my beer into the kitchen, having a few swigs on the way. I opened the cupboard under the sink and lowered myself to my knees. I leaned into the cupboard and began rummaging around for candles when I had a strange feeling someone was behind me. I pulled myself out of the cupboard and turned around. Jade was right there.

"Whew, you scared me! I didn't hear you come in from the living room."

"What's this?" She was standing beside me now, looking at the note on the counter.

"Oh, I found it in this weird little cupboard. Must have been from the previous tenants. The landlord told me they were always hosting parties and didn't pay rent on time."

"*'I hope you are brave and not superstitious. This house is full secrets.'* Sounds like they were having some weird things happen to them. Maybe they gave notice and had enough. Were they mad you were moving in?"

"Not sure. They weren't here when I did my viewing, so I never got to talk to them."

"Hmm, creepy. Maybe they're the ones making the sounds in the house. You know, coming around and trying to scare you. Either way, you really are having some bad luck these days."

"Yeah, well. Things haven't come easy. This is no different. I just want to finish this year of school and graduate. Here, found some candles," I said.

"Let's go to the living room," Jade said and started into the living room.

We sat in front of the window seat, which looked out onto darkness. An eerie feeling crept over me.

"I'm not sure about this, Jade. I have to keep living here—alone. I won't be able to sleep if anything weird happens.

"Come on. I'll stay over tonight. This is perfect. Full moon. Halloween night. One of the oldest houses in the city. Where's your sense of adventure?"

"All right, but let's make it quick. I don't even know what to do."

"Light the candles and I'll start."

I flicked a lighter and held it to the wick of the four white tea lights I had found under the sink.

We sat in soft, eerie light. I noticed the fireplace was filled with cobwebs that I hadn't noticed in the daylight. The inside was stained black; I wondered how many fires it had seen. How strange it would have been to make a fire for heat rather than turning the dial on a baseboard heater. A shiver ran down my back. I pulled up my hood as Jade began speaking.

"I call on whatever spirit or entity is in this house to bring your energy to our circle. I respectfully ask that you honour us with your presence this evening. Whatever you are, give us some sign. Make yourself known."

How did Jade know how to do a séance? The longer I knew Jade, the more surprises she revealed. I wished she had eased us into it a bit, started with something smaller—not asking it to make itself known. But there was no easing anything with Jade.

I looked at Jade; she looked at me. Then I glanced around the room but didn't notice anything out of the ordinary. No noises. No sounds at all, other than the light pitter patter of rain that must have just started.

Then something happened. A shiver ran up my spine and I noticed a drastic change in the temperature.

"Nothing is happening," I said. I decided I didn't want to continue.

"It is, though. It just got super cold in here. It takes the spirit some time to make itself known. Spirits are just bundles of energy. Let's give it a minute." Jade's eyes were wide. She was loving this, while I wanted to be anywhere but here. I did not know how I was going to sleep after this.

"Let's make popcorn and watch a scary movie on my laptop." I didn't want to admit to her how scared I was.

"We need to wait." Jade's eyes were even wider.

Still no sound. Just the growing pitter patter of rain on the roof.

"If you're here, make yourself known. We mean no harm."

A car whooshed by on the street. Then a breeze blew through the house. The flames flickered slightly. The lace curtains swayed a little. I was suddenly even colder. I wondered if the draft came from the fireplace when it was windy outside. If this breeze was normal, I didn't notice; I never sat on the floor and had been avoiding the living room completely since all the nonsense smells started coming from here.

But nothing totally dramatic happened. I was fully creeped out now and ready for this to be done. "Nothing is happening. Let's make popcorn."

"Okay, in just a minute. I want to ask one thing: Spirit of the house, answer one question. If it's a no, tap once. If it's a yes, tap twice. Is there something you want from us, something you need to continue your journey to the next life?"

No sound. No breeze. Not even the sound of a car outside.

"Nothing more is happening. Movie time," I said.

"Ugh, okay," Jade said. "Let me close the séance."

It was then that we heard a tap. Three seconds later, we heard a second one. They weren't loud taps but definite sounds.

"Thank you, spirit. Please move on, now. You aren't wanted in this house. Go on to whatever is next for you. Thank you for that answer of yes. Now, move on. And I thereby close this séance," Jade replied.

"What was that noise?" I asked, immobile and rapt in fear.

"Definitely something outside. We should go investigate."

"I don't think I can. Let's just watch a movie and forget about it."

"I want to know, though. I've never actually had a spirit answer back during a séance before."

"All right, but let's do it quickly. I want this Halloween to be more lighthearted."

Jade stood up and started walking across the living room. I blew out the candles and followed her to the front door.

Chapter 14

Hannah

November 7, 1887

I held the photograph to the light. It was a portrait of Tristan beside the living room fireplace. He showed a toothy smile and stood straight with his hands behind his back. It was good to see him smiling. His smiles had been less since losing his father.

I stood in our living room, behind a table I had turned into a makeshift photographic workspace. The black box camera sat on the table, as well as vials of developing chemicals and a thick-spined brown book.

I purchased it at a bookshop downtown for thirty-five cents. It was all about photography and was the best thirty-five cents I have ever spent. It had solutions for all my photographic problems and answers to my photographic questions, and it kept me interested and motivated to keep learning photography. Best of all, I could open it at night once the children went to bed. It was ready to teach me whenever I had ten minutes to spare.

I made notes in my red notebook of things I learned and wanted to easily recall. For example, I learned that putting a dark cloth over my head while taking photos kept light out of the viewing area and let me see the picture more clearly.

The children adored being my subjects, and they were the best subjects one could ask for. Emerson and Tristan enjoyed posing, and

Alice gave me ample practice with movement. She did cartwheels, handstands, and even when she was meant to be sitting still, she moved. It gave me the practice I knew I would need.

Late one night, I taught myself to produce a positive image by contact printing the negative image to sensitized paper sheets. I worked in the kitchen by lamplight. My book was propped open in front of me with the help of a recipe stand; the camera was on the table next to it. When the image of Emerson on the kitchen chair came clear, shivers came over my arms. I had done it. I could finally operate the camera.

I found great pleasure in shooting photographs. My mind settled; my world shrank. All that existed was me, my black box camera, and the subject. The satisfaction of developing the images was a reward almost greater than taking the photographs. I wanted my photographs to be different and catch the viewer's eye. All I wanted to do was to shoot more photographs. If I could make money doing it, all the better. Taking photographs made me more than a widow—I was an artist. I must find a way to keep taking photographs.

I could finally check off the first box on my list of steps to getting a photographic parlour. Now onto the next step: finding a building to use as studio space.

≈

The next morning, while the children were at school, I decided to find space to rent and transform to a studio space. I had been taking photos every spare second, and my work was finally good enough to sell. I was determined to make a living taking photographs. I would do anything it took to make that a reality.

I set off toward the Doveport Harbour. It was a fall day, where the sun had just enough energy to keep me warm. I had dressed in my most traditional dress. I wanted to be taken seriously.

I gazed at the ocean as I walked toward the harbour. I never tired of watching the ever-changing blue mass of water. It was different every day and gave me a sense of calm. It brought me back to the moment and shut out thoughts and plans that cluttered my mind. Today, the ocean was whitecaps as far as the eye could see.

I walked briskly and was soon at the boardwalk that was Doveport's main area of commerce. I walked along and entered a shop that had an empty storefront next to it. It was a butcher shop and the smell of dead meat hit me in the face when I entered. I tried to keep my face neutral as I went to the counter.

"How do you do today, sir?" I asked the red-faced pudgy man behind the counter.

He barely looked up at me as he cut into the body of a pig. "Been worse. What can I get for you today?"

"I'm hoping you could tell me who owns the building next to you."

He didn't look up at all. "That would be me."

"Is it for rent? If so, how much?"

"Who are you asking for?"

"Myself. I am starting a photographic studio, and I need to rent space." The tinny smell of blood was now stronger. The space lacked ventilation and was uncomfortably warm. Lack of windows added to the crowded feeling.

"Hmph," he made a sound dismissively.

"Well, how much is it to rent?"

"I'm not really renting it. I might expand my butcher shop and am waiting to see if I need it."

He didn't look up as one beefy hand covered in shiny blood held the body of the pig and the other pulled a knife through its flesh.

I straightened the front of my dress, brushed my hand down to remove any creases, and adjusted my hat to sit straight. My whole body felt warm, and angry thoughts invaded my mind.

"Thank you, sir, and good day," I said, though I did not mean it. I would not show him my annoyance. I held my head up high, brought my shoulders back and strode out of his shop.

My body still felt hot, and my heart raced. My head felt pressurized, like it might explode. Never had someone dismissed me in such a rude fashion. I took some deep breaths and tried to let the anger dissipate in the cool air. I was grateful to be away from the stifling air of the butcher shop and its repulsive smell of dead animals.

I continued along the boardwalk and thought of the butter that I could not buy. I thought of Emerson's thread-bare trousers. I thought of Alice's round brown eyes and the way they crinkled when she smiled, and I thought of the photograph of Tristan smiling in front of the fireplace. I would keep trying.

I walked along the boardwalk until I saw another vacant shop. This time, the shop next to it was the local newspaper. I stepped in. A man sat at a desk with a typewriter, smoking a cigarette and looking out the window.

"Afternoon, ma'am. What brings you in today?"

"I'm looking to rent a storefront and wondering if you know who owns the one next door." His eyes moved down my chest, to my waist, and back up to my chest. When he met my eyes, he gave me a sheepish look.

"The man who owns it also owns the general store five blocks down the boardwalk." His hand moved in slow motion as he brought the cigarette to his mouth.

"Thank you," I said, feeling lightheaded from the cigarette smoke that hung thickly in the air. I turned on my heel and left through the door as quickly as possible. My shoulders drooped. Finding space felt impossible. Why would nobody rent to me? I took a big breath of sea air and kept walking down the boardwalk.

When I arrived at the general store, I looked up at the sign. This was not my usual general store, as I found their prices high and their products unnecessarily high quality. They didn't carry standard brands, but only higher-priced ones.

I straightened my dress, put my shoulders back, and entered the store. It smelled of expensive perfumes and was bright with lights. A jukebox in the corner played music so loud it was hard to think. I couldn't see anyone at the counter but made my way there. I stood at the counter and noticed someone crouched under it.

"Good afternoon," I said.

Nothing for a moment, and then the man slowly stood up. He had grey hair and a white apron. His nose was big, and his cheeks streaked with tiny blue green veins.

For the third time that day, I stated my business. "I'm looking for a store front to rent. I'm inquiring as to the cost of the storefront down beside the newspaper. The man in the newspaper shop said it's owned by this store."

"Yes, it is. I'm not sure of our plans for it yet, so it's not for rent." His beady black eyes bore into me.

"When will you know the plans for it?" I asked, wondering if this was indeed the truth or if he simply didn't fancy renting to me.

"I don't know. My son is doing most of the management work. I don't know when we will decide. Perhaps try inquiring down at the ravine for a building to rent."

My cheeks burned. The ravine was a low lying, muddy tidal flat and a short walk from the tidy boardwalk where we stood. It was filled with seaweed, garbage, and other refuse that people had tossed. The ravine held several rickety wooden houses without foundations that often flooded with ocean water at high tides. Many leaned sideways. Worst of all, many of these dilapidated buildings were brothels.

"The ravine will not be suitable for my purposes," I said as I turned and left the store. My ears burned, and my head ached.

I strode along the boardwalk the way I had come, hoping to put as much distance as possible between myself and the store. When I was far enough away, I sat on a patch of grass to collect my thoughts. Why was this so difficult? I never had this much trouble with practical things when Richard was alive. Why now? Did some bad omen overcome me when Richard died? Was some evil force at work?

I looked out at the water in the harbour. It was now royal blue colour, and the white caps had grown bigger. While musing about Richard and our trip here and interactions I had with men while with him, a thought came to me. I was not cursed or having any bad luck. I was having trouble renting space because I was a woman and I did not have a man with me.

The realization hit me like a sack of flour. That was it. I was not being taken seriously because I was not a man. Anger welled up in me. This was not something I could change. Richard would have been angry about this too, but he was not here. No matter how unjust it was, there was nothing I could do. This was an unchangeable part of the world in which I lived. I stood up and began walking toward my house, which was safe, warm, and where I was looked upon as no less than anyone else because of my gender.

Chapter 15

Brooke

October 31, 2017

Jade and I faced the wooden door of the yellow house. The rain was harder now, the pitter patter louder and faster. The smell of sulphur from the extinguished candles hung in the air. We contemplated opening the door to investigate the two taps we heard after asking if there was something the spirit wanted to tell us. Two taps had meant yes. But yes to what? And why did Jade insist on going outside to see what had caused them?

"I wonder if whatever made the noise is still there," Jade asked.

I did not understand her detached curiosity. I was petrified. "I really hope it isn't, and I would really rather not know."

"We have to know. It's always better to know what you're dealing with," Jade said.

"I'm not going to sleep after this," I said.

"You'll be glad we investigated. When you face something you're worried about, it usually isn't as bad as you imagined it being," she said. We both knew she was talking about more than this incident.

"Facing things isn't my strength," I said, feeling vulnerable but the beer made me care less about what I said.

"We'll do it together. Let's go." Jade pulled the door open.

I followed her onto the dark porch. The air was cold and damp. It smelled of rain and felt lightly salty from the nearby ocean. I closed the door behind me; the handle was cold and smooth.

Jade's phone, set to flashlight mode, illuminated the front porch. Nothing was out of place: the chairs that I put there when I moved in were in the same place, the white railings looked the same, and we heard the same sound of rain.

"I don't see anything. Let's go back in," I said.

"Maybe the taps really were from the spirit," she said dreamily. "Maybe it tapped for yes and left the house. Maybe it's gone from the house for good. Maybe we've stopped all the crazy things happening in the house," she said, grinning.

I held onto the railing and looked over the porch. I spotted something on the lawn below the railing. "What's that white thing on the lawn?" I asked.

Jade took off down the steps and into the rain. I followed her until we were standing on the lawn, the road behind us, the house in front.

The cause of the taps lay on the grass in front of us. Eggs. Yellow yolks and clear whites with jagged white shells were splattered all over the house.

Someone had thrown two eggs at the house. My house.

One after another, and that was the taps we had heard.

My stomach sank. I thought I didn't want it to be the spirit, but now, I wished it was. Someone had egged my house. I felt violated, gross, and like the house was more hostile than ever. Somehow this rattled me more than the other happenings.

"Who would do this?" I managed to get out.

"I'm sure it was drunk people or random vandals," Jade said, but didn't sound convinced.

"Does Beverly know where I live?" I said, looking straight at Jade.

"I don't know. I hope she wouldn't do this. Let's, for the sake of worry, hope it was kids or teenagers and they're randomly egging houses."

"I hope you're right. Let's do popcorn and a movie," I said and started toward the steps.

We walked up the steps and stepped out of the rain and dark and back into the house. Before closing the door, I turned back and glanced at the empty street. Somehow, I was more scared than when I stepped out of the house minutes before.

≈

The next morning, I awoke in my bed with a dry mouth and pounding behind my eyes. Jade was on the floor on couch cushions and my extra blanket. She looked peaceful and happy and not thirsty or like she had a pounding head. I remembered the night before: the séance, the eggs splattered on the house, and the movie and beer that I now regretted. I still had to clean up the eggs and also had school work to do.

I had to get a handle on the frantic thoughts going through my head. I needed to stop worrying about whatever spirit was in this house. I needed to start going to classes. I needed to get my life back on track.

But I didn't know what I would say when I got back to classes and people asked me where I was. I didn't have a good excuse. I couldn't explain that I was rejected by a group of friends and that someone was harassing me; that wouldn't fly. This was university, not elementary school. Besides, nobody would believe me. The professors were under Beverly's spell as much as our friends.

I got up quietly, as not to wake Jade. I went to the kitchen and filled the kettle with water for tea. Then I put two pieces of bread in the toaster and opened the fridge for jam. I would figure things out today and go to school tomorrow; that was it. Tomorrow was Thursday and the perfect day to return. I felt better being decided. I would just say I was sick or something when people asked. I was mostly caught up in assignments now, so it would be fine. Then I would email my academic advisor and say everything is good and I'm back on track.

Just then the toaster light went out, and the fridge sputtered. I had blown a fuse. I went to the fuse box on the other side of the kitchen and checked for one that was switched. None were. Not this. Not now. Always something. Then something startled me. A jolt of adrenaline surged through me and I turned quickly around. It was Jade.

"You startled me," I said, clutching my hand to my chest.

"What are you doing?" Jade asked.

"Trying to fix a blown fuse."

"Oh, what a bummer. Always something with these old houses," she said.

"Yeah, but the weirdest thing is that none of the switches have been flicked. It must be something else electrical. I'll have to call Brian."

"Okay, well, I've got to go. Studying and all that."

"All right, see you later," I said, still squinting my eyes at the fuse box.

"Hey, you going to come to classes this week?" she asked, her brows furrowed with concern.

I turned away from the fuse box to look at her.

"Yes, I'll be there this week. It's just been . . . hard since, you know, everything with Beverly."

"Yeah, I know. But you're not hurting Beverly or anyone else by not coming to school. You're only hurting yourself," she said as she turned and left.

I watched as the door closed behind her, leaving me alone again in the yellow house.

≈

Brian, the home's owner, was on his way with an electrician to check out the electrical problem. I paced in front of the fireplace. My head swam with thoughts, and my headache morphed into a tiredness and a feeling of needing to do something but not knowing how to start.

I had just sat down at the kitchen table with a book, hoping to distract myself when a loud knock on the front door made me twitch. I walked to the door, let them in, and explained what happened. We went to the fuse box, and I showed them how none were flicked.

"Hmmm, strange," the electrician said. "Looks like it's the wiring. I'm going to have to saw into the wall in the kitchen to expose the wiring."

"All right," Brian said.

I remained with my laptop at the kitchen table to type an assignment.

The electrician went to his truck and came back a few minutes later with a drill and hand saw.

Loud drilling kept me from my typing. I looked up from my work to dust and paper coming out of the wall. He drilled in another spot also and repaired some wiring. Brian swept the drywall and dust into a dustpan and dumped it into a black garbage bag.

Fifteen minutes later, the electrician spoke.

“Wiring is fixed, but I found these.” In his hand, he held a small pair of brown leather shoes—a pair of boy’s shoes, much smaller than my feet. The inside material of the right one was completely missing. The grommets that held the laces had rusted and a few had completely fallen out. Those that remained were dried up and hardened.

“Strange, indeed.” Brian said. “Goes to show how old this place is. People did weird things back in the day. I’ll take them with me.”

I spoke without thinking about it. “Can I keep them?” I couldn’t believe I said it, but I had. My cheeks reddened, and a small surge of panic coursed through me and settled in my stomach. I don’t know what made me say it, but something about the small shoes made me want to keep them. They looked old, and the leather looked hard and dried up. I was strangely drawn to them.

“Sure,” said Brian, giving me a puzzled look.

The electrician put them on the floor in front of the fridge. I continued working on my paper, hoping my cheeks had lost their redness. Brian and the electrician didn’t seem to care that I wanted the shoes, but I was overthinking it, as I did with so many things these days. My mind ran wild with all the things they could be thinking about me.

Half an hour later, I was half done my paper and the electrician’s voice interrupted my typing and train of thought.

"All done. Some wonky wiring in these old houses. It's all fine now, and you shouldn't have anymore trouble."

Brian thanked him and so did I. Brian said he would come back next week to fix the drywall. He had swept up the dust, but it would need to be covered up. I followed them toward the door and said goodbye. Then I closed the door behind them. I felt a bit calmer now they were gone.

I walked back to the kitchen and picked up the pair of shoes that were on the ground. They may have been the oldest thing I had ever held. They were just as hardened as they looked. I felt warm fondness for them. I had never given much thought to having children myself, but holding these little shoes in my hands and running my hands over them, I thought it might be nice to have a child one day. I wondered who they had belonged to and why were they in the wall. I set them back down on the floor gently and went to my laptop.

I googled "shoes in house wall," and what came up was far from what I had expected:

"Shoes were put in the wall in the nineteenth and early twentieth centuries as magical charms to protect occupants against evil forces. These concealed or 'secreted' shoes are called 'spiritual middens.' Secreted shoes are often found in chimneys, fireplaces, under floors, or embedded in plaster halfway up walls. They're often found on the northeast corner of structures, as some occultists believe that is the side evil spirits attempt to enter structures. Children's shoes were more often used, as they were believed to be more innocent and work as better totems than adult shoes."

I suddenly felt cold. Anxiety that had lifted slightly when Brian and the electrician left came back like a quick breeze.

I read on: *"Concealed shoes have been found in different types of buildings, including houses, orphanages, pubs, railroads, schools, barracks, churches, and hospitals."*

I stopped reading and closed my laptop.

So someone had placed the shoes in the wall to ward off evil. Had this dwelling always housed a sinister presence? Did our séance somehow cause it to come out? What was this house trying to tell me? I hoped my Internet search would give me answers, but it gave me more questions. The worst one: Was the evil of the house related in any way to the trouble with Beverly and my recent avoidance of school? What kind of evil was I dealing with and what should I do about it?

Chapter 16

Hannah

November 22, 1887

The realization that I could not acquire a rental space for my photographic studio because of my gender bothered me for weeks. I thought about it while wringing clothes over the washing board. I tossed it around in my mind while chopping vegetables for supper. I pondered a way around it when I lay awake at night, searching for something to occupy my thoughts. My father back in England had always treated me the same as my brother. Richard had never thought me less intelligent or competent than him because I was a woman. I did not want to believe that those men thought of me as less than them. Over many cups of tea, I thought of a way around it and tried to devise a way I could secure rental space.

One Tuesday, when the children were at school, I was tidying the kitchen cupboards and found a book. It was called *She: A History of Adventure*. Holding the blue book in my hand and admiring the gold writing brought back memories of Richard sitting beside the fireplace reading. He could make himself comfortable anywhere, but he looked especially at home reading beside the fire. I opened the book. On the inside cover, in Richard's handwriting, was his name: *Richard Hatherly*.

Reading his name at first caused tears to well, along with a wave of sadness. Then reading his name gave me an idea, the answer to the question that I had been turning over and over in my head for weeks—

the solution to renting a space for my photographic studio. I knew how I would get around my problem of finding a place to rent.

I would rent space under Richard's name. That was it.

I would tell them I was renting the space for my husband. I would pay for it through the bank account that I used and that was still under his name. Brilliant! A surge of energy came over me. I suddenly felt like I could do it, that I could get my own photographic studio. I could do the next steps, too. That is what I would do.

I went straight to my room and prepared to leave the house. I put on the same black dress I wore the first time I searched for a space to rent; it was my finest dress. I clipped my hair back and put on a plain black hat. A dash of lipstick, and I was ready to go. I left the house and headed down the street. I tried to ride the wave of excitement and push any doubts out of my mind. There was no need to worry today. Today, I wasn't a woman looking to rent a space. Today, I was a woman running an errand for her husband.

As I walked toward Doveport's main commerce area, potential problems lodged their way into my excited mind. I hoped to God nobody recognized Richard's name from the newspaper of men who had died in the mine explosion. I also hoped they didn't want him to sign any papers in person. I planned to bring the papers home, get them "signed" by Richard, and deliver them back to them. I also realized that my sign would have to say Richard Hatherly, rather than my name. So many details. I hoped it would work out. I was not usually a desperate woman, but my situation was becoming more desperate by the day.

It was early afternoon when I arrived at the boardwalk. The sky was overcast, and the sea was calm and glassy. The harbour was a perfect mirror image of itself on the ocean water. I walked past the butcher shop, past the newspaper shop, and pushed the door to enter the store. A bell jingled to indicate my arrival.

I strode to the counter. This time nobody was behind the counter. I looked around. The cash register stood tall and imposing in front of me. Stacks of papers lay haphazardly beside it. My grocery store did not carry fancy things, but it was tidy, tidier than this place.

I heard footsteps coming down a stairwell. Someone was coming to greet me. In my mind, I hoped it was the man's son; it was not. The grey-haired man with the big red nose said, "Afternoon, ma'am."

"Afternoon, sir. I am here because I left out some important information last time I was in. I was actually here on behalf of my husband to inquire about the space next to yours."

"Oh? What kind of business is he trying to start?"

"A photographic studio."

"When is he hoping to start renting?"

"As soon as possible."

"Hmmm, all right then. I will ask my son?"

It made my blood boil with anger that I was getting so much further when I was asking on behalf of my husband, but I felt slightly closer. "Thank you, sir. Here is my husband's contact information if you need to reach him," I said, handing him a piece of paper that I had neatly written "Richard Hatherly" and our street and house number on.

I left the store feeling a shred of hope but also some resentment that I set foot back into his store after his comment about the ravine last time. I had done the right thing, though. I had to move in the direction of my dream and that meant putting my emotions and anger aside for the sake of finding space for a photographic studio.

I thought about going back to the butcher and trying my new plan on him but thought otherwise. Instead, I decided to take a momentary break and watch the boats. For a few precious moments, I enjoyed myself. I pushed thoughts from my mind and focused on the boats.

A sailboat with tall masts came through, followed by a fish boat strangled with nets. A very costly looking wooden boat cruised past me. Aboard was a man in a black suit and bowler's hat and a woman with a dramatic feather-filled hat, lace-lined dress, and purple parasol twirling in the air. Bowler hat leaned over and kissed feather hat. It did not make me angry to see people so evidently in love. I wished what happened to me on nobody, but I vowed not to turn bitter or angry about it. Besides, bitterness would not help me attain a photographic studio.

I watched the sea and tried to enjoy the moment. I tried not to think that my fate was now in the hands of the store owner's son. I tried not to think of the laundry and wood chopping waiting for me. Most of all, I tried not to think of being five dollars short on each pension check. Living like this was wearing me thin.

I decided to take a different way home, so instead of walking on the boardwalk, I took the dirt road directly behind the boardwalk. A wooden sidewalk paralleled the street. My shoes made a clipping noise with each step, and I was careful not to catch my shoe on loose boards. A black horse pulled a carriage with a man, a woman, and two children on board. Another carriage passed me pulled by four black horses. One reared up slightly as it passed me, the carriage wheels bounced on the dirt road. The carriage itself was filled to the brim with wooden boxes of supplies, no doubt bound for some store. I hoped the horses were not strained with the effort.

I gazed into the shop windows, imagining what it would be like to have a tiny fraction of extra money to purchase something frivolous for the children, and the look on the children's faces if I surprised them with a bicycle or a shiny toy car.

Then a hand-written sign in a narrow shop window caught my eye.

For Lease.

Small second floor commercial space.

Suitable for small shop.

Must be clean and reliable.

At first, I could not believe it. It was exactly what I was looking for. But I had stopped looking for the day. Sometimes, I think I pushed too hard at a goal; that the harder I pushed, the further I got from it.

I leaned my head back to better examine the building. It was a wooden building, painted white. A long and narrow sign read "Erskine's Boot and Shoe Emporium." Without further hesitation, I exited the wooden sidewalk and entered the door off the street. Inside was impeccably tidy, even more so than Tong's General Store. The store was narrow and made narrower by the neatly stacked boxes of what I assumed were shoes and shoe supplies. Glass bottles filled with black liquid were stacked on some of the boxes. "Shoe Polish," read the labels.

At the back of the shop was a counter and cash register. At the front of the shop was a man sitting on a wooden chair. He was short and had a long but neatly trimmed white beard. He wore a white shirt with stripes, sleeves rolled up to his elbows. Suspenders could be seen underneath a white apron. He sat with his knees spread. Between his knee was an upside-down shoe lacking a sole. His hands held thick string and a large needle. He appeared to be redoing the sole. He was bald and his face was wrinkled, but his eyes were kind.

"G'day," he said simply.

"Good day, sir," I replied.

"You have some shoes in need of repair? The drop box is there." He indicated to a basket near the counter.

"I don't have shoes that need repairing at this time, but my husband is looking for space for a photographic studio. I'm inquiring on the price of the space you are renting above." I felt bad lying to the man. It felt wrong to lie to someone with such kind eyes, but I couldn't risk being rejected again.

"Ah, yes. It's quite small, and the entrance is through my store here and up those stairs. For those two reasons, rent is five dollars a month."

"I see," I said, trying to hide my excitement. Richard was always telling me not to show excitement about buying something. I was so expressive, though, so this was difficult. "May I take a look?" I asked, adding, "so I can let my husband know."

"I suppose so," he said as he put the shoe down on the counter. He climbed the stairs and I followed him. He moved a curtain sideways at the top of the stairs and we stepped into the upstairs space. High ceilings and big windows greeted us. Light streamed through the window, and a light breeze blew in. The windows looked over the street and out toward the long green mountain, Mount Alfred, that dominated the skyline behind Doveport.

"I think it should work for my husband's purposes," I said, once again hiding my excitement at the ideal nature of the space while also feeling guilty for lying. The space was perfect. I was already planning how I would decorate it so that people would quickly forget the walk up the staircase.

"Will he mind that the entrance is through my shoe shop?"

"No, he won't mind. The space will suit him fine. May I take a contract of sorts to him to get him to sign at home?"

"I don't have no contract. Payment due on the last day of the month for the following month and a ten-dollar deposit for damages."

There were ten days until the start of the next month. Ten days to get ready.

"Can I bring the money, his money, by the day before the month?" I asked, hoping he would say yes. I would not have enough until the next pension cheque arrived.

"I'm afraid I can't hold the space until I have the money in my hand. This month of it being empty has been hard enough as is."

"Very well, then. I will give you the money from my husband in the next day or two. Please, sir. Keep me . . . my husband in mind for it until then."

"No guarantees, but I'll remember you came by," he said as the door jingled, indicating a customer.

He started walking down the stairs and I followed him.

"Good afternoon, ma'am."

"You, also, sir. I didn't get your name."

"Harold Erskine."

"I thank you, Harold. My name is Hannah Hatherly and my husband is Richard Hatherly." Once again, guilt panged me at the lie, but I needed the space.

We descended the stairs. At the bottom, he went to the customer and I left the store, finding myself once again on the dusty sidewalk.

The sun had emerged from the grey clouds while I was in the store. I felt a burst of hope. If I could come up with the money, I had a photographic studio. It was a small victory, but a victory nonetheless. Little did I know then that my work had only just begun; the larger obstacles were yet to come. Had I known this, I may not have had such a pleasant walk back to my house.

≈

Two weeks later, I hammered the last nail into my sign: "Richard Hatherly's Photographic Studio." I stood back, hands on hips, and looked at it. A wave of excitement ran through me. My excitement was laced with fear and doubt, but I tried to focus on the excitement. I felt unqualified and even fraudulent, but I pushed those thoughts away. If I was going to do this, those thought would not serve me. I had been open a week—the first week of owning my very own photographic studio.

I went into the storefront and walked up the stairs. As I finished unpacking my things and had hung a photograph of an old barn on my wall, a man appeared from behind the curtain.

He stood very close to me while I sat my desk. I stood up and took a step toward him. He remained where he was.

"Your sign says 'Richard Hatherly,'" he said.

"It does," I replied.

The man had a gun with him that was pointed into the air. I hoped the safety was on. He was bald, with a moustache and beard. I would guess him forty years old. He smelled of whisky.

"I don't see no man here."

"My husband isn't in today. I am doing the photographs today. I think you will be pleased with the result. Are you interested in a portrait session?" I asked.

"Eh, second thought, I don't need no photos. I'll come back another time." His leather boots were undone, and he stumbled before starting down the stairs.

I exhaled a big breath and went to the window. I watched as the man left the shoe store below my studio and stumbled to the pub across the street. A crowd of men stood smoking outside, and the man with the gun, who had been in my studio moments before, pushed through them and disappeared into the darkness of the pub. I sighed again. This was the second time this had happened today. And it had happened several times a day since I opened. The novelty of a photographic studio was noticed, but men were unwilling to have their photograph taken by me.

In my planning, I overlooked the fact I would be unable to hide my gender once people came up the stairs. I hoped that most people would be more interested in their photographs than who was taking them. I hoped they wouldn't mind when they saw the quality of their photograph. But many people gave up when they saw me. Or left the store when they found out I was the photographer and not the assistant.

Thankfully, the shoe store owner had not yet mentioned my absent husband. I hoped he was too busy with his own business to notice that Richard had never shown up, or that he noticed but didn't care.

He had approved of my sign, which had been dreadfully costly—so much that I had to put that week's groceries on credit at Tong's General Store. I hated that, but Tong did not mind. I couldn't help but think that I was indebted to him somehow or that he might think less of me for needing to put it on credit.

Money was tighter than before, but I tried not to lose hope. I tried to feel proud of myself for keeping the household running while being out of the house most of the day. I was doing a lot and managing to keep afloat. But I wasn't sure how long I could keep this up for. My overhead expenses were more than my revenue. If I didn't get more paying customers, I would not be able to keep this up. I needed more customers—but how?

Chapter 17

Brooke

November 22, 2017

I awoke to rain driving sideways against my bedroom window. Relentless drops hammered the house and raced down the glass of my bedside window. I lay snug under my covers and watched rivulets of water start at the top of my window and stream down. Like liquid worms wiggling their way with gravity. The rain hitting the roof made a rapid pitter patter. I pulled the covers up and over me and tried to fall back asleep. Usually, I loved listening to rain from the coziness of my covers, but not today.

Today, I thought about school and my inability to find joy and comfort in my world. These days, as soon as thoughts of school entered my mind, I felt a headache begin and a stomachache start. Thoughts darted around my head like bats in a dark cave, and I felt an urgency to do something that would remedy the uneasy feeling. Sometimes, I tried to type assignments, but today, I stared at the blinking cursor on the white screen.

I sat up, swung my legs over the bed, and placed my feet on the floor. I would start my day. I would push through the headache and stomach pains and keep going.

It was November, and I was struggling. Avoiding school became routine. I couldn't remember the last time I attended. I submitted papers from home, but I was failing two classes—classes where assignments or in-class workshops compromised the mark.

After Halloween, the séance, the egging, the shoes in the wall and vowing to go to school, my struggles got worse. The first school day after Halloween, I had planned in earnest to go to classes. I had set my alarm early, and when it went, I picked up my phone and shut it off. I hoisted myself out of bed and started my usual morning routine. I couldn't find my notebook, and it took me ten minutes to locate it. I also had failed to lay my clothes out the morning before, and the outfit I initially chose wouldn't work. The sweater was frumpy; the pants dated. I changed three times. When I checked the clock, I was five minutes behind schedule. I imagined walking into the lecture late but decided not to go to school after all.

To say November was a tough month was akin to calling a whale large. Each day was darker than the last and the rain was relentless; each day strung together like one long dark dream.

I wandered to the kitchen, then bit some toast and poured hot water over a tea bag. *I'm not going to attend today,* I thought, *but I will get lots done from home*. That was what I told myself every day. I poured milk into the red-black tea. Milk welled up from the bottom and turned the tea cream-coloured. Once my toast was gone, I turned on my laptop and checked my email. This turned gnawing worry to a nauseous constant. Today was no different. But I needed to check my email for assignments I could do from home. Five emails showed bold in my inbox: two from my academic advisor, two from professors, and one from Jade. I clicked on the one from her.

Subject: Escape Christmas

> *Brooke, want to escape Christmas this year? I just found out my family isn't leaving town at Christmas after all, so I'm free for Christmas break. There's this gigantic white sand beach hours north of Doveport, with a cabin we can stay at. It's paradise. You'll love it. Long hike to get there, but beyond worth it. I have hiking boots you can borrow. Come with me? Xo Jade*

I closed the email and shut my laptop. I took a big sip of tea and pondered the email. At first, thinking of leaving Doveport over Christmas made me frantic with worry. My mind started racing with things that could happen. I didn't have hiking boots. I had never done a hiking trip before. What if I was bad at it?

But the subject of Jade's email was comforting and appealing. It made me curious. *Escape Christmas*. That I could get behind.

Christmas had always been a grim time for me. The entire season was loaded full of societal expectations and family focuses. The focus on family brought all my complex feelings about my parents, or lack thereof, to the forefront. At school, the constant focus on family drained me. The older I got, the better I navigated the Christmas season—with its expectations, traditions, and in-your-face ways—but I still didn't enjoy it. Plus, the strange happenings around the house were weighing heavily on me. I still didn't know what it was. Maybe some distance, both literal and figurative, would help me formulate a plan, give me some insight on what to do next.

I thought about what would happen if I said yes to Jade's invitation. I would have to pack things in a backpack and leave town. Drive somewhere I had never been. What if I was awful at hiking? Worse yet, what if I hated it? The thought of saying yes and packing a backpack made my heart race. I wouldn't go. That was that. I opened my laptop and replied to Jade's email, saying I couldn't go. Then I opened a paper on Shakespeare's *The Tempest*. I typed away on my laptop, trying to put the cabin on the big beach out of my head.

I felt calmer after declining, but I also felt worried. Because if there's a worse feeling than knowing you're missing out on something amazing, it's the feeling that you know you'll miss out on something without knowing just exactly how amazing it could be.

≈

It was two in the morning and something was tapping on my bedroom window. Since the séance, I hadn't heard any sound or seen anything strange. I desperately hoped the séance had worked and that whatever was torturing me in the house had listened to Jade's words and moved on.

My heart pounded in my chest as I assessed my options. I could try sleeping through it and hope the sound stopped, although it was unlikely I would find sleep now that I was awake and fear coursed through my body. I could go to the living room, but the thrift store couch there had hard mattress wires that made sleep unlikely. The third option made my stomach sink: I could pull back the dark blue curtain and investigate the source of the noise.

I played out the options as I pulled my blanket over my head and listened to the constant taps on the window beside me. What did the spirit want? What on earth was it trying to tell me? Or ask me? On a whim, I decided to investigate and confront the sound head on, not at all my normal plan of action for things that scared me, but I desperately craved sleep.

I took a long, smooth breath and sat upright. I was now directly beside the sound. It was a foot beside my head. I wiggled over and brought my arm out from under the blankets. I moved my arm slowly toward the curtain, the way you move your hand toward a hot stove or a spider.

I grasped the cream-coloured fabric. It felt scratchy on my hand. After seemingly an eternity, I pulled the fabric sideways so I could see outside the window. My heart was now pounding in my chest, my mind racing. At first, I couldn't see outside the window, but after a moment, my eyes focused in on something out in the inky blackness. It was small and brown and hit the window repeatedly.

It had wings, furry legs, and was the size of my hand. A moth! A chest full of air left my mouth that I hadn't realized I had been holding in. A moth—big for a moth, but nothing sinister or supernatural.

Maybe the spirit was gone after all. I wondered what kind of moth it was. I knew it was not smart to look at my phone at night and expose my eyes to light that would hinder my chances at falling back to sleep easily, but I needed something to distract my mind from my residing fear. I reached to my nightstand for my phone and laid on my back. Holding the phone over me, I typed in "white and brown moth North America." I scrolled through the photographs until I found one that matched what I saw. A giant silk moth: *Antheraea polyphemus,* my phone said and named for the silk that they spin into their cocoon.

After reading about their life cycle and evolution, my eyes got heavy and my breathing became even again. It was then that the tapping started once again, except it was different this time: the taps were further apart in frequency and softer sounding than before. I sat up and pulled the curtains back again. This time, there was no furry brown moth, only nothing but blackness outside my window.

Strange, I thought. *It must have flown away.* Perhaps it startled off when I pulled the blinds away. I lay back down and closed my eyes. Then once again: tap, silence, tap, silence. I sat up and pulled the curtains back again. Still nothing. Just the blackness of the middle of the night.

I sat up and swung my feet over the side of the bed. I would go outside and find the moth. Hopefully, I could shoo it away and go back to sleep. I padded to the front door, unlocked the deadbolt, and stepped outside. The world was still and black. I turned on the flashlight feature on my phone and looked over to my window. The white pane was clear and in front of me. There was no moth anywhere to be seen. In fact, there was nothing around, again, nothing but cold and darkness.

Was it Beverly messing with me? Or was it whoever threw the eggs at the house on Halloween? A dark wave of worry washed over my body. My heart started racing, and I tried my best to think of some realistic thoughts to counter the scary ones. Maybe there was a moth and I couldn't see it. Maybe the moth left. Maybe it was my mind playing tricks on me.

I didn't believe myself and my mind was still racing with what-if thoughts. My body was cold, my arms speckled with goosebumps. I wrapped my arms around myself. I entered the house, went to my room, and climbed back under the covers. I was nearly warm again and was getting my breathing back to normal when I heard it again. Tap. Silence for a few moments. Tap. Silence again. Tap. The lightest rapping on the window. Or was it on the wall beside the window? *It's got to be the moth,* I thought. *But why wasn't it there when I went outside?*

I repeated my before actions, shining the light on my phone toward the window pane. Once again, nothing. Nothing. Panic overcame my body like a storm. My throat tightened, my neck tightened, and goosebumps spread over my body. I startled and turned around and looked behind me. I was sure I had heard something. I shone my light onto the porch behind me and onto the lawn to see nothing but grass on the lawn, nothing but wood boards on the porch.

Again, I went inside and again crawled into bed. The tap, tap, tap sounded on the wall beside my window. I thought of the email from Jade inviting me to that cabin in a few weeks. I decided I would email her and tell her I had changed my mind. I would join her. A hiking trip to unknown wilderness was better than whatever was going on in this house.

Chapter 18

Hannah

November 30, 1887

I sat in my desk in my studio and gazed out the window. Outside, fog hung like an enormous ghost. Buildings across the street were invisible. My building was socked in. I sat at my desk with my elbows on it. I pondered how I could draw more business. I needed to attract more customers. One customer a day was not enough to pay the bills. I could not go on like this.

I looked around and felt a surge of energy and happiness at what I had done with the space. I had found a backdrop from an old theatre hall and pulled a round tea table from a dumpster behind the studio. I covered its scratched surface with a tablecloth and placed a grey fur rug below the table. Eva Ling gave me a rectangular mirror that she no longer needed, which I placed above the tea table. A space of my own.

The trouble was I needed customers. Most people who did come in did so on a whim after seeing my sign. I needed another way to get customers in my door, and I needed to get them talking to their friends and families so more people would come. My photographs were good; I knew they were good, but I was hesitant to go door-to-door after the rather hostile reception I got when I went seeking a place to rent.

I was in the middle of thinking about a newspaper advertisement when I heard footsteps coming up the stairs. Perhaps a customer? I stood up and straightened my dress, then took a quick look around the room. It was immaculate.

When the curtain moved and revealed the visitor, my heart sank. It was the cobbler and my landlord from downstairs, white beard and white apron.

"Afternoon, ma'am." He had been formal with me since I had moved in. I found it charming, but I was put off by it now.

"Afternoon, sir. How is business?" I was nervous now. Why had he come up? Had he found out I ran this business, not my husband? Was he about to confront me about it? I braced for an argument; I was prepared to fight for this place. I had put so much effort into it already. I would not give it up.

"Business is fine, thank you. I have a matter to speak with you about," he said.

"Of course. Do sit down. Would you like a cup of tea?"

"No, thank you. I won't be long. Only a quick matter. As you know, rent is due in two days."

"Yes, and I'll have it for you," I said, hiding my fear the best I could. Was he going to tell me I wasn't welcome here? Was he going to call me on my lie? I held my breath but did my best not to let my fear show.

"Well, I will be away tomorrow. That is the matter I wanted to speak to you about."

"Oh, all right." Relief washed over me, and I tried not to let it show.

"So, you can pay rent the day after tomorrow. My wife and I are going out of town for a night, and I'll be back the day after."

"Yes, of course," I replied.

"Also, I trust you will lock up the shop at the end of the day tomorrow."

"Absolutely, sir. I will be sure it's locked when I leave at the end of the day, and I will have rent to you the day after."

"Very good, then."

He hadn't mentioned my husband. I couldn't believe it.

"Of course, sir," I repeated, not knowing what else to say.

Then he continued talking.

"And you can put your own name on the cheque. Renting to you don't bother me none." With that, he moved the black curtain out of the way and started down the stairs. I watched the curtain settle into place in disbelief.

And so began our unspoken agreement of me running the photographic studio under my dead husband's name. I was deeply grateful it wasn't a lie anymore—and very relieved. I revelled briefly in this small victory.

Then, disappointment replaced the gratitude and relief. That was one problem solved, but it didn't fix the customer one. The studio was pointless if I had no customers. None of this space mattered without people. As the day progress, no one but my landlord had come up the stairs.

My situation was becoming increasingly desperate.

≈

"What about a newspaper advertisement?" Eva asked. We were drinking tea at her kitchen table the following Sunday. Her children and mine were outside in her back garden. From her kitchen, we could see them and hear their happy squeals and shrieks, but they could not see us.

"I thought of that, but I have no money for it," I said, feeling dejected and exposed in talking about something so deeply personal with Eva. Until now, our relationship had been built on the superficialities of dinners, children, and Doveport events. Now, we talked of a real-life problem—and mine, at that.

"Well, you might have to spend money to make money. It might sound counter intuitive but might be necessary."

I sat up straighter at her table and straightened my dress. I felt a rush of defensiveness, as if I couldn't handle things myself.

"I don't want to put anything on credit. Aside from groceries some weeks ago, I have never used credit in my life. It was always so important for Richard and I to live within our means.

"Well, you're a business owner now. Maybe that's different."

"There's nothing different about it. Credit is credit, no matter how you look at it. It's me owing money to someone else," I explained.

Eva looked at me and tilted her head sideways. I could tell that she cared, but I was becoming irritated with her incessant suggestions and ideas. I was clearly against putting a newspaper advertisement on credit.

"Is it because Richard wouldn't want you to or is it for yourself?" she asked, interrupting me from my irritation.

"For myself," I said quickly. "Richard wouldn't mind putting something on credit. Few things bothered that man; he was so good natured. I don't want to put it on credit because it's like needing help. I'm not the kind of woman who needs help, and I don't want anyone looking at me in that way."

"What's so wrong with needing help?"

"It's weak. Pitiful. Not at all how I want to be seen. I want to do this all on my own. Without the help of a bank or a lender." I suppose I got this trait from my mother, who was stubborn beyond measure. Once she walked around all day on a broken foot, refusing to see a doctor.

"Well, suit yourself," Eva said, pushing her chair back, the scraping sound against her floor being the only thing between us. "But let me ask you this: Is not asking for help worth losing your business over?" She stood up from her chair, opened the stove, and pulled out a steaming casserole.

I sat and didn't answer. I was thinking. I thought about it for a long time before answering. I felt something between anger and sadness. I so badly wanted to soften and accept the help and say I would put it on credit. But something inside me, a burning kind of anger, was stopping me.

"I'm not sure the answer to that," I said finally.

≈

In my studio, I held a photo far out in front of me and admired it. It was magnificent.

I was the subject of the photograph, but there were five of me. Five images of me on the same photograph. Multiple exposure, it was called. I had read about it in my photography book and, after many attempts, made it work.

In the photograph, I wore my best outfit: a black blouse with puffy shoulders, white spots, and a large white bow tucked into a black skirt that ruffled out at the bottom. The blouse and skirt combination flattered my waist. I had spent more time on my hair than ever before: bangs free on my forehead and curls pulled back with hair pins.

The five images stood alongside each other, each of me slightly overlapping. In each image, I held a different pose

The photograph felt playful. It was a pleasure to look at and different than any other photograph I had seen.

This is the one, I thought to myself. This was the photograph I had waited for. This was the photograph I would use to advertise my photographic studio. *This one will get me noticed. People will stare. People will wonder—and people will surely want a photograph like this one of themselves.*

But how would I show this photograph to the customers who would want it? I could enlarge it and attach it to the sign outside my shop. No, far too costly. And besides, I needed to reach people who were walking places other than just my street.

I could bring the photograph to nearby shops, but then I thought of the time it would take to walk it there and the time it would take to make a sales pitch. No, far too time consuming and not worth it. Besides, some people were not happy to see a woman with her own business and even less happy to see a woman marketing her own business. I needed a way to reach more people. My eyes glanced around my studio and landed on a folded newspaper that rested on my desk.

An advertisement in the newspaper—like Eva had suggested and I resisted because I didn't want to put the money on credit, which was the problem I came to when I played out the steps necessary to get a newspaper advertisement. No, too costly also. An advertisement would be so costly that I would have to put it on credit. But without an advertisement, I was losing money. The children and I were going without many things we usually had—butter, sugar, and fresh apples. Those things were simply not within my budget. The children sometimes complained but were mostly fine. Children were so adaptive; they adjusted to change much better than adults. This was not how I wanted to live.

The key question played in my mind: Would a newspaper advertisement draw enough customers to be worth putting on credit?

I walked to my desk and carefully placed the photograph down facing upwards. I then picked it up again and paced back and forth across my studio pondering a newspaper advertisement.

The novelty of the photograph instead of a painting was what I hoped drew people to my photographic studio. As far as I knew, there were no other photographic studios in Doveport. And if there were, I highly doubted they were experimenting with multiple exposures. Multiple exposures were new technology, and it was highly difficult to do well. To do it, I had captured myself in each position, rotated the lens cap, and moved myself to a new pose.

I continued pacing back and forth as I thought of the dreaded interaction of putting something on credit and the person knowing you didn't have the money for the transaction and that you had to pay it off. I thought of the gnawing feeling I would have in my stomach knowing I had to pay the money back and the heavy feeling in my stomach of knowing that I owed someone something that I couldn't pay for by myself.

I sat down at the round tea table in my studio and placed the photograph on the tablecloth. I remembered Eva Ling's voice asking me if it was worth losing my business over not being able to ask for help.

I picked up the photograph and again examined it. I admired the dreamy, surreal quality it had. It was like nothing I had created before. I then knew what I needed to do—keeping my photographic studio was worth asking for help. I collected my purse, pulled the curtain away, and headed down the stairs and to the newspaper shop.

≈

It wasn't until I was outside the newspaper shop that I recalled my interaction with the smoking, piggish newspaper man the first day I searched for space to rent: the way the man's eyes had scanned my hips and bust, and the way he had looked me up and down. I nearly turned around, but I had made up my mind; I won't change it now. I hoped I could talk to some other staff and not the smoking man.

I straightened my hat, took a full breath, and pushed open the door.

It was not my lucky day. The air was so full of smoke I almost could not see the man at the desk. But even through the smoke, I could tell it was the man with the moustache.

"Morning, ma'am. How you do?"

"Fine. I would like to purchase an advertisement. What sizes do you have and what do they cost?" I wanted in and out of there as quickly as possible.

"Oh, an ambitious one. What are you advertising?" he asked, as if no woman had come in inquiring for an advertisement before.

"My husband has a photographic studio. What are the prices for advertisements that include a photograph?"

The man looked at me puzzled and brought his cigarette to his moustached lips, took a drag, and blew it out. He didn't seem to notice when I stepped back to avoid the onslaught of smoke. He took his time answering.

"There are three sizes. The smallest is twelve dollars and runs for six weeks. The prices go up from there for larger sizes."

This was more than I had even expected. That was just over a week of the pension payment I was receiving and that would be before paying any of my bills. "Are there any possible for fewer weeks?"

"No, ma'am," he said, his eyes lingering on my bust. He took another lazy drag of his cigarette and blew it into my eyes.

"I'll do that one, then," I said quickly. No going back now; I had to do something.

"What shall it say?" He slowly brought a pen out from somewhere under the desk.

"It should say, *'Mrs. H. Hatherly, photographic artist and dealer in all kinds of photographic materials. Fine portrait photography and surreal images including multiple exposures. 127 Wharf Street, Doveport.*'"

Moustache had not brought out any paper, so he had not written anything down. "I'm afraid I can't write that, ma'am." He put the pen down.

"Why is that?" I was starting to feel dizzy from the smoke in the air. I needed fresh air. I looked at the closed window, wishing it was open.

"Because our company does not permit a woman's name on a business advertisement." He took two faster drags on his cigarette, which he had not put down since I entered the store.

"Fine then, the first line can say Mr. R. Hatherly instead of Mrs. H. Hatherly. And here is the photograph that should be included." I placed the multiple exposure photograph onto his desk and slid it toward him, dodging a puff of smoke. Even upside down, I admired the uniqueness of the multiple images of the same person on one photograph.

"Hmmm, that we can work with." He started scribbling onto a paper that had appeared from below the desk. When he was done, he showed it to me so I could check it. I nodded in approval.

"How will you be paying, then?" he asked as he picked up the photograph and his eyebrows furrowed into an expression somewhere between confusion and irritation.

"On credit," I said. I pulled my lips closed. The dreaded moment had arrived. For the first time in my life, I would pay for something with money I didn't have. A wave of worry came over me and a fluttery feeling left an unsettled feeling in my gut.

"Sure thing, ma'am." He rang it through, then handed me a paper receipt.

I took it from him, wished him good day, and turned on my heel.

I left the shop and stepped onto the boardwalk. I took in as much cool, clean sea air as I could. I rubbed my eyes, which had begun to itch. I looked out at the sea. It was grey, just like the sky that went about it. I hoped my plan worked.

The cost of the advertisement could have bought a lot of flour, oats, and potatoes. And I still had to pay rent in several days. Alice desperately needed a new dress. To top it off, the date was December 6. In nineteen days, presents needed to be under a Christmas tree. Christmas was going to be heartbreaking, as it was the first without

Richard, but I vowed to maintain as many traditions as possible—turkey, presents, chocolate, stockings stuffed with nuts and fruit—and those traditions required money.

The advertisement had to work. I didn't know what I would do if it didn't.

Chapter 19

Brooke

December 22, 2017

It was the Friday evening of Christmas vacation, and Jade and I drove out of Doveport. Jade drove and I sat in the passenger seat worried about all the things that could go wrong on the hiking trip. We were in Jade's dad's white pickup truck. The truck bed held our hiking packs, and the small cab held us. We passed houses with windows illuminating families decorating Christmas trees, mall parking lots overflowed with cars, and crowded intersections. People were like ants, frantically moving from one place to another with intense urgency. We, on the other hand, were headed to the wilderness. We had nowhere to be and no obligations. Just an empty road ahead of us. Two hours outside of Doveport, the highway was almost bare. In four hours, we would reach the trailhead. We would sleep in the truck there.

"Well, are you excited?" Jade asked once we were nearly out of Doveport.

"Ugh, bit excited, but mostly nervous. I don't want to slow you down. I've never been on a hiking trip before."

"Brooke, I wouldn't bring you if I didn't think you could do it. You walk kilometres and kilometres a week. You're fit and strong. You'll be more than fine. And the beach! You're going to love it. I promise it will be worth the walk. Paradise." Jade smiled and looked at the road.

"All right, I'll try to remember that. I just worry about things going wrong, like a branch falling on us or rogue wave or something."

"Well, worrying about those things isn't going to stop them from happening. If it's going to happen, it's going to happen anyway. No sense in letting worry take away from the fun."

Jade was so practical. I couldn't help but feel a bit calmer.

"That's true. I wish I could stop worrying so much. Maybe time in the wilderness will melt away some worry."

Jade and I talked to pass the time. We talked about school, about friends, about where we were going. Jade had been there many times. When someone talked lovingly about a place, it made me want to go there. Sense of place is powerful that way. Now, as Jade talked about the beach and the cabin, the rainforest, and the rivers, my worry melted and was replaced with hesitant excitement.

Before meeting Jade, I had been lonely. I had no experience with friendships before university, so the process of getting to know someone was something I learned late in life—at university. It was something I learned mostly from watching other girls in my residence interact with each other. I was quiet and didn't talk much, but I was very good at watching, something I learned from the multiple foster homes. I learned the norms of the household, the way people talked to each other, and interacted, where the shoes got put. I found it easier to blend in with the culture of the household than go against it. And I learned it all by watching.

Jade was the first friend I confided in about my deep feelings of abandonment, deficiency, and unwantedness that bouncing from home to home had left me. I admired and envied Jade's sense of identity and the solid foundation her family identity had given her. Growing up, I lacked the support and identity parents provided. I was without a compass or starting place when inventing my identity.

Though Jade and I were opposites, our conversation in the truck flowed freely. Hours passed, and eventually, we were past any traffic lights, just our truck and dark road. We enjoyed each other's company. Jade was like Doveport's Mount Alfred: solid, strong, and intentional, always sure of her next step. I, on the other hand, was like the water in the ocean east side of Doveport: fluid, unsure, and going where I was pushed. Jade was brave and confident and everything I wished I was. She was comfortable in her own shoes, whether they were gumboots or flip flops. She made decisions and went for them with a vengeance. She loved people, could chat up anyone, and effortlessly made friends with strangers. She loved people, and people loved her. She somehow didn't care what others thought yet had the uncanny ability to know how others were feeling. It was as though she could see right into people.

I tried to read people like I read my novels, but still fumbled with my words and struggled to connect. Jade embodied all the characteristics I wished I had. She had a loud voice; I was soft spoken. She gained energy being around people, while I recharged while alone. Jade carried conversations effortlessly, while I was anxious and awkward. She was the kind of person who gave you her undivided attention, making you feel very important and like you could tell her anything.

As we drove north on the dark highway, our conversation moved to family.

"I love my siblings and all, but sometimes, I think my parents expect too much of me. Always making me look after Florence. Ugh, I'm so excited for a few days away." Her brow furrowed as she spoke and drove. "The day we return from the trip, I'm helping my cousin move houses. Always seems to be something I need to do with family."

I felt a pang of jealousy for the close relationships she had with her immediate and extended family. Then I felt guilty for being jealous. Feelings were complicated.

"Yeah, must be different having a big family. The closest thing to family I gave is Derek and David, the last foster family I had before I aged out of foster care and moved out on my own. It was quiet, just the three of us, but it was the first time I felt like I had a family."

"They sound like the best. I want to meet them sometime."

Derek and David were family to me. Two dads. Each teaching me things I used daily in my adult life. Derek taught me how to fry eggs, stir fry vegetables, and write down dentist appointments in a day timer. *"Leave more time than you think you need to get to places,"* he would say. *"There's no sense in being rushed."* That nugget of advice did wonders to make me less worried when I got somewhere and helped me land every job I had landed in the past year. David taught me to ask for a raise, parallel park, and merge onto the highway.

Derek and David were key to turning my life around and finishing high school. Both taught me to trust, that I didn't have to do everything alone. Even if I could do it myself, I didn't have to. They both taught me trust through actions; that was more powerful than any verbal promises anyone had made me. There was deep comfort in knowing two people had back my no matter what. Living with Derek and David was my first time experiencing that feeling of comfort. It rooted me but also let me soar. Like an eagle soaring, I flew because I had people who cared about me.

Derek and David didn't have a lot of money, but they had time, which they gave without hesitation. For the first time in my life, I was gifted with attention—something I had craved desperately without being aware of it. Suddenly, I wasn't alone in the world. I was welcomed. Mostly, though, I was wanted.

After four hours, one gas station stop and many kilometres down a bumpy unpaved logging road, Jade announced, "Here we are. The trailhead."

We stopped in a dirt parking lot. Giant cedar trees surrounded the parking lot. The forest stood impenetrable around us. Thick ferns grew beneath the cedars. It began to rain. I felt on edge and nervous at the thought of packing everything in one pack and keeping up with Jade and her long strides the next day.

We set up our sleeping mats and sleeping bags in the small cover of the white pickup truck. Jade's breathing was smooth and deep the moment after she said good night. I mulled over worries in my head, trying to be excited, but I was nervous of the many uncertainties of the next day of hiking. What if I sprained an ankle? What if I hated it? Did I pack enough wraps for lunches? The light patter of rain took to the background as I tried solving each worry. At some point, to the soft sounds of rain on the truck's roof, I fell into sleep.

≈

The next morning, I nearly forgot where I was. I awoke expecting the dreaded fear of the yellow house but, instead, saw the roof of white pickup when I opened my eyes. I rolled over to say good morning to Jade, but her sleeping bag was empty and she was nowhere in sight. Panic seized me as my body quickly transitioned from the calm of sleep to a rapidly beating heart and feeling of uncertainty. I pulled on a fleece jacket and scrambled out of the truck. Frost sparkled on everything and mist hung in the air, showing just peek-a-boo views of mountains that surrounded the parking lot. The place would have been breathtaking if I didn't think I was alone.

"Morning, friend!"

I swung around. Fifty metres behind me and the truck was a covered picnic shelter with a cement platform and picnic tables. Jade was under it, in a tuque with a pot of something steaming on a camp stove.

I walked closer and smelled coffee. I didn't usually drink coffee, as it made me jittery, but on occasions, I would. This was one of those occasions. Jade could not go without it. The smell of cinnamon and apples wafted together with the coffee aroma as I neared.

"Morning, I didn't know where you were. I didn't notice the picnic shelter for some reason."

"Internal alarm clock woke me at the usual time. Coffee and apple cinnamon oatmeal is ready to go. I'm so excited to get hiking."

Once we were fuelled, we crammed the final things into our backpacks. Hauled them on our back and started off down the trail. At first, nervous thoughts gnawed at me. I ran through the packing list Jade had given me and hoped I hadn't missed anything. I hoped the meal I was making for dinner would taste good. I hoped I could do it. I had never hiked fifteen kilometres in one day, like we were about to do. At one point, my worried thoughts left my head and turned to words.

"Jade, what if I forgot something?"

"At this point, if you don't have it, you don't need it. Plus, I could share anything essential. I'm stoked that you're here, Brooke. This is one of my favourite places in the world. Look at the mist burning off through those trees."

Jade was eternally optimistic. Sometimes, it bothered me, but this morning, it was reassuring. I tried to let the worried thoughts flow through my head and not take the temptation to land on them and give them my attention.

At some point, my worried thoughts departed naturally. Morning sunshine burned the fog off. The most beautiful forest I had ever seen overshadowed any remnants of worried thoughts. Every possible shade of green existed in this forest: fern green, cedar green, moss green, yellow leafy green, mud green. Moss grew on every surface. It covered the trunks and branches of trees. It hung off trees in beard-like tendrils. It concealed wooden boardwalks and paths. It grew thickly on rocks and stumps. In the forest, it grew in steps, one step for each year of growth, which Jade later told me. Frost melted and turned the earth from frosty to damp.

We walked over dirt paths meandering through groves of Sitka spruce and cedar trees. We meandered past huckleberry bushes long past their fruit-bearing stages. We crossed bridges with fast-flowing water below them, river stones that city landscapers mimic when they design natural looking places amid the cement and skyscrapers of cities. We climbed over blown-down trees and crawled under other ones. We walked past a lake that was one of the quietest places I had been. Nobody was out there but us. At home, this thought had been terrifying; now, in reality, being alone in this mystical forest was oddly comforting.

Throughout the day, rain was a continuum, ranging from light mist to pouring down in large droplets that sideswiped us, making our chins drip and infiltrating places between clothing items and wherever it could get in.

The ache of my backpack on my shoulders began as a dull ache and soon turned to a sharp, piercing pain, but somehow this didn't worry me. If anything, it took my focus from worried thoughts.

As we walked through the forest trail, thoughts meandered through my mind. With a detached curiosity, I sorted through the happenings of the past months: my move from the house of girls to the yellow house, Beverly's constant barrage, and the most recent act of hostility against me, where she commented on a piece of my writing. Thinking of that gave me a stomachache, and I tried to push it from my mind.

Being away from the house, away from Beverly, and away from Doveport gave me a different perspective. I examined things more objectively than when I was directly in them. Things were not going well this year. Something strange and possibly sinister was happening in the yellow house. Beverly's harassment was increasing, and I lacked the courage to confront her. I needed to tell someone but how? I needed to pass all my courses to graduate. I needed to find work after graduation. Or should I do a master's degree and continue my education? But that would mean no money, and eventually, I needed to buy a house. Houses in Doveport were becoming increasingly unaffordable. Maybe I would have a partner by then and we could pool our money together. I tried to rein in these ferocious worries of distant life events and tried to pull myself back to the trail in front of me. What was going on in the house? What was it and what did it want from me? Life was so complicated back home, but so simple here. Did I even deserve happiness? I had no parents, after all.

Mulling over the thoughts was orderly and comforting, despite many of them requiring no immediate actions. I tried allowing thoughts to come and go from my mind, like clouds passing in the sky.

I took solace in the wild green jungle around me: the tropical ferns jutting from the ground, the strong trees towering over me with white moss hanging from them like beards of wise old forest wizards, and the pillows of moss sitting high up on tree branches, with ferns sticking out of them like a giant green pincushion. Peace came over me for stretches of time longer than I could remember.

Six hours later, the forest trail opened and I stood on the most expansive sand beach I had set foot on. The earthy smell of wet rainforest mixed with the smell of salty ocean water engulfed me. The crashing of ocean waves mesmerized me and echoed over the beach. Jade and I were the only souls on the beach. I suddenly realized that I had walked here myself. Happiness bubbled inside me. I tried not to let it overcome me; I wasn't deserving of this happiness. I didn't have parents, so I wasn't deserving.

"We made it. I knew you could do it, Brooke."

"I wasn't sure I could, but I'm glad I did."

"Let's get to the cabin, take our packs off, and get a fire going."

With that, we headed down the beach to a wooden A-frame cabin with a chimney jutting into the sky.

≈

A few days later, I awoke, pulled on a wool sweater over my head, and walked into the main room of the cabin. Jade sat in front of a fireplace of dancing flames. It was Christmas morning and the third day of the trip.

Life had become deliciously simple. Walk. Eat. Sleep. We lived in the moment. We ate when we were hungry and did what we wanted. We read books, wrote in our journals, and beachcombed. Jade fished in the river beside the cabin. I read for my own enjoyment, rather than for school. No analysing. No reflecting. Devouring pages of words purely for pleasure. The only time I was worried was when my thoughts turned to Beverly and the yellow house. The distance from those two things made them easier to push from my mind.

"Merry Christmas!" Jade said, and handed me a cup of steaming tea. A mug of coffee was in her hand. She was buzzing. The tiny hemlock we'd cut sat in the corner with shimmering abalone shells and white cockle shells underneath it. Outside the large cabin windows, green waves crashed onto the beach and turned into white foams of water. The wind howled outside; the cabin shook.

"Merry Christmas," I said back. "This is for you. Thanks for bringing me here. I haven't felt so free and unburdened in a long time. Maybe ever."

It was true. The past few days had lessened my anxiety in a huge way. My mind had a break from the incessant stream of worried thoughts. My body was tired at the end of the day. I slept better than I had in weeks. Best of all, the yellow house and Beverly felt far away.

"Wild places centre me. Time away from everything city and time alone with my thoughts always clears my head and helps me put my priorities into order," Jade said, taking the present from me and wrapping her arms around me in a hug.

She pulled off the paper. It was a calendar I made of photos of our last three years in university, each photo a memory of our friendship.

"Jade, thank you! Here's yours," she said, handing me a rectangle wrapped in white tissue paper. I pulled off the tissue paper and found a hardcover turquoise journal.

We cleaned up and left the cabin to walk the beach. Rain fell as if buckets were being dumped from the sky. It descended in sheets of water that made the forest misty and hazy. The trail was a river. We walked to a pocket beach with some sea caves and explored.

As we left the sea cave, Jade turned to me and spoke. “Have you thought any more about reporting Beverly to the university?”

“I’m not going to.” The darkness of the sea cave looked sinister and reminded me of the fireplace.

“What’s stopping you? Don’t you think it will just continue?”

“I can’t report her. They’ll never believe me. And I’m still dealing with the weird things in the house. All of it is just too much.”

“I think it will all continue until you act. I’m here if you need help with reporting it.”

“I appreciate that, but I’m fine,” I said, knowing it wasn’t true. “I’m glad to be here away from it all.”

Jade opened her mouth like she was going to speak and then closed it again. She sighed. “Let’s go back to the cabin,” was all she said.

Calm was restored between us. I knew she was right and that it wouldn’t stop unless I did something, but the fear of Beverly and confrontation was too much to consider. Worry welled up inside me. I pushed it down.

On December 30, a week after arriving at the cabin, we left. We closed the door behind us and walked the trail the way we had come, packs much lighter than the trip in. We arrived at the truck and unloaded the packs to back of the truck. It was delicious to be sitting as we started the drive home. The speed felt drastic after all that walking. I fell asleep fifteen minutes into the drive, exhausted, blistered, and with a newfound respect for people who had done the trail before me, pioneer people who walked trails like that without modern-day gear to protect them from the elements.

It was night when we arrived back in Doveport. Coming home from the cabin was strange. Parking lots were empty. Roads were bare. The Christmas typhoon had come through, and the city was quieter but still not quiet. The chaos had come and gone, but the city was always busy. Now, it felt unbelievably crowded. Everything was organized, regulated, and crowded. At the cabin, there had been no rules and only self-imposed regulations.

Jade pulled up on the street in front of the yellow house. "I'm glad you came."

"I'm also glad I came. I almost didn't."

"But you did it. Always worth pushing past the fear," Jade said with a cheeky grin before driving off.

I unlocked the door and walked into the house, refreshed in mind, yet weary in body. I put down my pack by the entranceway and unshackled myself of my hiking boots. I went to the bathroom and looked at my face in the mirror. It was narrower, my eyes clearer. I touched my skin and my cheeks were soft—maybe from being perpetually wet for five days. Perhaps sea air and rain were good for the skin.

I wandered to the living room and looked at my simple home décor items: a potted fern, a few pillows in the bay window nook, and all my books. I was acutely aware of how many house possessions were solely for looks.

Sounds and smells of home overwhelmed me. Sounds that were normal before—the fridge, cars driving down the street, and fog horns from boats—now sounded louder. Everything was stimulating, loud, and bright. At the cabin, sounds had been rhythmic, a white noise almost: the howl of the wind and the constant sound of surf and waves.

Being indoors was strange. I was satiated spiritually, but thirsty for water. *This must be the culture shock Jade was talking about,* I thought to myself.

Everything seemed too easy at home. A simple pull on a tap gave clean water, and the flick of a switch boiled water for tea. It felt strange to be constantly warm and dry. It was strange to have dry feet and to feel clean, to not have to put on a coat to go to the washroom.

City things competed for my attention. My phone buzzed for my attention, and emails had piled up. My body was tired. I examined purple bruises that adorned my hip bones, where my pack had sat. felt different. Satiated. Full. Fulfilled. Like I could do anything. Perhaps I should push past my anxiety more and maybe, just maybe, I would get through this year. Maybe I could put this Beverly issue behind me, move on, and figure out what's going on with this house. Even find the courage to move out if things didn't improve. The trip had made me see that I could steer my own ship, but to do that, I needed to take the wheel.

I walked to my bedroom, climbed into bed, and pulled the covers over me. Compared to the cabin cot, my bed was expansive, soft, and fluffy. My head landed on the soft pillow, and I heard whooshing cars and distant ambulance sirens instead of wind and crashing waves. The last thought I had before drifting into sleep was that I would have missed all of that if I had listened to my worry.

Chapter 20

Hannah

December 13, 1887

I moved a soft cloth over a camera lens at my studio desk one afternoon in December. Thumping footsteps coming up the stairs interrupted my cleaning. I looked up from the lens. The black curtain moved sideways and a man stood imposingly. He was tall, with broad shoulders, a trim waist and a shortly trimmed beard. His jaw bones dominated his face. I thought him handsome until he spoke.

"I'm looking for Mr. R. Hatherly," he said.

"He's dead, sir. Died in the coal disaster back in May." I could say it without tears piercing my eyes, but the words made a jabbing feeling at my heart.

"That's unfortunate. I am looking for a photographer to do some portraits."

"Yes, it is unfortunate, indeed. But I am the proprietor of this photographic studio and I would be pleased to take some portraits for you."

"Are there any photographers at this studio other than yourself?" he said as he looked me up and down.

"No, just myself." I hoped he was asking out of curiosity, but this interaction was too familiar. He wanted a man to take his photographs but wouldn't say it outright, which somehow made it worse.

"Hmmm, I'll be going then," he said, and grabbed the curtain to leave.

A flash of anger rose in me. It was going to go like this then; customers like this man came in more and more often. It was like a battle to convince them to keep their business with me. Sometimes, I won the battle; sometimes, I lost. I put on my mental armour and prepared to fight.

"Wait a moment, sir," I said quickly. "I think you might want to see some of my photographs. I have a rather impressive portfolio here. Customers have told me I have an uncanny ability to make someone look the best they can possibly look. Here, take a look." I handed the man a hefty brown leather photobook.

Usually with customers like this, appeasing their larger-than-life ego went a long way to keeping them as customers. I detested doing it, but I desperately needed the business.

The man's hand let go of the curtain, and he reached out and took the leather book. He held the book in one hand, as someone would a bible, and flipped the pages with the other. I watched as his eyes took in the photographs. His eyebrows rose on his forehead; his eyes widened. I wondered what photograph he was impressed with, likely the one of a man with the unloaded gun I had as a prop.

The spell was broken as he looked up and handed me the brown leather book back.

"I'm looking for a photographer who is a man. Best get that sign changed. It is false advertising and gives misleading information about your business." With that, he pulled the curtain aside and stepped through it. The sound of his steps descending the stairs was the last I heard of him.

Anger welled up within me. I had put myself out there, and he had turned me down. I knew my photographs were of high quality and so did he, but he would not let me take his photo because I was a man.

I sighed and put the photobook down on my desk. I picked up the soft cloth and continued where I had left off rubbing the camera lens clean. I wished this wasn't so hard. Every ounce of my mind, body, and soul was into this business, and so far, it had only been difficulty. I desperately wished for more customers. If I didn't get any, I would have to put rent on credit for the second time. I dreaded knowing how much credit I had with the bank.

≈

That evening, after dinner, clean up, and the children's bedtime routines, I readied the house for a spiritualism gathering. It was my turn to host, and I lit candles on the fireplace mantle. The children were in their rooms and tucked in for the night. The other "sitters," as they were called, would be arriving in an hour. I got into spiritualism as something to do instead of work. My life had begun to be a rotation of work, children, work, children. I needed something else in my life and spiritualism had always interested me. Truth be told, part of me became involved in spiritualism in hopes of contacting Richard; I yearned to feel connected with him. I closed the curtains by the big front window in the living room and lit a few candles on the fireplace mantle.

A flutter of excitement came over me. Spiritualism was a trend, and trendy things weren't usually things that interested me. But spiritualism was different. Spiritualism started in Upstate New York with a pair of sisters called the Fox sisters. Their experiences communicating with spirits spread across the continent, eventually crossing the ocean and arriving in Europe. Of course, it arrived in North America also. My spiritualist group met in someone's living room once a week.

A knock at the door signalled the start of the night.

"Come in," I said as I let them in the front door and ushered them into the entranceway.

Each person found a spot at the wooden table in the kitchen. Candles flickered on the big fireplace in the living room and at the table where we gathered. There were six of us sitters: three men and three women. We alternated men and women.

When everyone was seated and ready, we joined hands and I began to speak. "Spirits that be, let us contact the spirits tonight. Let them come to us and bestow upon us the messages that we need. Who is it with us tonight?"

The woman who was medium began speaking. "I sense a male spirit. Dark hair. Does that resonate with anyone?"

"My husband," I said.

"He is trying to tell me something."

I looked at her. All of us looked at her. This was the first time someone had contacted me. Every other time, it had been a family member of someone else or a random visitor that nobody recognized.

"He's trying to say something, something about bravery. I can't quite figure out what he means, but the word *bravery* keeps coming up."

My heart got heavy; I felt both grateful and weepy. I thought about the note on the shovel. *"Raise our children bravely,"* it had said. But it seemed now that it meant something different. I opened my eyes and looked at the medium.

"He's gone."

Sadness overtook me, and I quickly rubbed a tear from my eye. I would not let anyone see me cry.

After one more spiritual visitor, the medium closed the circle. I brought over a tea pot, and we moved from the kitchen table to the living room. The medium, whose name was Mabel, asked me something nobody had asked in a long time.

"Hannah, what was your husband like? You must miss him."

The question startled me. I hadn't spoken about Richard since his funeral and I had quickly moved the children off the topic when it came up. I knew I should speak about him more with the children, but talking about him made me weepy. I had it in my head that it was impossible to be weepy and emotional and a successful business owner at the same time. Plus, talking about him reopened the cut that was my longing for him. So, I never spoke of him.

"Richard was a good man. Honest, kind, and a hard worker. Yes, I miss him."

I could have spoken about Richard for hours. I could have told them the way he used to read to the children every night before bed. Or the way he would always be the first to start building sandcastles at the beach. Or the way he brushed the unruly bits of hair out of my face before planting a kiss on my lips. I could have told her that although I put on a brave face for the children, there were nights that I missed

Richard so much, it hurt and that the pain of missing him always transformed itself to tears running down my face until I fell asleep.

But instead I closed her out. I didn't add anything to my brief answer despite the open look on her face, evidence she was ready and could handle more.

"Oh, I see," she said. She was socially astute and realized I had slammed the door on the conversation. She did not try asking about Richard after that, and I did not ask about her departed loved ones. We kept our relationship superficial. Our friendship was like lily pads on a pond: pretty but always floating on the surface. There was nothing close or caring about it.

I was reluctant to let a group of people into my life. Perhaps, deep down, I was afraid if I got close to someone, male or female, they would leave me and I would be left feeling empty and grieving again. Perhaps I had enough grief to last a lifetime. I told myself that my business and my children kept me busy enough.

When the sitters had all left and the door was closed behind them, I couldn't help but think that I might be missing out on a good part of life by not letting myself get close to anyone—by barring anyone from the private realm of my thoughts and feelings. A thought came to me that surprised me. Perhaps Richard was telling me that bravery was facing things that scare us. For me, that was getting close to other people.

≈

A week after the man refused a portrait with me, as I sat at my deck, touching up a portrait of a baby with cherubic cheeks for a client who had come in the day before, the curtain opened abruptly, startling me. I had not heard footsteps ascending the stairs.

A woman with light blue eyes and dark hair stood in front of the curtain. She was heavily weighted down by jewellery and wore a fine black hat.

"Good day, ma'am." I said in greeting.

"I would like my portrait taken," she said shortly. She spoke in the way a person speaks when they can buy anything they like."

"Of course, ma'am. What style are you looking for?"

"High class. Make me look good. And my waist can be brought in if you are versed in those kinds of adjustments."

"I can do that, ma'am. Which backdrop would you like?"

She turned around the studio looking at all of them. "That one," she said, pointing at the backdrop of the smooth surface of the lake.

I brought a stool over and had her sit on it. For the next hour, I clicked photos of her. Though it took an hour, time nearly stopped. I was now adept at lighting checks and dictating poses.

She was a natural at posing—the ideal subject—and was delightful to work with. This flowy state of enjoyment was unnatural to me. Things had been such a struggle until then—like pushing something heavy up a hill. Now, I was flowing downhill with the wind behind me. I tried to enjoy myself but wondered when it was suddenly going to get difficult.

However, no difficulty came in that photo session. Afterwards, the woman said, "How much will that be?"

I told her the cost and she didn't say a word. She simply put a white gloved hand into a satin wallet and pulled out a handful of bills.

"Keep the extra as a tip. I think I will be very pleased with the finished product." With that, the woman pulled the black curtain behind her before descending the stairs the same way she had ascended them—without a sound.

I stood and stared at the curtain before counting the bills, in disbelief at the ease at which that customer interaction had taken place and that I had just acquired currency for doing something I found so enjoyable. After counting the bills, I was in shock. The extra was beyond generous, so generous that it would cover the next month rent completely. Perhaps, I could make my photographic studio a successful business after all.

Chapter 21

Brooke

January 15, 2018

Two weeks and two days after returning from the hiking trip, I sat the kitchen table in front of the large window. Light tried entering, but the day was overcast and grey; no rain, but the sky was trying for it.

I hadn't been to school in weeks—since well before winter break and not at all since winter break ended. My laptop sat open in front of me and a cup of cream-coloured tea sat beside me. Steam rose from it in a straight line, like smoke from a log cabin in the woods. The house was cold, and I pulled a wool sweater up to my neck and down my back so it covered as much of me as possible. I pulled a knit tuque down over my ears, then glanced at the door to the backyard where I had rolled up towels to stop the draft. I wondered if the towels made any difference.

Six emails sat unopened and in bold font in my email inbox. This was the worst part of my day, as it caused worry to well up inside me. Emails were necessary if I wanted to pass classes, but I hated it. I looked to the screen, assessing what emails would force me to confront that day. Three were from professors. Two were from the university communications with generic information for all students, and one was from a Harbourview University email address, but from a name I didn't recognize. I clicked on it first.

The email addressed me. My eyes scanned to the bottom to see who it was from—the dean of the creative writing program. My heart started to beat faster. What did he want? My mind shot to the worst-case scenario: Was I being kicked out of the program for my attendance? I knew the situation I had put myself in was bad, but I didn't think the dean would be the one to alert me that I was being given the boot.

I read the email in its entirety.

From: Mark Price <mark.price@harbourview.ca>

To: Brooke Daniels <brooke.daniels@harbourview.ca>

Date: January 15, 2018, 8:17AM

Subject: meeting

Dear Brooke,

This letter is regarding your second paper, turned in on 9 December 2017, written in fulfillment for the requirements of ENGL 425: Advanced Topics in Creative Writing. After receiving a report from another student and after reviewing your work, it has been determined that your paper titled The Real Nixie of the Mill-Pond *contains plagiarized material and is nearly identical to the work submitted by another student.*

This constitutes a case of academic misconduct. The course syllabus indicates the penalty for plagiarism is failure either for the assignment or for the course, and possible other sanctions regarding graduation. In consultation with your professor, I have determined that the penalty will be failure for the course. As you may know, this would make you deficient in one course toward your graduation this spring.

In accordance with The Student Code, *you may request a hearing with the Academic Misconduct Hearing Board. You have thirty business days to submit to me a written request for a hearing. If I have not received any communication after that, the said sanction will be imposed. The Community Standards staff are available to meet with you to review* The Student Code *and answer any questions you may have. You may reach Community Standards at communitystandards@harbourview.ca.*

Please note that a copy of this letter has been forwarded to Community Standards, who has the right to convene the Academic Misconduct Hearing Board to consider additional sanctions if you have a significant student misconduct history.

In addition to the penalty, I would also like to discuss this serious matter with you in person. Let me know if tomorrow at 1 p.m. works with your schedule for a meeting. It will take place in my office, in Building 410.

Sincerely,

Mark Price

Dean of Humanities

Harbourview University

Anxiety gripped me like ice cold hands that tightened around my neck. My throat constricted, and my heartbeat quickened. I rested my elbows on the table and enfolded my face in my hands. I couldn't believe what happened. I reread the email one more time to make sure I hadn't misunderstood it. My world slowed, and I realized I was in shock. Outside, rain fell like a drummer was on the roof. This could not be happening. I took a sip of my tea, but barely tasted it.

At first, I thought it must have been a mistake, that they got the wrong person. Yes, I didn't attend, but I would never cheat. Ever. I painstakingly cited everything. If anything, I overreferenced my work. I always made my work the best I could make it. They must have the wrong person. But the assignment's name was there—that was my assignment.

My mind then went to the student who reported it. Who accessed my laptop? Then a memory came to me. I remembered back in August, when I got back from viewing the yellow house and my laptop was open on my desk. I normally closed it but left it sleeping; it was quicker to get working that way. I remembered thinking it strange that it was open; this was right after Chatham had asked me out. Then a light went off in my head and the truth of what had happened hit me like I had been whacked in the chest with a backpack of textbooks.

Beverly stole the assignment from my laptop and reported me for plagiarizing.

A sick feeling overtook my stomach. Images flashed through my mind: a truck racing toward me on the road, the yellow smear of eggs on the house. I imagined Beverly accusing me of plagiarizing. This time, she had gone too far.

There was only one thing in this world that I had that Beverly didn't—a gift for writing—and that is what she went after me for. I got better grades than her, and she obviously couldn't stand it, so she took it from me. She submitted my assignment as her own and then went straight to the dean or Community Standards staff herself before the professor noticed that there were two identical assignments submitted.

I didn't have a childhood with happy photographs of beach days, amusement parks, lakes, and docks, smiling adults around me who loved me and who would do anything for me. I didn't have a pool, and I certainly didn't have two biological parents who liked my social media posts, called me to check in, helped me pay rent when I was short, and showed up in my life. I had no idea who my parents were or where in the world they were.

That assignment took me hours, probably close to twenty hours if I totalled the hours I spent on it. In the end, I had been so pleased. It was a re-telling of a classic myth from *Grimms' Fairy Tales*. The original story was *The Nixie of the Mill-Pond,* about a shapeshifting water elf. I put a contemporary spin on it and added my own complexities to the plot. It was readable yet thought-provoking; it made the reader feel something.

Anger welled up inside me. The Jack Kerouac comment on the social media near my magazine article had been upsetting, but this was heartbreaking and, somehow, more violating. It was like the character and the world I had dreamed up for the assignment had been ripped away from me. It was not fair. I knew life wasn't fair—that was something I had learned from a young age—but I couldn't accept unfairness in this context.

The statement in the second paragraph was the worst part of the email, though. *"As you may know, this would make you deficient in one course toward your graduation this spring."* My graduation was in jeopardy.

I could go to the Community Standards, but then they would question my attendance and probably not believe me. After all, how could someone who had stopped attending classes back in October produce something this good? I couldn't face them. What if they made me meet face-to-face with Beverly? I couldn't outplay her in a social situation like that. Surely, she would win and I would be on the defensive from the start.

I sat up in my chair and tried to think rationally about my next steps. I took a few sips of tea and looked at the fireplace in the living room. It was dark and menacing, like an evil grin. I wondered if it looked more cheerful when a fire was in it.

I could explain to the dean when I saw him tomorrow. I could tell him the situation with Beverly: that we used to be roommates and that she had stolen the assignment from me. I decided that would be my best bet and that was what I would do.

I took a big breath through my nose and placed my fingers on the keyboard. I hit reply and typed a brief response, saying I would be there tomorrow. I hit send and closed my laptop. I took the final lukewarm sips of tea and put the cup on the table. Rain splattered on the bay window and ran down the glass. The living room was dark, making it a gloomy cave.

I felt utterly alone. I could call someone but didn't want to. I didn't want to bother. My life was spiralling out of control, like a snowball racing down a hill. I wished there was a way to stop it, but I felt like if I put myself in the way of the snowball, it would cover and suffocate me. There was no point in even trying.

Chapter 22

Hannah

March 12, 1889

It was a clear-skied and chilly March day as I walked to work. I had just dropped the children at the one-room schoolhouse up the street from our house. Now, I had a full six hours to work before I had to pick them up. As I put one foot in front of the other, my dress swept along the ground and my mind replayed the past year. The newspaper ad had worked wonders. Several weeks after the advertisement appeared in the paper, people started coming up the stairs, people who were serious customers and wanted photographs. Aside from the odd customer who refused to work with me because I was a woman, most people were content and even thrilled with my work.

The brown bound book that was my portfolio burst with strange and outlandish photographs. Happy customers told their friends. Their friends became happy customers, too. I managed to pay the bank back the credit. Emerson, Tristan, and Alice had shoes without holes. Most weeks, I had enough money left over for butter once I paid rent for the studio. Things were starting to work out. I turned onto the boardwalk that circled the harbour before getting onto the dirt street my studio was on.

I settled into a routine of getting the children ready for school, followed by a long days at the photography studio, dinner, school work, and bedtime routines. It got tiring. I tried to carve a bit of time each evening for myself, but most of the time, I was so weary from the activities of the day that I fell into bed and was fast asleep moments later.

Every day, I missed Richard. Every day, we lived with an unfixable hole in our household, but we held together as a family despite the loss. Both aspects of my life—portrait work at my studio and the children at home—brought me satisfaction. Life had a rhythm that was both comforting and satisfying.

Morning light sparkled on ocean water as I continued along the boardwalk at a good clip. *Good morning, Ocean,* I thought, as I did every morning. I was grateful to live next to the sea. A fine layer of frost sparkled on the boardwalk. I hoisted my dress to prevent it from getting wet and took more cautious steps to prevent slipping.

Suddenly, a piercing cry came from under the boardwalk. It was a high-pitched screech—a living being in distress. It sounded like a child.

I crouched onto my knees and brought my face to the boardwalk. I tried looking through the cracks in the boards to see what caused the sound, but in the spot I knelt, the boards were too closely placed and I couldn't see a thing.

I decided to go under the boardwalk to see what was happening. I stood up and ran to the side. A steep and muddy embankment led to under the boardwalk from where the piercing cries continued. I had to try to save whatever was under there.

One step told me how slippery it was. My foot slipped and I fell down the bank. I put my hand out sideways to stop myself from sliding, but my palm hit something jagged. Sharp pain radiated from my palm up into my fingers. An oyster shell. It had cut my hand. I turned my palm over and blood oozed from a hold in my muddy palm. My dress was covered in mud, and my boots were soaked through, but I was now under the boardwalk.

It was dark, damp, and smelled strongly of salty low tide. Finally, I saw where the sound came from. There stood a large, tan-coloured animal with a small black animal in its mouth. A long tail flowed out behind the tan attacker, giving away its identity—a cougar, and a large cougar at that. The screams came from a black dog that dangled from the cougar's large and very toothed mouth. I had to do something—and fast.

I looked around for some tool I could use to hit the cougar. The only thing around was a wooden boat oar just up the bank, near where I had just come down. I scrambled toward the bank, but slipped back with every step I took. I finally reached the oar and grabbed it. It was heavy and cumbersome, and much longer than I anticipated. I slid intentionally this time, and when I was under again, I walked toward the giant cat with the oar out in front of me. I swung the oar at its head and missed. The oar was also heavier than I expected and hit the wood boardwalk. I aimed again, and this time struck the cougar on its back near its tail. It turned toward me, loosening its jaws enough to let the dog go. The dog limped up the bank; its cries ceased. Now, the cougar focused its attention on me.

Its head was giant and its body moved with characteristic feline grace. I held the oar out in front of me but was out of breath from the effort of swinging it. In one swift motion, the cat lunged at me. As it came at me, I swung the oar, but the cougar dodged its wooden blade.

The cougar circled around me, setting up a lunge from a different angle. I swivelled with it, wielding the oar like a knight with a sword. The huge cat came toward me, teeth bared. This time, I waited a second longer than when I had wound up to hit it the first time. My patience paid off, and the oar hit its neck. It fell sideways slightly, and for a spit second, I felt bad for it, but only for a second. It turned and ran under the boardwalk toward the forested area beside the harbour. Continuing to hold the oar in front of me, I waited until it was gone into the bushes. Would it come back? My efforted breathing was all I heard.

When the cat didn't appear, I scrambled up the bank and onto the boardwalk. The small black dog was nowhere to be seen and must have headed home. I propped up the oar next to a maple tree and picked up my leather satchel that I had abandoned on the frosty boardwalk. The sun was higher now, the frost all but gone. Already, more people were walking about. Several boats cruised out of the harbour. I made my way down the dirt road and to my shop, then let myself in the door on the street level. As every day, the cobbler wished me good morning but, today, looked a second longer at my muddy dress and bleeding hand. I returned his good morning and walked up the stairs and straight into the bathroom. I cleaned my hand and took as much mud off my dress as I could.

I emerged from the bathroom as clean as possible, given the events of the morning. I then readied the studio for a portrait shoot with a man heading to the gold fields in the Yukon. He wanted portraits for his family before he "struck it rich," as he said.

The run-in with the cougar gave me a surge of adrenaline—a burst of energy not unlike the surge of energy from a strong cup of black tea. In fact, I decided to withhold my cup of tea and felt awake enough to develop a few photographs from the previous day's shoot. I dipped the photographic paper into the developing chemicals and re-ran the morning's incident in my head. What a strange morning. Had it even happened? It was amazing that the dog was not injured.

All morning, as I worked away, I could not stop thinking of the morning's encounter with the cougar. I went over the size of the cat, the length of its tail, and how it got bigger and darker near the end of its grand tail. It was times like these—when I had something so interesting or exciting to talk to someone about—that I most longed for Richard to still be alive.

≈

The closest I came to romance happened at the bank later that month. I needed to make a deposit from a photo shoot for the wife of a wealthy Hudson Bay Company employee. Money was no issue for this woman, and I sat her on a regal wooden chair with white lace. I spent the day getting a likelihood of her that she was pleased with. She paid me in silver coins, and I didn't fancy having them left around; they had to be deposited.

A man I had never seen before sat behind the counter of my bank. I strode up to him and dropped my bag of silver coins. I didn't want this to take long. I wanted to develop her photos as quickly as possible, but the man who stood in front of me was in no hurry. His calm demeanor, combined with his kind blue eyes, made me think of Richard. No man had made me feel this way since Richard had died. I was unnerved, and my cheeks went hot. I hoped they had not gone red.

"In a hurry? You must own a business," he said.

"Well, yes. But why would you think that? Most people think I am an accountant for my husband's business."

"You have a business way about you," he said. The coins sat unmoved from where I had placed them.

"Well, I best be going. Deposit, please," I said, hoping he would get going with our transaction.

"What is your business?" he asked.

"I'm an artist—a photographer—and I work for myself." I stood a bit straighter.

"A photographer . . . a noble art."

"I suppose. It pays the bills." Would he ever stop with the questions and get on with the transaction?

He looked at me a moment with a slight sideways smile. "Your hat is unusual, as is your hair."

"Well, yes. Why be like everyone else when you can be original?" I said more as a statement and didn't expect a reply.

"I see what you mean. I have an intense dislike for artificial society. One should be able to lead a free life and do what one wants to do without interference or criticism from one's neighbours." With that, he took the coins and started to print me a paper.

I looked away, not knowing what to do. Now, my cheeks felt very hot. His words were like the thoughts in my head. I had a strange feeling that I had met him before, but that was impossible. I felt guilty for feeling this way about this man I just met. Though Richard was dead, it felt disloyal to have the slightest romantic thought about another man.

The man handed me the paper showing my deposit.

"Thank you and good day," I said.

It wasn't until I was out the door that I checked that he deposited the correct amount. I chided myself silently. Usually, I checked it at the teller's desk. Now, I skimmed it, checking the numbers. It was correct. But there were some words written in pen and in a free and scrawling handwriting that was the closest to my own that I had ever seen. It said:

> *It isn't the mountain ahead that wears you out—it's the grain of sand in your shoe. No person can be a failure if they think they're a success. If he thinks he is a winner, then he is.*
>
> *Cordially, Robert Service*

I stood on the street and stared at the words on the paper. The *t's* and *p's* were uncannily like my own handwritten *t's* and *p's*. There was something whimsical about the man, and something strange about how he made me feel. An "Excuse me, madame" from behind me broke my spell. I folded up the paper and put it in my pocket, then started walking at a quick pace back to my portrait shop. For the rest of the day, I wondered about the man. I wondered what he had said, about why he said photography was a noble art.

The handwritten words on the receipt paper the blue-eyed man wrote gave me a feeling like anything could happen, like I shouldn't fret every small detail and should try for anything I wanted in life. With that, I went to sleep and tried my best to stop thinking of the man in the bank and his sideways smile that made my stomach feel strange but pleasant.

≈

A few weeks, I stood outside the tall and imposing bank. I hadn't been in since the interaction with the teller that left me feeling more alive than I had felt in months. The way I felt after speaking to that man frightened me. Although I had felt so happy, I didn't want to feel that out-of-control way, but I kept the paper he had given me. I looked at it every so often and had even begun keeping it pressed in the book where I kept Richard's shovel message, though I felt a twinge of guilt placing it there.

The night before I stood in front of the bank, I laid in bed awake and missed Richard. Then my mind went to the man in the bank and I wanted nothing more than to see him again. I longed for human touch. I wanted to learn more about him. I made up my mind. I would bring my deposit to him the next day, just to see if he would be there, and I would gather information. Once I made my mind up about something, I always followed through.

I took one more look at the bank, strode up to the door, and pulled it open. I walked with a purpose through the bank and to his wicket stand. My heart fell when I got there. A portly man with a red face smiled at me and greeted me in a nasally voice. "Ma'am, what can I do for you?"

"Oh, hello," I said. "I have a deposit." I placed my bills and coins on the counter between us.

The man took them and began ringing them through.

"Anything else today, ma'am?" he said as he handed me the paper receipt.

"Yes, actually. The man who used to be at this stand. Dark brown hair, a talkative fellow. Is he in today?"

The portly man let out a high-pitched giggle. "Oh, Robert. What a bizarre fellow."

I looked at him expectantly, trying to be patient, and not seem overly eager. He noticed me looking at him and eventually realized he hadn't answered my question.

"He moved out of town. Said he was going to the Yukon. Went on about being brave and true, wanting the strange and new. Something about going places that were rough and tough and getting to the bedrock and meeting human people. Real odd chap, that one. Full of verses and rhymes. People been asking about him all day long since he left town. Why do you ask?"

"No reason, just wondering. Thank you," I replied. Then I lifted my dress, turned on my heel, and walked out of the bank. My stomach sank, and I wished I hadn't come in. What a silly idea it had been. I vowed not to be so thoughtless and foolish ever again.

That was the last time I even remotely considered remarrying. There was nobody after that. Besides, my business and children kept me busy enough. I had no time for romance.

Chapter 23

Brooke

January 16, 2018

I craned my head upwards to see the building number: 410. A raindrop fell into my eye and stung. I blinked, a feeble attempt to make the stinging subside. I looked down at my phone to double check the building in the email from the dean. I was in the right place. My phone said 12:52 p.m. In a few minutes, I would sit in front of the dean. I walked to the door of the building, pulled the handle, and stepped inside.

I hoped I didn't see anyone I knew on campus—student or professor. I dreaded having to explain where I had been the past few months. I was incapable of lying, but I didn't want to explain the internal mind struggles I was having. Nobody would understand. And if I vaguely said I hadn't been well, they would reply with, "You don't look sick."

If only I could avoid this meeting. But I couldn't. I could avoid classes. I could avoid emails. I could avoid workshops. But I could not avoid this meeting. My graduation hinged on this getting this resolved. I had to go in and fight for my truth.

If I didn't make the meeting, I wouldn't graduate in the spring. As of now, I was three months and five courses away from finishing my bachelor's degree—a feat I never thought possible until the last few months. This was something I had poured my life into for four years, something I had gone into burying debt for. Just months before, graduation felt close to reach out and grab; now, it felt out of reach. My dreams of graduating would be crushed if I didn't attend this meeting.

After a stomach-lurching ride up the elevator, I found the reception area to the dean's office. I checked in with reception and sat in a hard blue chair. His office reception area was on the eighth floor and was floor-to-ceiling glass and windows. I felt a bit of vertigo when I looked out. It was like a castle in the sky. I saw the ocean strait and coast mountains across the ocean but was in no place to relish the view. My stomach turned, and I felt dizzy. I told myself I had rehearsed what I would say. *You can do this*, I told myself. *You must do this. Do it for your graduation*.

At that moment, the receptionist called over her desk.

"Brooke Daniels, Mr. Price will see you now. You can walk down to his office. That way." She indicated down a hallway.

I got up from the hard chair and walked down the hall where she had pointed. The hallway was also floor to ceiling windows. I walked until I arrived at the end of the hall and entered an office with the door open.

"Hello, come in," he said, pointing to the chair across the office.

I walked to the chair and sat down. The positioning of my chair away from the door gave me an uneasy feeling.

"I'll be with you in a moment," he said as he clicked away on his keyboard. I sat with my feet firmly placed on the floor and my knees together. I tried to straighten my back. I glanced around awkwardly, not sure if I should say something.

"All right," I managed, and continued looking around.

After some more clicking, Mr. Price took off his glasses and addressed me. “Hello . . .” he looked at his computer, “Brooke.” He reached over to push the door closed. It shut with a loud bang.

“Hello, Mr. Price,” I said. He was a large man with a barrel chest and a very red face. I couldn’t help but wonder his liquor of choice.

“You’re here because of plagiarizing. It’s a serious academic misconduct offense, and you were set to graduate.”

“Actually, I want to tell you a few things.”

“What’s there to explain? You submitted the same work as another student. Pretty simple to me and not much you can do now other than make an appeal to the Community Standards staff.”

I swallowed and my throat tightened. My voice shook as I said what I practised at home that morning.

“Well, I do have a few things to explain. I think I know the student who reported me and we have a bit of a . . . complicated relationship. We used to be roommates, and I think she took the assignment off my laptop. I have all the papers here from my story outline and from writing the paper.” I held out a yellow folder bursting with lined sheets of paper I had pulled out of one of my notebooks.

The dean did not take the folder, which left my hand hanging awkwardly in the space between us.

I finally brought the folder back onto my lap.

“Nonsense. There is no way that student would have stolen your work. I know her father from business school and he is a stand-up guy. His daughter would not do such a thing. I won’t hear any more about this. The purpose of this meeting is to inform you that will not graduate because of this sanction.” His eyes then moved from me to his computer screen, and his hand moved to the mouse on his desk. He clicked something on the screen and began typing.

I then realized there was no point in explaining myself further or in trying to show him the papers that proved the story was mine, that proved I researched the story and worked on it for hours.

"All right then, I'll be going. Thank you," I said, and felt my face getting hot.

He didn't look up from his computer screen.

My throat was tight and my mouth as dry as after an hour-long walk with no water. I thanked the receptionist and left the glass room. I took the stairs this time, descending quickly and trying to focus on my steps rather than the thoughts that raced through my head.

I pushed open the door. Tears stung my eyes as I started walking home.

I should have known there was no point in defending myself or explaining. Beverly was so well connected and well protected. Of course, she had reported me in the most professional way, solidifying me as the cheater. Of course, she had stolen my work in a foolproof way, and of course, her father knew the dean. The dean wasn't going to listen to someone with no parents, no connections, and who hadn't attended classes in months.

I pondered how Beverly had done this. Did she have no remorse? How did someone have so much hatred in them? If I didn't like someone, I didn't feel the need to hurt them.

I walked home, heading across campus the way I had come. Anger washed over me like a wave of cold water. A nauseous feeling settled in my stomach as I descended the steps and swallowed the prospect of not graduating.

Chapter 24

Hannah

November 22, 1891

One November morning, I sat at my desk in my photographic studio. Morning light filtered through the big window, and I looked at my full schedule for the day. I noticed the date: November 22, 1891. The date stood out, but it took me a moment to figure out why. Then, it donned on me: that day marked four years, to the day, that I rented this place and started my photographic studio. A pleasant shiver ran over me, and I felt a tug of pride inside me for what I had done.

The first year had been horribly difficult, but each day had gotten easier. Now, I had regular customers and enough walk-ins to pay the bills, maintain the eaves of the house, purchase wood for the fire, and buy the children new shoes. Some weeks, there was even a bit extra. I missed Richard every day, but I had done the best with the hand I had been dealt.

I looked around my studio. Floating dust particles caught in the bright morning light gave the whole place a magical appearance. My eyes went to the round table, set for tea with the grey fur rug underneath. I recalled using it as an ideal backdrop for some multiple exposure photos that I had now mastered. The hat I wore that day sat on the desk in front of me. It was black velvet with a wide brim and adorned with a dramatic black feather. I had been so proud the day I bought it.

My bicycle sat in the corner. When my precious time wasn't taken up with the children or working in my studio, I rode around the park. I greatly enjoyed riding through the large park downtown Doveport. Trees and fountains flashed past me far quicker than I could walk. It was a thrill. Once, I spotted two baby fawns ahead of me. I stopped my bike and stood very still. I could see their white spots and black noses. One deer lifted its front leg and pushed its hoof onto the other fawn's back, which initiated a few precious minutes of the two of them bouncing around like two dogs playing. Eventually, they bobbed off into the undergrowth. The bicycle afforded animal and landscape viewing that I couldn't have dreamed of before owning one. Though I missed Richard, I had carved a good life for myself and for my children.

I finished setting out my lenses for my day of three portrait appointments. I then sat down at the big wooden chair and awaited my first appointment. A newspaper sat on my desk. I opened it and idly flipped the pages until an advertisement at the back made me stop flipping:

> *City of Doveport Seeks Police Photographer. Must be versed in newest photographic techniques, professional, and have keen eye for detail. Apply at the Doveport City office on Wharf Street.*

A police photographer! What a grand adventure that would be. The strange and unusual people you would get to meet, and guaranteed appointments every day. No more haggling customers trying to get your prices down so they get a deal. And, it would mean a new challenge and new things to learn.

My immediate thought was that I would apply, but after sorting through thoughts in my mind, I decided otherwise. Surely, many men would apply and they would get the position over me. I didn't fancy putting my name out there only to be rejected. Besides, I made enough with my photographic studio. I heard footsteps coming up the stairs. I closed the newspaper and stood up to greet my first appointment of the day.

≈

Later that day, I tidied my desk for my final appointment: a portrait session for a woman who was the wife of the governor of the great land on which we lived. I dragged over the greatest wooden chair I had and straightened up the backdrop. I moved a black feather duster over all the surfaces in the studio. The studio had to be impeccably neat and clean for this shoot.

After I finished tidying the studio, I sat at my desk and looked at my clock. I had ten minutes until the wife of the governor arrived. I decided to pass the time by organizing papers on my desk. I was doing just that —moving papers to piles to throw out and a pile to file away—when I came across a piece of paper in handwriting I nearly confounded as my own. My stomach got a fluttery feeling as I read the note: *"No person can be a failure if they think they're a success. If he thinks he is a winner, then he is."*

It was the note from the bank teller. Reading those words gave me a feeling of hope—a feeling that anything was possible. I thought about the police advertisement. Maybe I should apply. I wouldn't know unless I tried. I might be successful; I might not. But the only way I would know is by trying.

With that, I decided to apply. Reading the words about being a winner gave me an expansive feeling of possibility, a feeling that it might be worth the risk of not getting the position for the possibility that I might get it. I made up my mind. I reached over to my brown leather portfolio and pulled out a few of my best photographs. I spent the last minutes before my next appointment tapping at my typewriter and putting words into sentences to make myself sound like the best police photographer the city could hire.

Chapter 25

Brooke

January 17, 2018

The day after I met the dean, I woke up drenched in sweat, my heart racing. In my dream, I walked the graduation stage, but my diploma kept getting further and further away. What I wanted seemed constantly out of reach and I felt paralyzed. The dream felt so real that when I woke up, I had to think very hard about if it happened or not.

I threw off the covers and swung my legs off the bed. I pulled on soft sweatpants, slippers, and an oversized hoody, then walked into the living room. The fireplace loomed in front of me and the reading nook by the bay window sat empty and forlorn. Heavy fog hung in the air outside and I couldn't see across to the park, let alone out to the ocean. The greyness of outside mirrored my inner landscape of hopelessness, despair, and injustice.

I replayed the meeting from yesterday. It was unfair, plain and simple. He wouldn't even look at my notes or story outline that proved that I wrote the assignment. There was a timestamp on the computer document that showed when it was created and who created it, proving how long it had been on my laptop. There had to be some way I could show the university that it was mine, but was it worth putting myself out there again, only to be shut down when I wasn't believed because I didn't have some powerful dad in business who knew other men in positions of authority?

I startled to a strange sound from by bedroom. A light bang. Someone or something was in my room. I pulled up my hood and walked with trepidation back to my bedroom. I peered in and noticed the source of the noise on the floor next to my nightstand. It was only my phone. Its vibrating had knocked it off my nightstand onto the floor. It was still vibrating, indicating an incoming call.

I picked it up and answered it.

"Hello."

"Brooke! How are you? It's been ages. What have you been up to?" It was Jade, peppy, wide awake, and hammering questions at me.

"I'm all right . . ." I lied. It was hard for me to open up. I had this problem where I didn't want to burden anyone with my problems, and part of me thought maybe I deserved what was happening. Maybe I wasn't meant to graduate.

"Are you sure? I haven't seen you in classes. Everyone is wondering where you are. We're so close to graduating."

"Yeah, I've been doing my work at home these days."

"Hmmm, well, want to come out tomorrow night? Some people from school are going to watch a live acoustic show downtown. Want to play a game of pool at Hawthorne's and then head to the show after?"

I panicked. The thought of getting dressed up and facing people made my heart race. I didn't want to answer questions about where I had been.

"I can't. I have an assignment to do, and I'm not really feeling up to seeing a lot of people."

"Brooke, you'll feel better if you come out. Like the hiking trip, remember? You didn't want to come, you pushed yourself . . . and it was the best trip ever. You were so glad you came. Come on, I'll come get you and we can walk together."

"No, I can't. I'm really not feeling up to it."

"More the reason to come, then! Is there anything going on that you want to talk about? I'm always here to listen, and I won't offer advice unless you ask for it. Anything at all that you want to talk about?"

I thought about telling her about the academic misconduct, about Beverly's report against me, about being deficient one class to graduate, and about the meeting with the dean and how he didn't believe me. I thought about how it would be difficult to tell her, how I would probably break down crying, but how light it would feel after.

No, still not worth it. She would make me act against Beverly and the situation, and I couldn't do that. Best to keep everything to myself.

"No, nothing. I just don't feel like coming out." It was easier not to tell her.

"Are you sure there's nothing? It sounds like there's something there you don't want to tell me."

One more chance, but I didn't take it. I couldn't. "Not tonight. Maybe next time. But thanks, and hope you have fun."

"All right, well, let me know if you change your mind."

"All right, thanks." I was relieved she had stopped asking, but that meant the knowledge of my graduation status, the failed course, and the allegation against me was still trapped inside me. In a way, telling her would have been a greater relief.

"And, Brooke . . ." she said.

Oh no, what now? Was she going to continue to coerce me into going out tomorrow night? "Yeah . . ."

"I'm always here if there's anything you want to talk about."

There was my chance again, to tell her everything and put down the heavy, figurative backpack of worries and false allegations and injustices just for a moment, to take the weight from my shoulders and put it down for a break, the chance to let someone share in the weight and maybe support me. But I didn't deserve it.

"Thanks. I'll remember that." I couldn't do it. I couldn't tell her.

After some tea and toast, I climbed into bed, propped up two big feathery pillows, and pulled the covers up over my chest. I spent the rest of the day lost in the world of a science fiction novel. I had five assignments to do for school, including one for the creative writing course that I was once excited about. The meeting the day before sucked all motivation for schoolwork. There was no point anymore. I wasn't going to graduate, so there was no point in putting hours into typing assignments.

I pulled the covers up further and adjusted the pillow under my head. Curling up warm under the covers and getting lost in a story about a girl in space was comforting and easy. It was a safe place to be. But I couldn't stop thinking of a saying I had read in a book at one point.

The saying was something about boats in harbours being safe, but that wasn't what boats were built for.

≈

I awoke the next morning to the deep, long blow of a foghorn. Its haunting low wail echoed over the water and seemed to float into the yellow house. I wandered into the kitchen, made some tea, and sliced up an orange. The milk swirled in the tea, turning it cream coloured from the bottom up. I had a sick feeling that there were things I should be doing but wasn't, like the five assignments for my classes, like filling out the written request for a hearing or at least contacting Community Standards staff at the university and seeking advice, and like letting Jade know my recent struggles or seeking support from Derek and David.

I played it out in my mind calling Derek and David. They would be angry at the injustice and would advise me what to do. They would comfort me, but they would also make me act, and I couldn't bear to put myself out there to be shut down again. Besides, Derek's mom was sick and in hospital. I didn't want to add anything to their plate. I didn't want to be a burden to them.

Deeper down, buried under years of moving from house to house and not having a go-to adult, I didn't think myself worthy of their unconditional love and attention. They had already done so much for me. I couldn't repay them for the years of a solid home and love they gave me. The least I could do was not bother them with my problems now that I lived alone.

I spent the entire day with the science fiction novel. I tried ignoring the dark and sinking feeling that I had assignments to be working on or I only had twenty-seven business days left to submit a written request for a hearing with the Community Standards board. As the hours ticked away, the prospect of graduating slipped further from my reach.

≈

Later that day, darkness fell over the house and the ocean. I felt restless and anxious after another wasted day. I was anxious I would miss out on the night. Five times, I picked up my phone to text Jade back and tell her that I would go out that night after all. But each time I picked up my phone, I put it back down again. Texting her meant that I was accountable for showing up, and I wasn't sure I could do it. Would people ask me where I had been? Had Beverly told people I had plagiarized her assignment? I decided not to text but to go find Jade. I would put on a brave face and try to navigate the questions about where I had been the past months.

I left my phone on the fireplace mantle and walked to my bedroom to get ready. I pulled the doors open to the small closet in my room and looked at the few clothes hanging on hangers, the neatly stacked pants on the upper shelves, and a few pairs of shoes neatly on the bottom—mostly thrift store finds but cute ones. I picked a pair of jeans, a tight-knit forest green sweater that matched my eyes, and some leather mid-ankle boots. I wish I could say I was a trendy minimalist, but the truth was that I would rather spend my work money on the odd book from a used bookstore or put it toward my student loan. These days, most of my paycheques went toward this house.

I had a flutter of excitement of seeing people, but also a sense of dread. The truth was that I missed having a group of friends. University had been the first time I had felt like part of a group of friends and was automatically included in group plans. My social life was planned for me and I did whatever the group was doing that weekend. That was before Chatham decided to ask me out and Beverly started with me.

I heated up some leftovers for dinner and pulled out a beer that hid like a lone soldier at the back of the fridge. The fog had thickened and foghorns blared more frequently. All the boats coming and going quietly at normal times now made their presence known.

I grabbed my leather satchel, put on some lip gloss, and headed out the door. The night air was cold. I could barely see half a block ahead of me, but the way to downtown was one I had done dozens of times, usually with Jade but, this time, on my own.

I walked along the harbour toward downtown. I passed a wooden oar that a maple tree had grown around. A metal plaque said, "Feel free to use again to fight off cougars." I always wondered what the story was with that. Surely there was a story that went with the plaque.

When I arrived downtown, I felt another anxious flutter in my stomach. I pushed it away and peeked into Murphy's pub, where the show was happening. It was nearly ten, and the show would start soon. The pub had big windows that afforded a clear view of the entire pub. I stood on the street and peeked in. I saw the stage and the band members milled about getting ready to perform. I spotted Jade, her dark hair and long legs giving her away. But who was she with? I recognized a few people from the creative writing program, but they were crowded around someone I didn't recognize. Until I did recognize her—it was Beverly. They were crowded around her, looking at something she was showing them on her phone. Anger bubbled up in me. Anger mixed with anxiety. I didn't want to be seen. I couldn't go in. Beverly would surely make a scene if I entered the pub. My plans to be social for the night were ruined.

I couldn't believe Jade was with that group, the group that kicked me out so easily—one day I was in their ranks, the next I was out because of Beverly's tight grasp on people.

Suddenly, I felt reckless, like nothing mattered and nothing I did made a difference, but most of all, like I didn't care what happened to me. I turned away from the window and started toward Hawthorne's. I would go there alone and play pool.

When I arrived in Hawthorne's, multiple pairs of men's eyes turned and assessed me. Though I didn't sport revealing clothing, I still seemed to get attention from men; I didn't know why and I certainly didn't deserve it. I was an orphan and unlovable, and I wasn't going to graduate university now.

I walked straight to the bar.

"I'll have a double rum and Coke," I said. I usually drank beer, but I wanted a quick buzz tonight, anything to get me to forget my life, forget Jade standing in the same circle as Beverly.

"Coming right up," the bartender said.

I sat on a barstool and watched him pour the clear liquid into a glass, add ice, and then the syrupy brown soda. He handed it to me, and I took the longest sip I possibly could from the straw.

It was way too sweet, and when I took my mouth from the straw, I felt dizzy and numb.

"Having a rough night?"

"You could say that, I guess."

"Up for a play a game of pool?"

I wasn't up for a game of pool, but I was horrible at saying no.

"Sure, why not?"

He came around from the bar, and we took over the corner table by the window, the same table Jade and I always played at. It had a light over it and there was a plant sitting in the corner by the window. I missed Jade and our easy conversation. I sipped on my rum and Coke.

"What happened?" the bartender asked as he broke and sank a solid red.

I circled the table and assessed my choices with the stripes. "Just problems with university," I said, not wanting to get into it. I sunk a yellow stripe into the side pocket, followed by the orange into the corner.

"C'mon. Let me know what's going on. Nothing I haven't heard, being a bartender and all. People tell me their stories all the time."

"A girl stole my paper and is making my life miserable," I finally divulged. As soon as I said it, I regretted it.

"Well, I hope it works out for you."

After that, I kept the conversation superficial. The bartender was moderately interesting, but I wouldn't let him get close physically or emotionally. Finally, I left Hawthorne's and walked toward the yellow house. Even though I didn't do anything with the bartender, I felt empty and dirty. I realized that I was associating anything to do with romance with Beverly's harassment. This was going to become a major problem and would guard me from any romance in the future, but I didn't know what to do about it. I walked past the wooden oar being eaten by the maple tree again. This time the writing on the plaque was blurry and illegible. At last, I turned down the street leading to Winfield Crescent. My head was foggy and thoughts drifted away before I could process them.

When I got into my house, queasiness washed over me. The house felt hot and stuffy, and the fireplace creeped me out. I went out the back door and out to the backyard, then sat myself on the bench directly outside a big vined tree that grew over the archway. I wondered why someone didn't clip it back. I thought of how good things had been a month ago and how devastating they were now.

As my thoughts spiralled down a tunnel of gloom, caught my eye—something through the kitchen window moved. Before I thought it was nothing, it moved again. Something was in the yellow house. I stood up from the bench and stepped sideways. I couldn't see anything when I looked inside. *Perhaps a raccoon,* I thought. Perhaps it got in and rummaged around looking for garbage. Or maybe it was a rat. Being near the port, rats abounded. I walked closer to the back kitchen door but saw nothing. *Must have gone on its way, whatever it was,* I thought. That, or my eyes had played tricks on me.

I turned to head into the house. When I nearly reached the door, I saw what had caught my eye in the kitchen. A woman. There was a woman seated at the kitchen table, a woman wearing an old-timey long black dress with puffy sleeves. Her hair was very curly and pulled back. She was straight from an old-fashioned painting. She looked at me with a sully expression. Shivers went down my spine. I backed up from the kitchen door and felt my heart beating in my chest. I looked down so I wouldn't slip on the uneven ground of the lawn. When I looked up at the back kitchen door, the woman was gone. The table was vacant; the house, empty.

There had been a woman sitting there, her legs tucked under her—I was sure of it. But as the seconds wore on, I became less sure of myself. Did I really see it? Now, I couldn't be sure. I already had enough going on; now I was seeing things that weren't there. I wished Jade was here.

Then I could have known if there had truly been something there. If she saw it, I could have confirmed it in my mind and crossed off "potentially hallucinating" to my long list of current worries.

I finally summoned my courage, open the back door to the kitchen, and went inside. I filled up a glass of water as quickly as I could and walked to my room. I crawled into bed and sleep engulfed me quickly.

Chapter 26

Hannah

January 6, 1891

The day the phone call came, I was in the middle of a portrait session with three children. The mother sipped tea at the back of the studio while I snapped shots of her children. When one screamed, she looked up and then went back to powdering her nose with the powder case and mirror she held up in front of her.

The phone rang and rang, but I didn't pick it up. I was at a crucial point where I had just got the infant comfortable and looking over to the camera. I walked slowly back to my camera and clicked the button. Whoever was calling would have to wait. I walked from the children back to the camera several times and hoped for some good shots. This was a first-time customer, and I wanted to leave a good impression. Over the years, I found that word of mouth was a more valuable way to advertise than any other.

Five minutes later, the phone rang again. I looked at it and thought I'd better answer. I worried it might be the children's school and that something had happened to one of them. Since Richard died, my mind tended to leap to the worst-case scenario. It had never done that before Richard's death.

"Hello, photographic studio," I said while pulling my mouth into a silly grin and opening my eyes in a funny way toward the children, in hopes it held their attention.

"Hello, I'm looking to speak to Hannah Hatherly."

I stopped pulling the face. "This is her," I said impatiently.

The mother looked over at me and then at her watch. This was, after all, her photographic session that time ticked away upon. I would have to explain to her that I would reimburse her the time at the end.

"Yes, this is Benton Fowler calling from the city."

"Yes, hello, sir." I looked to the mother and held one finger up—trying to communicate to her that I would be but one minute on the phone.

"How are you today, ma'am."

"Fine, thank you." I wished people would get on with things. I didn't have all day to be muddling away with small talk. I was in the middle of a portrait session. The children already wiggled and moved from positions I spent minutes coaxing them into.

"I'm calling because we were very impressed with your application regarding the position at the city."

"I'm glad to hear that," I said, now very curious as to what was coming next.

"And we would like to offer you the position as Doveport's official police photographer."

I was flabbergasted. It had been five weeks since I had brought in my application. Three weeks ago, I had lost all hope, thinking that surely they had found someone else. I had decided against calling them to confirm I didn't get it. My pride had been injured enough as it was.

"I'm delighted," I started with. "I am pleased to be offered the position. What are the next steps?"

"Come to the office tomorrow at ten in the morning, and we will start the process of getting you hired on. Welcome to the team, Mrs. Hatherly. I think you will find that working for the city has a great many benefits and that you will be compensated finely for your work."

"I very much look forward to it. Thank you, sir. I will be there tomorrow."

I hung up the phone and went straight back to snapping photos of the three children. The rest of the photo session went by like the flash of my biggest camera. I couldn't believe I was selected for the position. I knew I was exceptionally good at my trade, but I didn't expect them to recognize that. I thought they would hire a man for the position for sure. As it turned out, someone knew what was good for the city. I was grateful for whomever that person was. The words from the bank teller must be true: you truly are a winner if you believe you are.

≈

My studio as an official police photographer was on the ground floor. It had a proper door that closed and even a sign nailed to the door with my name on it—not Richard's name, but my name. *Hannah Hatherly, Doveport Official Police Photographer.*

In many ways, it was more convenient, but I sometimes missed my old studio. Overall, my job as a police photographer gave me great satisfaction.

I stood in my developing room thinking back to how far I had come—from the days that I couldn't buy shoes for my children to the day I realized for the first time in years, I could purchase something frivolous, something for myself. Every day, I tried to raise the children bravely as Richard had written on the shovel. I think he would have been proud of me.

Over my developing tray, I worked at putting two photographs on the same negative. I had been at it for weeks and felt I was a moment away.

As I just about had it, two policemen brought in a curious looking suspect.

"Arrested criminal for photographing," one officer said.

"All right, bring them on in," I said, moving the developing solution aside on the counter. I wondered who it was today.

Nothing surprised me in this job. People of all kinds had their portraits taken. I never knew who would show up at my door: people who stole a can of beans from the corner store, someone who broke into another's house, a stowaway on a ship who looked like he had not showered in days and whose rankness I smelled from the door, and so on.

But this time the convict brought to my studio door surprised me.

I adjusted the settings on my camera while the police officers loosened the cuffs on a petit woman with light brown hair and the lightest of blue eyes. She stood with two officers wearing their black officer hats and black officer coats with shiny buttons down the front. She was beautiful beyond measure yet cold and aloof.

I was equal parts enthralled and wary of her.

"Hello, ma'am. Have a seat," I said, and motioned to the stool by the backdrop I used for mug shots. Against the backdrop, I noticed her flamboyant hat, all ribbons, and bows.

"I didn't mean to kill him," she said in a dreamy voice, her face blank.

"Kill who?" I asked her, as I adjusted the mirror beside her head. I was experimenting with a new technique that would be revolutionary if I could make it work. The positioning of the mirror was key to the plan working.

"I got in a fight with my boyfriend. I meant to just push him away, but I killed him by accident," she said, and continued looking blankly ahead.

I nodded my head but said nothing.

The officer piped in then. "Tried decapitating him with a razor. It's looking like five years for manslaughter."

The girl continued to stare blankly ahead.

"Oh," I said. "Move your head sideways," I told her. Her head had to be positioned just so for me to get the profile shot correctly.

I walked to the photo and shot away. The girl barely blinked.

"All finished," I said when the photographs were taken.

The woman didn't respond as she was led out of the room. I felt sorry for her, bound to be behind bars, but I had a goal in mind and wanted to complete it before I went home. I had thirty minutes before the police chief would be gone.

I took the photos to my dark room and got to work.

When I pulled the photo out, I was delighted and had to show someone. My plan had worked.

It was five minutes to five o'clock when I strode down the hall and knocked on the chief of police's door. The door opened, and he stood questioning me.

"I have something to show you, sir." There was no need for small talk with the chief of police. I knew how to work with him. No nonsense; cut straight to the point of the conversation's purpose.

"What's that?"

"A new way of taking photographs of convicted criminals that hasn't been done yet. Here." I handed him the single photograph.

He took it from me and placed a pair of finger-printed and slightly bent spectacles on his nose, then moved his eyes to the photo. A slight grin came over his face as he noticed what I had done.

"Clever. Both the full face and the profile view on one photograph," he said.

"Yes, and I can reproduce it easily." And I could. I had done it. What started as an idea in my head had become a reality. I put the full-face mug shot and the profile on the same photograph. To do it, I hung a mirror behind the person, so the person's full face was in the main part of the photo and the profile was seen in the mirror. Two photographs, one piece of paper.

It was an efficient and conscious use of resources.

"It will save time and materials," I added.

"Well done, Hannah. You were the right person for this position."

I walked down the hall toward my office, then placed the photo on my desk and allowed a wide grin to spread across my face as I grabbed my coat from the rack. A warm feeling of pride welled up in my chest. I had reached the zenith of my career. I felt like this new way of taking photographs was a culmination of everything I had learned as a police photographer. It was practical but allowed me to flex my creative muscles. It had taken many hours to plan and then to make it work in practice.

I collected my leather satchel, pulled the door closed, and glanced at the plaque bearing my name before I walked toward the door. I wouldn't get Richard back, but my life had taken some unexpectedly positive turns. Life was as good as it could be, all things considered.

Chapter 27

Brooke

January 19, 2018

I awoke the next morning in my clothes from the night before. My head pounded. My mouth was as dry as a bird cage's and tasted like one, too. I recalled the events of the night before. It all came back to me: Jade with Beverly, me at Hawthorne's, the double rum and Cokes, the bartender and the woman in the old-timey dress at the kitchen table.

I sat up to reach for my phone on my nightstand, and a wave of nausea washed over me. I thought I might throw up, but the wave passed once I was upright position. I looked at the time: just past eight a.m. I put my phone back on the nightstand and reached over to close the gap where my curtains and window didn't fully meet.

Using a hand on each curtain, I pulled them together, trying to move them from the top. Stubborn daylight streamed in every time I took my hand from the curtain. I yanked again, harder this time, hoping if I got the fabric to slide from the top that they would meet at the bottom and stop light from getting in, but they would not come together. Frustrated, I gave one more yank. All at once, the curtains came crashing onto me, followed by the metal curtain rod. It impacted the top of my head and sent a jolt of pain through my already throbbing forehead. I looked up and saw that the force of my pull had also broken one of the metal brackets. It must be in the mess of the curtain or in my bed somewhere. Now, daylight streamed in uninhibited, increasing my headache and giving a jolt of nausea. I thrust the curtains and curtain rod onto my floor and lay back down. I pulled the covers up over me and put a shirt over my face. For a while, the world spun and then I was back asleep.

I woke up to my phone vibrating. I pushed the shirt out of my eyes and looked at my phone: 12:15 p.m. The incoming call was Jade. I let it ring. I couldn't face her. It was silly to be mad, but I felt betrayed. I turned the phone over, and it soon stopped buzzing. The silence was a relief but also lonely. I should have picked up. I should open up to her. She was my best friend, after all. But I didn't think I could handle going over everything that had gone on. I thought I might break, and she would force me to do something about everything. I had no energy for that. The swimming nausea had subsided, but my temples still pounded. I needed water.

Slowly and without sudden movements, I got up and padded to the kitchen. Walking slightly hunched over felt better and less like I was going to throw up. I pushed toast down in the toaster and flicked on the kettle. I looked across to the kitchen table where I saw the woman last night. Did I really see her? Was it possible that the bartender put a hallucinogenic drug in my rum and Coke? I should have been more careful. Normally, I was vigilant beyond measure about my drinks while out. Last night, I was reckless. What was possibly going on in this house? I seriously considered giving a month's notice. It had such a charm to it in many ways. That clawfoot tub was a dream. I needed to use it more—treat myself to a hot bath. I was terrible at doing nice things for myself; I needed to work on that.

The smell of sweet, toasted bread wafted from the toaster and I was suddenly hungry. I spread peanut butter over the toast and poured a few thin lines of honey over the peanut butter layer. I poured hot water over a tea bag and splashed some milk over it to make it a satisfyingly cream colour. I took both to the table.

I slowly bit at my toast and sipped my tea. Then I flipped my phone over. The white calendar square on the interface showed me the date—twenty-six business days to send in the written request for the appeal. But was would be the point? It already felt too late.

I was certainly not up to checking emails. To see everything I needed to do? No, thanks. I felt less nauseous after eating and revelled in the few moments of feeling normal. Oh, how I took feeling normal for granted on a day when I wasn't ill from drinking. I noted to try to be grateful for just feeling good more often. The subsiding of the nausea didn't last long, though. Soon enough, a wave of queasiness came over me. I left the dishes on the table, slowly walked to my bedroom, and climbed back into bed. I dozed off, feeling physically and emotionally sick, guilty for all the things I should be doing but was not.

When I finally awoke, it was after five in the evening. I still felt sick, but it wasn't as violent. I could sit up without being ravaged by nausea. Thoughts swam through my brain. I should call Jade. I should call Derek and David. I should write a letter of appeal. I should mediate and start a yoga practice. I should eat less toast and more green smoothies.

Thoughts bounced off everywhere in my brain. They were out of control, like a wild horse. I racked my brain for a way to feel better, something in my toolbox of things to take care of myself, and ideally something that worked fast.

Walking. I would go for a walk.

For the first time that day, I dressed. Then I put on running shoes and my raincoat and locked the door behind me. Rain came down in sheets as I started down Winfield Crescent. I passed the white building that

Jade had told me was a mine rescue building back in the day. There had been some horrible mine explosions, and that was where the rescues happened. Today, the white building served as a food bank. On Tuesdays, there was a line nearly down to my house of people waiting patiently to pick up food. It broke my heart to see it, and it broke my heart to think about it now. Alcohol made anxiety a hundred times worse, I mused. I shamed myself for going last night. What had I been thinking?

I tried my best not to think of the past and not to let my mind take flight to the future. I tried to notice my surroundings to keep myself rooted in the present.

Raindrops landed on puddles like countless stars flickering in an inky black liquid sky. Streetlights shot a pillar of yellow light downwards as a million diagonal droplets careened sideways toward Earth. An occasional large droplet fell from the yellow light.

Down a steep side street, black rivers of water fell in waves like fish scales, little waves slipping down the street in order, forever one after another.

Four blocks from my house, I settled into the present moment. Out of nowhere, a putrid smell made its way to my nose. I looked over at the houses, wondering which one was the source of the offensive odor. Something dead or decayed? Compost maybe? Luckily, I would be away from it soon. But half a block later, the smell still lingered. Almost so much that it felt like it was up my nose. Fowl and strong, there was only one thing it could be: dog poo. I had stepped in it. I silently cursed the person who hadn't picked it up. I wiped both shoes along the pavement, hoping to rub it off, but it only served to broaden the smell, making it worse. Just when I thought things couldn't get much worse, I now had dog poo all over the sole of my shoe. I gave up rubbing it off and pulled my sweatshirt up to cover my nose, then tightened up my hood to hold the material up.

I arrived back at the yellow house. It smiled in a sinister way in the darkness. In the day, the storm shutters gave it a cheerful, character-house feel, but at night, they showed it as the spirit-filled, ancient house it was. I tried not to breathe in my nose as I unlaced my shoes and left them on the porch. I turned the key and entered the house. My clothes were soaked through; I peeled them off, starting with my coat. I thought what a waste I had made of the day that was when my phone buzzed from the kitchen table. The buzzing startled me out of my thoughts.

I walked to the kitchen table and flipped my phone over. Jade again. I reached for it and hovered my thumb over the green icon that would answer it, but I couldn't face her. Even after my walk, I couldn't explain things any better now and I still couldn't take any actions I needed to even though I knew they were what was best for me. For the second time that day, I didn't answer a call from my best friend. My life was spiralling into a dark place, and I felt helpless in doing anything about it.

Chapter 28

Hannah

October 19, 1937

I'll always remember the day I died. Like a birthday, the day that I died was etched into my memory, both for the day that it was—October 19, 1937—and for its details.

The day had been cold and clear. The moon glowed off the window of my hospital room, throwing off a brightness that lit up the room like sun did in the daytime. It was a bright full moon that made you gasp with awe and made you feel small and insignificant—a grain of sand in an infinite universe. Moon shadows played off the flowers and cards that my children and grandchildren had brought me. A heart attack landed me in the hospital a few days before. Then the doctor told me I had to stay so they could keep an eye on my vitals.

Hours earlier, shortly after I had eaten soup and a hard bread roll off the hospital tray, the nurse appeared at my door.

"You have some guests, Mrs. Hatherly. Would you like me to let them in?"

"Yes, dear, let them on in."

I sat upright and ran my hands through my thin hair, trying to make it less frizzy.

The nurse disappeared and I looked expectantly at the door. In walked Alice, Tristan, Emerson, and Emerson's wife, Olive, who had fit into our family like a puzzle piece to a puzzle.

"Mother!" Alice called out and bounced in. It never ceased to amaze me that the children's personalities changed little from when they were young.

Tristan next, reserved as ever, came to my side and kissed me on the cheek. "Hello, Mother." He bent over and wrapped his arms around my body in an embrace.

Emerson and Olive had a bag in each of their hands. They plopped the bags down and embraced me—Emerson first and then Olive.

Alice was buzzing around the room and was now rifling through the bags like a bird on breadcrumbs at a park. She pulled things out and began some elaborate set up on the small round table next to the window of my tiny room.

"How are you feeling, Mother?" Emerson asked with a creased brow. Since Emerson had been a very small boy, he had always been inquisitive; he had always looked at you like he really cared about your answer to his question.

"Just find, dear," I said.

Truth was, I wasn't feeling fine. The pain in my chest had not subsided since the first heart attack and I felt dizzy on and off.

"How is the studio?" I asked, changing the subject away from myself.

Five years ago, I handed over all my photographic equipment to Emerson and he took over as the official Doveport police photographer. The year before I retired, I taught him all that I knew.

"Well, Mother, the new police chief just started, but he is handling things well. It was very busy this past month, mostly petty crimes."

"Glad it is going well for you, son. You have done well to keep the Hatherly name going as police photographer."

It had been easier than I expected, giving my position to Emerson. I could have kept working for a few years more but felt it important that the younger generation get a chance at it, and who better than my own son? I had enjoyed a hardy career. I had slogged through the start-up of a new business. Eventually, I had supported myself and my children doing something I greatly enjoyed. I had mastered portraiture of all kinds—from baby portraits to mug shots. I could say with every confidence that I photographed everyone in the town at one time or another. I had pushed the limits of the day. I took my art as far as it could go. I was pleased when Emerson took over.

Alice continued pulling things out of the bag, now arranging tea cups and saucers on the tiny table. She pulled out a large carafe and poured boiling water into the tea pot I had brought from England.

"Mother, we're having a tea party," she announced. "We figured you would have missed your cups of tea, so we're here to give you some good tea."

With that, Alice twirled the bag around in the pot, let it steep, and poured cups for all of us. Once we all had steaming cups, Alice sounded a spoon on the side of the cup.

"Mother, this is a toast to you. To all that we did as children. A celebration of you your life and to all the future good times we will have together in the coming years. Cheers to Mother!"

Alice then held her cup in the air. Our cups met in the air, clinked together, and then we sipped. Alice spilled hers and giggled as she wiped tea from her nose.

"Let's tell our best family memory," Alice said. "For fun. I'll start. My favourite memory was the days at the beach that we watched the sun go below the horizon."

Everyone smiled. Tristan spoke next.

"My best memory is playing in the backyard with all those different sized containers you gave to us, Mom, making mud out of them, making different 'food' out of the mud. I remember Dad would come and join us sometimes. He would make the best shapes out of the mud—sculptures almost."

The mention of Richard gave me a small wave of sadness, but an equal one of love. I still heard his voice and remembered the things he did forty years later. He lived on in our memories.

Olive spoke next. "Mine was the Christmas we helped you deliver your Gems of Doveport photos to the customers during that big snowstorm, and we had a big snowball fight when we got back to the house." She and Emerson grinned at each other and then turned their grins to us.

Emerson went next. "By far, my best memory was picnicking in the woods at that lake we used to walk to. It took so long to get there, and we would be so hot and covered in bugs when we did. You told us it would be worth it, Mom. And when we got to the lake and submersed ourselves in the cool, clear water, every second of the walk was worth it."

We laughed and nodded of our heads. Then Tristan looked out the window, perhaps filtering through his own memories of the picnics in the forest.

"What about you, Mother?" Tristan asked.

I had been readying my answer. "Ah, there are so many: days at the beach and letting a kite play in the wind, turning sand into houses or building driftwood forts, or the street fairs and neighbourhood events with Eva Ling and her children. But my favourite memory is a series of memories that happened daily during the summer months. After dinner, once plates were washed, we would go into the back garden. Emerson and Alice would usually play in the back, where the trees overhung the yard, making a little forest. They would play make-believe games of all sorts. Tristan, sometimes you would join in too, but more often you were devouring the pages of a book while sitting on the wooden bench under the wisteria tree. Your father and I would talk about our day, sometimes sipping our glasses of wine. Your father would sometimes join in the play. It's a simple memory, but we were all together." Those days were lovely in their simplicity. We were home. There was nothing complicated or fancy about them, but we were together.

And so the evening went on in that way—laughter, stories, and memories flowed along with cups of tea.

At one point in the evening, I sat back and sipped from the teacup with delicate blue flowers that had been my own mother's from England. I savoured the bold taste of a properly brewed cup of tea. I looked around at my three beautiful children, who were now full-grown adults, with children, houses of their own, and their own lives. Those moments were ones I wished I could trap and put into a frame, like a photograph, or trap in a terrarium, to be saved forever. But moments can't be captured. They are fleeting. Only be savoured in the present in their ephemeral glory. Moonlight still shone into the room like a wild round lamp outside the hospital window. Before I fell asleep that night, I thought to myself that perhaps that evening, in those moments, I had been the most content in all my life.

≈

The next thing I recall was feeling very dizzy and like I was floating. I heard voices, but they were foggy and muted—a bit like when you are underwater and hear voices above or like trying to hear people talking on the other side of a thick door. I vaguely made out the words being spoken.

"She had another one. Myocardial infarction in Room 201. Calling the doctor immediately."

"Looks like a big one this time."

And even more muted now: "We've lost her."

Then more dizziness, like I was swooping down a tunnel in a car. Where was I going? I was confused and felt nothingness. The sharp pain in my chest and arms was gone, and my stomach no longer pained me. What was happening? The last thing I remembered was going to sleep after a lovely party with my family. Now dizziness and swooshing.

I tried moving my lips to say something, to ask what was going on, but nothing happened when I used my brain to make my lips form words and let them leave my mouth as sounds.

"She's gone. God bless her," said the voice of someone very far away.

Again, I tried moving my lips but couldn't. The train tunnel racing swooping began again and lasted a very long time.

The next thing I remembered was being in my beloved house. I knew it was my house because the cups and saucers still sat in the china cabinet. My photograph of the waterfall outside of Doveport hung above the fireplace, which was cleaned out of soot just as I had left it. I peeked into the bedroom. The bed was made in the unmistakable way I made it every day—the covers pulled up and then folded over with the sheet. This was my house, and it was most definitely just as I left when I was rushed to the hospital.

I moved to the living room, to the window seat. I looked out the window. The view looked as it always had: white porch, black street, and the park with big trees where the eagles nested. I tried ignoring the strange and air-like quality I felt as I moved to the mirror by the front door and looked in it. What I saw in the mirror shocked and horrified me. What I saw in the mirror was nothing. Just the other side of the living room—no reflection of myself. I was invisible. *Impossible,* I thought.

It was then that the eerie thought crept into my mind: *Maybe I am dead.* Or maybe I should have died but didn't. Perhaps, I was a spirit being or I was in purgatory, purgatory in the form of where I lived when alive, but now I was an otherworldly creature; I had not made it to heaven or hell.

My thoughts spun around my head. *That is not a possibility. When you're dead, you're dead.* I didn't truly believe that, though, or why would I have spent that time attending seances? A belief in the afterlife and spirits was a core part of my spiritualist circles and something I had spent much time believing in during my living life.

I touched my arm. I didn't feel anything. It was as if I was touching air.

I was a being of no flesh and blood.

I had an idea. I would leave the house and try going wherever it was that spirits went to. I would try to move up. I would figure out a way to get myself to the afterlife, get myself to Richard.

I moved to the wooden front door. I stood in front of it and moved my hand to the handle. Although I willed my hand to move wherever I wanted it to, the door handle did nothing when I turned it.

I could not move things. I could not manipulate the world around me.

I went to the kitchen and looked for an open window. Then I went up to the children's old room—now storage for photography equipment—and looked for an open window. None were ajar.

As much as I tried, I could not leave the house. I was trapped. Panic rose inside me, then a feeling of dread. I was in completely uncharted territory, and this was a problem I couldn't overcome with hard work, immortal grit, and an unwillingness to give up.

I was stuck, completely and utterly trapped. I couldn't go forward and couldn't go back. I couldn't leave 701 Winfield Crescent. Since I had moved into the house thirty years earlier, the house had been my safe place, a domain of my own. It had been a place of refuge from the outside world and the place I had lived, loved, and raised my children.

But now, the house was now my personal prison.

Chapter 29

Brooke

February 8, 2018

"Hello, Brooke speaking." It was a grey and soggy morning, and I was working at the bookshop. It had almost been a month since the hideous night at Hawthorne's. Though I felt physically better, I remained emotionally flimsy. I hadn't been to class at all since. I left the house only for work and groceries.

No customers were in sight, inventory was done, and the shelves were freshly dusted. My phone rang and I answered it. I prayed it wasn't the dean. I had six business days to send the written appeal, and it was gnawing on me. I deeply hoped it wasn't the Community Standards staff reaching out to me. I didn't know what I would say to them. I equally hoped it wasn't Beverly upping her harassment to a phone call. I wouldn't put it past her to up her ante if she didn't receive the reaction she desired.

"Hi, Brooke, this is Sarah from the Doveport Wildlife Rescue Centre. We had your number down from when you rescued the eagle."

I breathed a sigh of relief. Not at all who I expected, but nothing to fear.

"Oh, yes, I remember that." Truth was, I hadn't thought of that eagle in months. It felt like so much had happened, and the eagle rescue was a distant memory. Things weren't so messed up when I found that eagle. I was still attending classes, I was still set to graduate, and I still had some semblance of a social life.

"I'm calling with good news."

"Oh? What's that?"

"Well, the eagle you rescued has spent the past months rehabilitating from its severe bullet wounds. His recovery has gone remarkably well, and he's set to be released next week." The young woman spoke a mile a minute.

"Wow, that's great." It was good news, but I wasn't sure where she was going with this.

"We're wondering if you want to be the one to open the cage and let him go free. Do you want to do the honours? It's super last minute, but he's being released tomorrow. He healed up quicker than we expected."

My first thought was no. "I'm not sure I'm able to."

"Are you sure? It really won't take long."

"Isn't there someone else who wants to?"

"Of course, someone will if you aren't able to. But it's important for us to give the opportunity to the person who rescued the eagle in the first place. So, will you do it?"

"Sure, I'll do it." I heard come out of my mouth without consideration. It felt weird to commit to being somewhere. Other than work, I hadn't committed to being anywhere in months.

"Great, *Doveport Newspaper* and Doveport News will be there to get photos. We'll meet at the end of Cameron Road. From there, we'll go to where you rescued him. See you tomorrow."

When our call was over, I put my phone away in my backpack. A sense of dread hung over me. I didn't want to be on the news. What if Beverly saw me and put some awful comments under the news social media accounts? Or worse, what if she was there and told people awful things about me? I felt nauseous thinking of the day and of the attention that would be on me.

But I had committed to going. There was no getting out of this now. I walked around the store and gathered books for the window display. I tried keeping my mind focused on finding books on new beginnings and tried not let my mind construct what-ifs of what could go wrong on the day of the eagle release.

≈

The next day was overcast but not raining. I waited at the end of Cameron Road and watched the river pass by me. I had a hideously anxious feeling in my stomach, as if a storm brewed inside me. Earlier that morning, I forced myself to leave the house. I treated the eagle release like a work shift I couldn't miss. That was the only reason I grabbed my coat, gathered a few things in my backpack, and closed the door behind me.

I waited for the rescue centre to arrive. I was glad to be early. It gave me a few minutes to centre myself and become less nervous. I was always less nervous when I was early somewhere. There was nothing worse than being nervous and a minute late. I had walked, hoping the exercise and the fresh air would ease my worry. While walking, I felt fine, but now my mind raced. What if I tripped? What if Beverly would come? I only had five days now to get the written appeal in. As of this second, I was not in a place to graduate.

I knew I should reframe the experience as something fun. Something that was out of the ordinary and exciting. After all, it wasn't every day that you got to release an eagle, and I was grateful the eagle had healed. When I had seen the dark, blood-filled hole in its wing, I worried it wouldn't make it. After this re-frame in my head, I felt a bit lighter, but then I remembered that the newspaper and local cable company would be there too. The rumbling feeling in my stomach was back.

At that moment, a white mini van with Doveport Wildlife Rescue Centre on the side rolled up beside me in the parking lot. A young man and woman got out and went to the rear of the van. The door lifted to reveal a large blue dog crate, with holes in the side. It held the eagle.

"Morning, Brooke!" the girl greeted me.

"Morning," I said, doing my best to feign cheerfulness.

"Excited to release this bad boy into the wild?"

"Actually, I'm a bit nervous." Something made me be honest with the girl. She was one of those people who automatically made you feel comfortable.

"Oh, yeah, fair enough. Some people don't like cameras and media stuff. But I'm sure you'll do great, and we'll all be here with you. It's not like you'll be a one-woman show or anything."

With that, the dog crate was lowered onto a wagon. A van that said "Doveport News" on its side and a small car pulled up at the same time. It was the cable company and newspaper.

We walked down the trail toward where I had found the wounded eagle. I led the way, followed by Sarah, the wagon carrying the eagle, and a young man.

After walking for ten minutes, I said, “This was the spot.” We had reached the dark clearing, surrounded by wide cedar trees and next to the river, where I had found the eagle last fall.

“Perfect, we’ll set up here,” Sarah called out to the camera crew and newspaper reporter, who trailed behind us.

Eventually, the camera was on me, and my heart began to beat rapidly as I awaited the questions.

“Brooke, can you tell us about last year?”

“Last fall, while I was walking down here, I found an eagle that couldn’t fly. It had been shot in the wing and was sitting on this log with a pool of blood below it.”

“What did you do?”

“I wrapped the eagle in my coat and this nice older woman gave me a ride to Doveport Wildlife Rescue Centre. Doveport Wildlife Rescue rehabilitated him, and I got a call yesterday letting me know the eagle was going to be released. I’m excited he survived and will be set free.”

“What do you think people can learn from this eagle’s story?”

I didn’t expect a philosophical question from this man with sweat stains under his arms and a belly bursting the buttons on the front of his button-up, collared shirt. The depth of the question left me surprised. Then something came to me that was honest and that I hadn’t thought of until that moment. “Um, perhaps that we can do more than we think, that we’re stronger, braver, and tougher than we think we are . . . and that we’re all more resilient than we think, too.”

Sarah gave me the thumbs-up signal we had agreed upon beforehand, which meant I was to open the crate. The camera followed me as I stepped toward the crate and pulled the handle that moved the door forward so it was wide open. Then I stepped back.

A few moments passed, and no movement came from the crate. I was worried the eagle wouldn't leave. Maybe he wasn't healed after all. I would look foolish if he didn't leave the cage. The worry pit returned to my stomach.

Then a rattling noise came from the crate, and a moment later, the eagle was on the grass in front of the crate. It stepped out in a swift motion. Its body was magnificent—all dark feathers and a massive yellow beak. Our eyes met, sending a shiver down my spine. Then it hopped forward, hopped forward again, spread its wings, and lifted off into the air. One wing was lower than the other, but it still could fly. Its wingspan was impressive—nearly the height of me.

The eagle landed high atop a cedar tree. It started making chortle noises. A feeling of wonder and warmth swept over me. The eagle was healthy and free. I kept my eyes on it. We heard a more distant chortling noise, and I turned around. In another cedar tree on the other side of the river was another eagle. They were communicating.

All of us stood in silence. I felt connected to the natural world in a way I never had. We stood in silence for a few moments, savouring the moment.

The news anchor man eventually broke it.

"This will make a terrific news story," he said.

I didn't care about the news story. I could care less how much attention the story would receive. But the eagle lifting off had left me in awe of so many things—the other-than-human world, what happens when you let someone help you, and the power of pushing past fear.

A foreign feeling made its way through my body. It started at the base of my spine, moved to my heart, and landed as a buzzing feeling in my head. It wasn't until part way through my walk back to my house, while I mulled over this strange feeling that had faded but not completely gone, that I was able to identify what it was—hope.

Chapter 30

Hannah

May 17, 1945

At first, being a casual observer in the house where I had once lived was intriguing. In my living days, spying on others would have been a thing I would have marvelled at—being invisible or a fly on the wall, discovering what people did with their time at home. But now, my fate as a casual observer had become tiresome and monotonous.

People moved in and moved out of the house; I couldn't keep up. It seemed like every first of the month there were new people carrying boxes and bags through the wooden door. My life was a never-ending Ferris wheel, going around and around with no sign of stopping and letting me off. I had enough. All I wanted was to be reunited with Richard and the children, who were now long dead, and escape the endless monotony.

I never thought I would wish such a thing, but I wished I was dead. The afterlife was what I desperately wanted, but there was no map of how to get there. No way that I knew to speed up this endless purgatory. Nothing I could do to escape it.

So, round and round I went, watching people move into the house and people move out, carrying their belongings in many trips, like ants carrying grains of sand. Every day, I tried leaving the house, through doors or windows left open, even up through the chimney once. But nothing worked; I was completely trapped in the house.

To amuse myself, I read books. I browsed shelves and read mysteries, classics, and books about other peoples' lives. I studied the supernatural when I could. But no matter how much I read, I couldn't escape. The house had me in its jaws.

≈

It was midday, and the people of the house were at work. It was grey outside, and I was snooping around for something to read for entertainment. This couple had no books. Of all the rubbish they purchased and brought into the house, they had no books. On their kitchen table that they did not eat at and that was piled high with papers, unopened shopping hauls, unopened kitchen junk, I noticed a newspaper opened to a page with a gigantic camera on the front. I couldn't resist. I had to see what the article was about. I read through the article and marvelled at the new cameras of the day: lenses long and almost like a pirate spyglass, and cameras so small you could hold them with one hand.

Then my own name in the text caught my eye: *"Hannah Hatherly: Police Photographer and Woman Ahead of Her Time."* Goodness me, I had made the paper—and fifty years later and in a Seattle newspaper at that! I read on: "*. . . her photographic work . . . excelled after the brilliancy of her self-portrait created in 1878 . . . expression and harmony of effect . . . She is recognized as one of the foremost representatives of the profession in the country.*" The article lifted my mood. I wished I could save the article somehow, pull it from the newspaper and somehow preserve it. But I could not, so I read it over three times more and tried filing it away in my large and crowded bank of memories.

Books distracted me from my inability to escape the house and be reunited with Richard and the children. Books let me travel to white sand beaches of the Caribbean, or houses of the royalty, back in England —the old country where I had grown up. Books carried me to distant shores and deep forests, all the while I remained trapped in spirit in the house where I had lived in for my entire adult life. Books gave me something to think about in the hours and days, months and years that passed.

What I had in abundance was time, so I thought and thought and thought of the predicament I was in. Over decades, I carefully examined all my options, and they came down to two main choices: I could be miserable or I could try to figure this out by taking small steps, make the most of a bad situation. Like bad things that happened in my living life, I wouldn't let this ruin me. I would keep reading books. If I was trapped, I might as well learn as much as I could. I would read until I could figure out some way to get myself out of here.

Over many hours, days, months, years, and decades, I constructed a plan. I would get myself out of this house somehow. Once out of the house, I could find a way to heaven or the afterlife and finally be reunited with Richard and the children. My plan was clear: when the time was right, I would make myself known to someone who could help me get out of here for good and move on to the afterlife I desperately desired.

Chapter 31

Brooke

February 10, 2018

The day after setting the eagle free, I woke up in my bed feeling more rested than I had in days. Relief flooded me. I was proud of myself for not avoiding or cancelling; I had shown up and done it.

But then dread rose in my chest as I remembered the appeal letter. I looked at my phone. February 10, a Saturday. I had until the Tuesday to submit an appeal—two business days; four full days including that day. It seemed pointless. Yes, I faced my fears and showed up for the eagle release, but the eagle release had been handed to me, something that didn't require me to stand up for myself. Writing a letter to the dean and the Community Standards board involved explaining myself, fighting for myself. Both things turned my body to an overflowing vessel of anxiety.

I rolled onto my back, logged onto my Instagram account and saw a private message from Jade. It was a news article and it was titled *Eagle Queen: Weeks After Rescuing Eagle With Bullet Wound, Harbourview University Student Releases Eagle Back Into Wild*. The article told the story, finishing with a description of the eagle's lift off to freedom.

The photograph was of me and the eagle, taken from behind. I was purposely out of focus and my hair flowed down my back. I stood relaxed posture in my jeans and moss-green sweater. In the background of the photo, but in focus, the eagle took its first wing flap after lifting off the ground. Its enormous wings were on an upswing.

Is that what I really looked like? I thought. If I didn't know it was me, I would have found the person in the photo quite pretty. But in my head, I was always mousey looking, with my long, straight hair that was the colour of sand. But in this photo, I looked hip. Maybe I looked like that all the time, despite my ugly self-image.

Then I remembered the horrific comment from Beverly below my Jack Kerouac article and got worried. I scrolled down to the comment section: three comments, all positive. They were commenting on how it was a great story and about the great work that the rescue centre does. One comment was about how brave it was to carry the eagle in a jacket. If only they knew how very un-brave I was, I thought. But it lifted my mood to see my photo and such a bold headline about it. *Eagle Queen*. I liked that.

I had one more unopened private message and clicked on it. When I read it, my stomach dropped and a sickly, sinking feeling came over me. It was from Beverly: *"You're still an orphan slut no matter what you do."* She included a selfie of her and Chatham kissing.

The photo had no effect on me. She could have Chatham. My few brief times around him had been unmemorable. He talked about football and his lake house. None of his stories had any pith. His personality was bland; his conversations, as tasteless as stale toasted bread topped with nothing. For the hundredth time in the past months, I wished he hadn't taken a liking to me. He had not been worth an ounce of the trouble he had brought me.

But Beverly's words stung. They cut into the place deep inside me that hadn't healed, the place that hadn't made sense of my parentless life.

It was pure callousness, and written with intent to hurt.

She must have seen the Eagle Queen article. She wouldn't have been able to handle it. She loved the limelight, lived for attention, affectionate words, and gestures poured on her.

I considered my choices: I could ignore the message or I could use them as a catalyst to stand up for myself once and for all. The first choice was easy; the second made me feel exhausted and nervous. It would take many steps. It would be tiring in a practical way and an emotional one. I didn't know if I could do it. The pros and cons of both options swam inside my head. To act on the message would involve appealing the accusation, going against Beverly to someone at the university, doing my assignments, and graduating.

Getting a university degree had been my goal since Grade 12. Graduating was necessary for a real adult job—a way to a comfortable life and a way to break the cycle of poverty—which had also been my goal since Grade 12. Graduating was the way I could avoid the kind of life my parents may have had and the way I could avoid whatever circumstances my parents had that didn't allow them to care for a being that was their own flesh and blood.

The times Beverly had provoked me before—the apple core, the comments, the graffiti—I had not acted. I had sat back and let her get away with them. I had pushed them away and tried to forget about them. I tried to push on despite them, but this time what Beverly said could not be forgotten. This time, Beverly had gone too far. It was like a switch went off inside me that activated me into swift action.

It donned on me suddenly: I was the only one who could do something about my situation. I was the only one who could change my fate. My university graduation was solely in my hands. Nobody was going to help me. Nobody was going to tell me what I needed to do. Only I could stand up for myself.

I had to graduate.

I suddenly had never wanted anything more in my life. Graduating would be worth the challenging actions ahead and worth risking everything for—even worth trying and losing.

But I was running out of time.

I thought of the eagle lifting off. I thought about how he had healed from a bullet wound and flew again. An image came into my mind: eagle wings plying the air and lifting him higher into the sky and then landing in the tree. If he could heal from a bullet wound, I could get through this.

I sat up in bed. Using my finger and thumb to simultaneously push two buttons on my phone, I took a screenshot of the message and saved it onto my phone.

I swung my legs over the side of the bed and prepared myself to fight. I was done with letting anyone dictate what was happening with my life. It was time to take things into my own hands.

≈

A few hours later, I sat perched at the bay window and furiously typed the last paragraph of the appeal letter. That assignment was mine. *No more sitting back passively; no more verbal withholding and suppressing how I felt,* I thought. When it was done, I proofread it five times, saved it as a PDF document, attached it to an email, and pressed send.

I began packing my leather satchel for campus on Monday when I thought of something I had to do. I grabbed my phone.

"Hi, Jade," I said when she picked up on the second ring.

"Hi, stranger. Long time no hear. I tried calling you the day after the concert. How have you been?"

I took a deep breath. It was hard for me to tell how I really felt, to let people in.

"Not so good, actually."

Then I told her about Beverly and about her accusing me of plagiarism. I told Jade about the comment on the Kerouac article. I told her about the shoes in the wall and Beverly's Instagram message. I told her about the eagle release and my plan to start fighting back to save my graduation.

"Brooke, I had no idea it was so bad. Why didn't you tell anyone? I thought it was you avoiding everyone and everything. If I had known it was all those things, I would have walked with you through it all."

"I was scared. Since I was a kid, I've not felt deserving of help. Or love. Or support of any kind. It's hard for me to reach out to people, and I didn't want to stand up to Beverly. I was scared."

Tears fell down my cheeks as I finished. It felt terrifying and terrific at the same time to have shared my struggles. I felt exposed to be telling someone so much—even if she was my best friend. I also felt an immense sense of release, like putting down a backpack you've been carrying for a long time. I tried taking some long, slow breaths.

"I'm so sorry. I can't believe you were going through all that. What can I do to help? Can I bring some food by your place tonight?"

"Yes to food. That would be amazing. And for help, did you happen to take a photograph of the graffiti in the washroom at Hawthorne's?"

"Sure did, girl. I was hoping you would use the photograph sometime. That was over the line."

"Can you send it to me?"

"Yes, sure thing," she said.

"Thanks and see you tonight," I said. I was about to hang up the phone when Jade spoke.

"Brooke, one more thing before you go."

"Yes . . .?" I said, eager to get off the phone and get going on my long task list.

"I'm proud of you. I know you can do this."

Chapter 32

Hannah

February 5, 1985

It was 1985, and a young couple inhabited the house. I sat at the window seat watching them for amusement. It was just past five in the evening, and darkness already fell outside. Rain pattered the roof the exact way it had when I inhabited the house while alive.

The couple had returned from work and were in the kitchen. He chopped peppers and onions while she poured oil into a pan.

"Well, that was the worst day ever," the woman said. Her voice lacked its usual cheer, and her shoulders and head drooped slightly.

"What made it so bad?" he asked, moving the knife quickly over the vegetables.

"Well, my lesson flopped, and then I didn't finish preparing for tomorrow's lessons. Teaching two grades is so much harder than one, and coaching basketball adds so much onto my day. I don't know that I'll ever master this job. It's an impossible profession."

Ah, so she was a teacher. I had heard her talk about school but didn't know her role.

She put down the small spoon she'd used to measure spices. Tears rolled down her cheeks and she leaned over, her elbows on the counter.

The man put the knife down next to the pile of red peppers. He walked toward her until he was in front of her and placed his hands gently on her hips. He then wrapped his arms around her like a bat wrapping its wings around itself. She wrapped hers around his waist so they became a mess of arms and bodies and hair.

"We're in our house. This is our safe place. Tomorrow is a new day. You're an amazing teacher. You're not alone in any of this; I'm right here with you."

She kept crying softly, and her arms tightened around him.

Eventually, her crying got softer, then stopped all together. She went to the bathroom, and I heard the tap come on. Then I heard water being splashed on her face.

When she emerged, her eyes were red, but her body was more upright and she had her usual pep back in her step.

The man added vegetables and chopped cubes of something firm and white to the frying pan. He then added the spicy sauce concoction that the woman had mixed. Sizzling and popping sounds from the pan drowned out their voices.

After this vignette, an emptiness in my heart opened. There was something about this couple, the way they looked at each other, that reminded me of Richard and myself.

I envied their love. I envied their life. They were so alive. I was so unalive. I was as unseen and unimportant as a shadow. I was a shell of a human—if even that. I was a shadow of a woman. Not noticed, nonexistent to anyone but myself. Not needed by anyone. But worst of all, not loved, not loved by anyone and with nobody to love but myself. I was trapped in a purgatory of my own making.

I missed my flesh and blood form. At certain times, I missed it more than other times, but I always missed the solid bones. I thought back to when I was alive and how I cursed the small dimples on my buttocks or the soft flesh around my hips. I deeply regretted the minutes and hours I spent wishing my waist smaller, my bust larger, or my skin free of blemishes. What utterly wasted time that was. It hadn't mattered then, and it didn't matter now. Why had I wasted minutes and hours on earth worried about such trivial matters? All that mattered in my life was loving, being loved, and the joy I experienced in life.

I had had a strong and healthy body, a strong vessel for life. It had given me three children—little beings who had made all the difficult days of work worthwhile, who had made every day better. My hands and arms had allowed me to make food for the children and make money to clothe them. My legs walked me to work and pedalled my bicycle to waterfalls and past forests with morning light streaming through them. My body allowed me a fulfilling life. Yet while alive, I had shamed it. Now, I would do anything to have it back. That, or be free and with Richard and the children in whatever after life existed.

Questions swirled around in my head like currents out at sea. What had I done to deserve this? I had filtered through my life events to try to find something I did that justified this punishment but found nothing. I desperately wanted to move on to the afterworld. Though I didn't know what that was, it had to be better than this existence.

After the couple finished their plates, they left them on the table and the woman took the man's hands and led him into their bedroom. I moved from the window seat to the kitchen and tried my best not to think about Richard and the pit in my stomach that had been pulled wide open.

Chapter 33

Brooke

February 12, 2018

I caught my breath after several sets of stairs and looked around. It was early afternoon on Monday when I arrived on campus. Students milled about. Some sat on the grass and soaked in the first sun in weeks; others ambled to their next class. A grey bunny ate French fries from a cardboard tray on the grass.

I felt a great relief after getting off the phone with Jade on Saturday. I spent all of Sunday putting together an outline of everything that happened with Beverly. I felt backed up and understood, like I could do this, like I could assert myself, prove I didn't plagiarize, pass all my classes, and even graduate. While walking here I had felt prepared, but now I felt nervous. I hoped I didn't see anyone I knew. I didn't want to explain anything to professors or other students until I had matters under control.

I headed for Building 210—the Student Affairs building. I would speak to the Community Standards staff. I had also planned to visit Building 410 to confirm receipt of my appeal letter, but a confirmation receipt email made the trip unnecessary. I was glad I didn't need to ascend to the strange, cold building where light bounced in all directions from glass windows. I walked into Building 210. A large half-circle counter greeted me. There were four of five different computers, and I scanned for Community Standards. I spotted its sign on the far right and walked to the desk. I felt flighty, like I couldn't do this. I thought about turning around. The unsure voices in my head brought up all kinds of scenarios that might happen. What if they didn't believe me? What if Beverly had also spoken to someone here? What if this didn't help and I failed the class anyway? The what-if scenario party in my head was interrupted by a voice.

"Hi, how can I help you?"

The voice came from a tallish, sandy-brown haired guy. His arms bulged with gym muscles and despite a frat-boy demeanor, his smile of big, straight white teeth was genuine.

"Um, hi. I've written a request for a hearing with the academic misconduct hearing board. I was advised that I could check in with Community Standards if I had any questions." My face became hot and red after explaining what I wanted. What kind of person would he think I was? He probably dealt with lots of people who were dishonest slackers, those who stole work and passed it as their own. Maybe they wouldn't even talk to me.

"Sure thing, let me see what times we have available," he said, and started clicking around and looking at his screen.

I breathed out and was surprised at his nonchalance toward this. Maybe I built things up too much in my head.

"We have a one thirty with Yvonne if you want. She's great and will be able to answer any questions you have."

"One thirty today?" I asked without thinking about it. I thought I would have more time to mentally prepare. I looked at my phone. It was 1:20 p.m.

"Yes, one thirty today. There was a cancellation, so you lucked out. Would you like to take that one? Otherwise we have a three p.m. tomorrow available."

My first thought was to take the appointment tomorrow. Anything to push it further away. I felt myself being pulled down the long dark hallway of anxiety. I didn't want to do it now. I could avoid it for another day.

"I'll take the three p.m. appointment tomorrow," I said quickly.

"Okay, no problem. Student card, please," he said and started tapping away at the keyboard.

I dug my student card out of my wallet and handed it to him. As he typed, I looked at my phone and the date: February 12. In one week, I would fail the class if the appeal letter was rejected. Time was running out.

"Actually, I'll take the one thirty appointment today," I blurted as my face flushed and a hot wave of embarrassment washed over me. I felt panicked and unprepared saying it, but I had to move quicker. If I was going to do this, I would do it right. Time was tight.

"Sure, that's fine. I heard him click the backspace button a few times and continue looking at the computer.

A few moments later, he reached his meaty hand over the counter and handed my student card back.

"You can wait at the couches, and Yvonne will come and get you when she's ready."

I returned the student card to my wallet and took a seat on the couch closest to the counter. The couch was very firm but comfortable. I put my leather satchel at my feet and looked around. The building was full of windows but held a completely opposite vibe about it than the dean's office. Posters on the windows made it seem less serious and several baskets held condoms with signs that said, "Take me." It had a much more student-centred feel to it.

Two girls sat near me and discussed a party from the previous Saturday. They both seemed happy and carefree. Why couldn't I be like that? I thought. Why couldn't I care less about everything?

I realized I was wringing my hands together as I sat. I placed them on my knees instead. I hadn't brought a book, so I continued looking around. I tried rehearsing what I would say to the Community Standards staff. How I would explain my situation. I was on my phone finding the written request for a hearing when suddenly a woman with long grey hair stood above me and said, "Hi, you must be Brooke?"

"Uh, yeah. Hi."

"Hi, Brooke, great to meet you. I'm Yvonne. Follow me."

I followed her down a hallway that went behind the half-circle counters where I had made my appointment. Yvonne wore flowy pants, the kind that are tight on the waist, baggy on the legs, and tighten again around the ankles. An equally flowy scarf adorned her neck. She smelled of something both earthy and floral.

"Come on in." She gestured at a couch in a small office at the end of the hall. She lowered herself into a weathered armchair beside the window. The chair looked more living-room worthy than office decor.

"What brings you in?" she asked.

"Well, I . . . ugh, I'm having trouble with one class." I felt blocked and nervous, like I was too vulnerable to explain. I didn't want to burden anyone. She might not be able to help, anyway; maybe there would be nothing she could do.

"Can you tell me more?"

"It's a fourth year English class and I need it to graduate," I said and looked down. Shame came over me. There was a small dark pebble at the bottom of my brain that said I deserved to be caught cheating, that I didn't deserve to graduate.

"You seem nervous, dear. But to let you know, Community Standards staff are here to help. We want to support students in any way we can. We're on your side. Can you tell me more about what happened with that one class?"

I looked at her kind face. She wore no makeup and seemed like the kind of person who went camping in the forest alone and volunteered walking dogs at shelters—unafraid of anything. I wondered if I would ever be unafraid.

"I wrote an assignment for that class called *The Real Nixie of the Mill-Pond*. I have all the notes from it here, including a detailed outline. I submitted it for my creative writing course and then I got this letter from the dean that said I plagiarized."

I handed her my phone with the letter pulled up from email. I paused my story while she looked at the screen.

"I think a former roommate of mind took if off my laptop. I remember a time when I found my laptop open in my room when I used to live with her. We were also in conflict, and I think she did it to retaliate against me.

"What caused the conflict with this other student?"

"The guy she had been dating asked me out. She was livid and did all she could to make my life hard. She wrote graffiti about me in the washroom of a bar. She turned my friend group against me and even threw an apple core at me in class. I have some nasty comments she wrote below some of my writing online, and she's been texting me awful comments, making fun of me for not having parents. Growing up, I was always in the foster care system, and she's used that against me."

I blinked back tears and sat there feeling naked and vulnerable.

"Do you have photographs and proof of any of the things you mentioned?"

"Yes, most of them."

"Wow, Brooke. This is a lot. I can help you with your academic appeal. You're going to need more than your notes, though. You're going to need to go into your word processing program and take screenshots of when you last edited the document and if you made copies of it, along with the writing process, and I would make copies of those too. I'll do my best to help you out, but we don't have a lot of time."

"Yes, I know," I said. "I feared reporting anything, and to be honest, I'm scared for my safety still. On one occasion, she drove at me in her truck and I fell over while jumping out of the way. I have no proof of that, though. And I'm scared people won't believe any of it."

"Well, we don't know the outcome, but it's worth a try. I'll do all I can to help with this appeal process, but I want to recommend a few other places on campus for you to check out."

"What places?" I asked. I was picking at the cuticle on my middle finger. I stopped and put my hands on my lap.

"I think you should go to the University Harassment board and put in a report. They're in Building 525, at the very top of the hill. And I think you should consider speaking with a counsellor. They're in Building 600. It sounds like the past few months have been hard and it can be helpful to have someone to talk to."

"I don't want to get her into any sort of trouble. I just want to pass that class and graduate."

"You deserve to be treated with respect and to be free of harassment anywhere on this campus, and that includes online. Can I take photocopies of your outline and your notes for this assignment?"

"Of course."

"All right, I'm going to give you an appointment next week, and we'll know more about the process then. I'm glad you came in. Will you consider seeing harassment committee and a counselling appointment?"

"I'll think about it," I said.

When I had my notes back, I left the way I had come. I tucked my notes and outline back into my leather satchel.

I stepped outside and stood still. The wind had picked up and any bit of gentle warmth was gone. I zipped my coat and planned my next move.

I didn't want to go to the Harassment Committee. I didn't want to get Beverly in trouble. But I did want to graduate. As I went back and forth in my head about what to do, Beverly's words came into my head. *Orphan slut*. And I thought, *If it's her or me, I must put myself first*. I needed to graduate. I had spent too much time and money on this degree to let it go. I could feel it slipping from my fingers as the minutes passed.

I headed up the stairs, toward Building 525 and toward the Harassment Committee's office.

≈

I stood outside Building 525 and nearly turned around. The thought of retelling my story again that day made me feel sick to my stomach. I looked down the set of stairs where I had come, and then I turned around and opened the door to the building in front of me.

There must not have been many people reporting harassment because the reception area was empty. Someone saw me right away. I questioned if my harassment was enough.

"What are the events leading up to this?" she asked when I was in an office.

I explained everything, starting with the text messages and graffiti and ending with the plagiarism report and the recent Instagram private message.

"Do you have documentation of all of this?"

I handed them my phone with the screenshots.

"Can you forward this to me?"

"Sure."

They kept typing something on their computer.

"And have you spoken to them yourself and asked them to stop?"

"Yes. When it first started, I spoke with them in person. Since the messages started, I haven't gotten into it with them. It's caused my anxiety to get quite bad. I've not attended class in quite some time." I looked down.

"Are you talking to someone about that?"

"No. This my second time on campus in months, to be completely honest."

"Up to you, but the support of a counsellor could help."

"Okay, I'll consider that."

"Leave this with me. I'll be in touch in the next few weeks."

Few weeks! By that time, my chances of graduating could be gone.

"Is there any way it could go faster? I'm on academic probation now, and if I can't pass that creative writing class, I won't graduate. A lot is hinging on graduation, and my post-secondary educational funding support from the government for being a child in care in the foster system runs out this year. It would be super helpful if it could be as fast as possible."

They looked up at me. Their face was expressionless, one of those faces that was impossible to read.

"I'll see what I can do. I'll do my best to expedite the process, but no guarantees. Sometimes these things are quite a lengthy process. And they don't always work out the way you hope."

Chapter 34

Hannah

September 1, 2018

It was fall of another year, and I was desperate to escape the house. There had been times throughout the years that I had felt a deep yearning to escape. But this was desperation. A constant need to leave.

Today a girl moved in. I heard a key turn in the lock. I moved to the living room and watched as the front door slowly opened. A face with very big green eyes opened wide peeked into the house. She then stepped in and put down a backpack and leather bag. She walked to the centre of the living room, where the midday autumn light poured into the room. She put her arms out and spun in two circles without saying a word. She then went straight to the bay window, kneeled on the window seat, and put her face very close to the window glass. She looked outside. As she rubbed her hand over the wood of the window seat, a hesitant grin came over her face. It wasn't an open mouth, toothy grin, but a closed-mouth, reserved smile. Her hand then moved to the wood between the windowpane and touched it gently, examining the white paint that was peeling ever so slightly to reveal pale blue underneath. *Who was this girl?*

Then she stood up, stepped back to the door, and disappeared outside. When she returned, another girl was with her. The other girl was taller, louder, and easier to read. I pegged her as a friend. Most people who moved into the house had boxes crammed with colourful material of some kind. Not wood but shinier and very manmade. It didn't appear the friend was moving in, but helping the girl with the honey hair move in. The girl lived alone. I was curious for the first time in years. Most people moved in with at least one other person.

This girl had only six boxes and two backpacks. Surely, that couldn't be it. There was something different about the girl with the honey-coloured hair, but I couldn't decide what it was.

I watched her for a few days and, on several occasions, made myself known in subtle ways. I hadn't decided yet. *What is unusual about her?* Then it donned on me: she was able to be alone. For the past ten or so years, anyone who moved into the house—whether young or old—could not be alone, not alone with their own company, alone with their own body, or alone with their own thoughts. This girl seemed to prefer it. I liked that about her. It reminded me of my stubborn resistance to marriage when I was alive, although young people were not getting married until well into middle age at this time period. But still, she could be with herself. And I liked that.

The girl with the honey hair had an openness about her. She looked wise beyond her years. She unpacked her books right away and preferred to be in silence, as if noises scared her. Or maybe she liked her own thoughts. Perhaps she was like Tristan in that she got overwhelmed when there were many sounds going on around her. She was an artist, that I was sure of. I wondered what kind. I would observe and find out. But there was something strange about the girl. She was passive. Hesitant. I would learn that she needed to be pushed. She needed to stand up and fight for herself. She had this strength under her that I don't think she realized she even had.

She was by far the most beautiful person who had lived in the house. I discovered her art was writing. She was a storyteller with words. This realization gave me a fondness for her and a connection to her, for I had been a storyteller too but with photographs and images instead of words. I thought of the girl and I as brethren of sorts. She had a sharp wit, and I loved reading her writing. From it, I learned she had no parents and that she had a dark fear inside her. I found out that she liked fairy tales. A few of her stories were retellings of *Grimms' Fairy Tales* that I used to read the children.

Her tales did what good ones should do—they took my mind away from my unwanted situation, of being trapped in this yellow wooden prison box. They took me to other lands, always with some brave character. I could imagine the places perfectly in my mind: the ponds with water fairies or the forests with Red Riding Hood as she willingly led the wolf to her grandmother's house. She knew what she was getting herself into when she let the wild in.

The papers she left around nourished my curiosity and my mind. When she left, I would devour them like some sweet dessert that I couldn't get enough of.

≈

Then one day, the girl stopped leaving the house. On the very rare occasion that she left, she would be gone for a shorter time than before. I was intrigued at her actions. The freedom to go wherever she pleased, but she stayed in the house. I would have given anything to leave the house, but she stayed here on her own will. Then the girl started spending more time sleeping. I wanted to shout at her. I wanted to set an alarm for her to wake up. I wanted to hug her. I wanted to tell her that she should be out living her life, not lying around under the covers.

I wanted her to know I was there. I wanted to talk to her. I wanted to push her to improve her life. I wanted to awaken her to her own power. I wanted to know her because I thought she might be one person who could get me out of this place once and for all. So, I started using all the things I had practised over all the years to make myself known to the girl in the house.

Chapter 35

Brooke

February 26, 2018

I sat at the bay window and tapped furiously on my laptop. I typed an assignment a journalism course. *Will it even matter?* I wondered. Sometimes, I was happy to have a focus—a list of assignments and reports to write—that kept me busy throughout the day. I had started going to lectures again. The counsellor and I had worked together to make a goal of attending two lectures a week. The next week, I would try attending four. I realized small steps were key to reaching goals, but I hoped it wasn't too late. Other times, doing assignments and slowly returning to lectures felt futile. My fate was in the air. My fate was being decided by someone in a tall glass building.

Overall, being occupied at a task felt vastly better than doing nothing. It kept my mind occupied and left less time for worried thoughts to jump from one what-if to another, like a wild monkey jumping from branch to branch.

I finished the paper and went to the next assignment on my list. The list of assignments was now fifteen—fifteen things standing in the way of me graduating. Well, that and a sanction against me that could cause me to fail a class I needed to graduate. But I was determined to try to think positively hope it would work out. It had to come together. I didn't have enough money to finish university if the government tuition support for foster care students stopped. If I didn't pass that class, I wasn't sure what I would do.

I checked my email; there were three new ones. I first clicked on one from a job search I had registered for. One of the jobs caught my eye. I couldn't believe it when I looked closer. My dream job—a position at the Doveport Public Library. At first, I was excited and hopeful. I read through the description of qualifications and skills: someone professional, responsible, adaptable, and a quick learner. Then I was disappointed. Surely, I would never get it. They would find someone else with more experience than me. I wouldn't bother applying.

The next email was from the dean. Hope fluttered up in me as I clicked on the email. It said my appeal had been rejected. My heart fell. It didn't give reasons but was filled with jargon. My cheeks went red and anger fumed through my body. How could institutions be so corrupt? His buddy-buddy relationship with Beverly's dad was preventing my graduation. Putting myself on the line and all my work with the assignments and the counselling that was helping me get back to classes was for nothing. I felt numb.

The third email was from the Yvonne from Community Standards. She too told me my appeal had been rejected. It gave no reason either. She said I could try the Human Rights Council, but if the dean rejected the appeal, there was little more she could do.

I wrote her a reply, explaining what the dean told me about he and Beverly's father when I explained my situation to him. I then wrote the reply in a separate document and made it as official as possible. I explained that there was conflict of interest and that the dean was a personal friend of Beverly's father. I wrote and rewrote it several times, making sure it was professional and clean sounding and that it stuck solely to facts.

I sent it to Yvonne and to the university's Human Rights Department. I also sent it to the Harassment Committee person I had spoken to previously. I needed as many people in my court as possible. I didn't know what was going to happen, but I would fight as hard as I could for a positive outcome. I was focused on graduating.

I sat back and looked at the books along the fireplace mantle. I wished I could escape into one of them, instead of toiling away on assignments that might not matter. I thought about my grim situation. I had gone to the top—the university's Human Rights Council. Now, all I could do was wait.

≈

Later that day, a knock at the front door of the house startled me and caused my heart to race. I had been typing a persuasive essay about whales in captivity. It wasn't my usual type of paper, nor my preferred one, but there was a narrow range of topics for this course. After I got the email from the dean, I went into my bedroom and climbed into bed with a book. I slowly felt myself heading down the long dark hallway of anxiety. I was tempted to walk the hallway and stew in worried thoughts. I caught myself and eventually got up, went to the window seat, and typed a paper.

When the knock came, I got up from the window seat and answered the door. Jade stood there. In the disappointment and shock of the email from the dean, I had completely forgotten that we had made plans tonight. We had planned a final séance. One of my bookstore boss's friends, who was a medium, was going to join us. A sense of dread came over me. I wished I hadn't agreed to the séance. Though I wanted things in the house to stop, confronting it at the same time as the Beverly issues seemed way too much for me now.

"Weird weather out there," Jade commented and came in. "Electricity in the air almost. Like it might rain, and this weird yellow light like before a tornado."

"I don't know about this, Jade. I'm sort of having second thoughts."

"What do you mean? We're all ready to go, and we even have a medium coming. Foolproof way to get rid of whatever is in here."

"Well, I just don't think there's a point. Maybe I should just deal with what's going on and not force anything."

"Brooke, you need to take control of this, just like you're taking control of the Beverly situation."

"Which isn't going well, by the way," I added, and explained that the appeal had been rejected.

"Well, one thing at a time. Let's continue with this. Candles first. The medium will be here anytime."

"Yeah, you're right. Okay. I'll get the candles." It was time to confront whatever was making strange smells and sounds in the house.

We set candles on the living room floor and on the window seat. Since Jade had arrived, it had become apocalyptically dark in the house. The candles flickered and threw shadows around the house's dark corners. I shivered and wished I hadn't agreed to this. I suddenly didn't want to know what was in the house. Now, the prospect of living with the spirit seemed a better option than confronting it.

I lined up a few candles on the fireplace mantle. It made the fireplace even darker and scarier than usual. I looked outside and the sky looked angry. A few drops of rain started hitting the window. I felt unprepared without a Ouija board or a planchette, the little arrow used to communicate with spirits, which I had read about at the bookstore one day.

My boss, Edgard, had insisted we didn't need anything. I had asked him a week ago for recommendation on a medium to help with the spirit in the house. As I did so, I couldn't believe I was having a casual conversation with my boss about mediums and spirits. Edgard Frost was the only person I could talk normally to about a spirit. He was happy to help and set the whole medium meeting up for me. "Have candles ready, and the medium will arrive at eight sharp," he had said.

It was two minutes to eight. Jade and I paced around awkwardly, waiting for the medium.

"I wonder what she'll look like," Jade said, her excited mood contrasting my dreading one.

"Hmmm, yeah. Probably like the people who come into Passages. Maybe even a customer of Passages. Edgard said he's known this medium a while and they're excellent."

Three firm knocks came from the front door. I looked at Jade, trying not to let fear show on my face. Then I went to answer it.

When I opened it, I tried not to let shock play across my face.

A man stood at the door who looked only several years older than myself and Jade. I put him at late twenties and six feet tall. His dark brown hair had been done with product so it stood up in the middle. His hair was well trimmed on the side. He wore well-fitted dark jeans with a simple black leather belt. His shirt was a black button-up; the rolled-up sleeves showed his forearms.

"Hi, Brooke?"

"Yeah, hi. Thanks for coming." I hoped my surprise didn't sound in my voice.

When I thought of what a medium looked like, this was not it. I expected a woman with waist-length grey hair, flowy clothing, and crystals hanging around her neck. The man standing in front of me looked like an accountant or realtor, not like someone who spoke with spirits.

"I'm Tanner," he said, smiling to show off straight teeth. I could not help but think that he resembled an Abercrombie & Fitch model.

"Great to meet you," Jade said, coming over and rescuing me from awkwardness. "I'm Jade."

A breeze almost blew the door open as he stood on the porch. He waited outside the door until I said, "Come on in."

He stepped into the house and slipped off his black leather shoes, which matched his belt. "Thanks. Weather is really kicking off out there." His voice was rich and deep and made me think of dark roast coffee with cream in it. "So, what's been going?" he said once we were seated cross-legged on the living room floor.

I relayed the things with the lights, the sounds on the window and the shoes in the wall. I even told him about the note in the kitchen and about the women wearing old timey clothes in the kitchen.

He didn't seem phased. He simply nodded his head.

"What do you think it is?" I asked.

"Different people would have different answers. To me, it sounds like a spirit—a mutated form of the human being. I think of spirits as disturbed bundles of energy—as beings just like us—but without this inconvenient outer shell that we have and fuss over so much," he said, motioning to his own body. He was matter-of-fact, as if he was talking about something he saw on the news that night.

"Why is it here?" I replied.

"My belief is that some souls remain earthbound if they have unfinished business to attend to on Earth, or they can't release their earthly bonds and remain stranded on this level. Other spirits won't leave Earth because of their connection to their family, so they stay on the level closest to their former life. Others have a lesson to learn on Earth. Once their lesson is complete, they can be free. What I'm aiming to do in this séance is speed up the process of learning, help them leave this level and allow their energy to change realms. Sometimes they just need some help progressing to their next life or realm of consciousness."

I struggled to focus on his words as the soft glow of the candles played off his dark hair and even darker eyes. I nodded my head.

"What happens to the spirit when it moves on?" Jade asked.

"Different mediums would also have different answers to that question. I believe souls exist on planes of consciousness. I think sometimes souls will incarnate again, sometimes going through hundreds or thousands of lives—living a different experience each time. I believe groups or families of souls sometimes reincarnate until they are together again. Some could get stuck in one cycle and need help from someone in the world of the living to help them get freed and move on to a different plane of consciousness—the plane of consciousness they desire. That's what I'll try to do for the spirit in this house. Should we get started?"

Jade and I nodded, and he started talking again. "Dear departed soul, we come to you with the utmost respect. We want to honour your presence and help you move to the next realm if that is what you want."

The tapping of rain started on the roof.

“Do you want to make your presence known to us?”

Nothing happened. I looked at Jade. Tanner sat cross-legged with his hands placed upwards on his knees. His eyes were closed, and he looked peaceful, as though he were mid yoga session.

Nothing happened, so he continued.

“What is it you want?” he asked. The rain got louder until the pattering was interrupted by the crack of thunder outside. Thunder storms were rare in Doveport, so this was unsettling.

“Hmmm, I’m getting that they miss someone. Or that they missed out on something some time ago. They missed some connection. They’re missing some part of their family, like there’s one or even two people they want to be reunited with again.”

I couldn’t help thinking about my lack of biological parents and how I grew up feeling I was missing something. He could have been talking about me. It creeped me out, and I pulled my hoodie over my head.

“I’m also getting that they feel that there’s some great fear underlying everything. Fear of not getting free and fear of something in this physical world.”

Again, his words resonated with me and the fear I had battled for months. The room lit up as lightening shot outside. I had never seen lightening so bright before.

I looked to Jade, who looked frightened. I had never seen Jade look scared, which added to the fear that was making a home in my stomach.

“Do you want us to help you move on?” Tanner asked with a real sense of caring in his voice. I still couldn’t help but think that he could be telling me about my investment returns or talking about the kitchen backsplash in a two-bedroom house in some suburb.

A boom of thunder made me jump. Tanner looked like he was concentrating very hard. His eyes were still closed, although his eyebrows were furrowed now, as if he was trying to solve some problem.

"I'm getting that they feel like they're not worthy of our help. Perhaps they have a lot of trouble accepting help or think it makes them weak to accept help. What's that? Oh, they don't feel deserving of the help, support, or to move to the next realm."

"What do we do now?" Jade asked, seeming like she wished she hadn't agreed to come.

"I'm here to tell you, spirit, that you are worthy. You always were worthy and you still are worthy. Your worthiness is present in you simply by being. You have nothing to prove, nothing you need to do or accomplish to go wherever you want to go. It's great to strive, have goals, and move forward, but I'm here to tell you you're worthy, despite the outcomes of these things. Let us help you get where you want to go."

Part of me was drinking in the words and taking them in for myself. I was surprised at how much his words meant for the spirit resonated with me. Perhaps no matter the difference in space and time, people had similar struggles, as if we aren't that different after all. This thought was comforting, and for a moment, I felt peaceful and comforted, like you do after eating a turkey dinner.

Then a bolt of thunder hit again; this time even closer than the ones before. The lightening bolts and thunder booms were getting closer together. I once heard that the closer the thunder boom was to the lightening, the closer the storm cell was to you. I shivered and hoped the séance would finish soon. Tanner was not phased by the storm and kept going.

"Powers of the universe, let freedom come to this earthbound spirit. Whatever powers may be, give this spirit the freedom they deserve. Give them awareness of their worthiness. Set it free in whatever way that happens."

The light that was on in my bedroom suddenly went out. The lightening storm had knocked out the power. I drew in my breath. A shiver came over me, and goosebumps came up on my arm.

Tanner opened his eyes and broke the silence. "I'm sensing a shift of some kind. I'm not sure it's gone, but something is different."

With that, the séance was over. I hoped with all my will that it had worked.

Chapter 36

Hannah

February 26, 2018

One night the girl sat on the floor of the house's living room with her friend and a dark-haired man. I couldn't tell you the day, month, or year. Time had lost all meaning. Space was arbitrary; it was unchanging since I had died. My house was the only place I moved about.

Then they were summoning me, this I was certain of. It was as if someone was calling my name, but they were very far away. I was sure it was me they were trying to reach.

I tried calling out to them, but my voice didn't work. I tried yelling louder, but I could not make a sound. I tried manipulating the thin string-like snakes that brought energy into the house, but it didn't work. Sometimes, I was able to do this, other times not. This time it was futile. I tried influencing the small flickers of candles, but my power waned. I was unable to make them brighter or extinguish them.

I was unable to make my presence known.

I became frustrated. Why were they trying to reach me?

I hovered on the ceiling trying to figure out what to do. It seemed they were trying to tell me something very important. I wanted to know what it was. I was desperate to receive their message.

After the passing of an indeterminable amount of time, I saw a glow in the distance. At first, I thought it was a candle, but it wasn't. It was more like bright sunlight at the end of a long hallway. The oval of shimmering light was very dim, but I thought I might get to it. I went toward the oval as fast as I could. The tunnel was narrow, and I moved quicker and quicker down it.

A whooshing sensation came over me, and I lost all control over my own being. I was heading toward the vortex of light at an alarming speed. I was being pulled along by some unknown force. I was close to the light, but also far from it. I was at the mercy of some strong and unknown force. Finally, I surrendered and let go of trying to get to the light.

Then, as immediately as I began the journey down the tunnel, it was over. A warm wave of energy swept over me. I was bathed in golden light. A buzzing sensation surrounded me. I felt heavier than I had ever remembered feeling.

I was acutely aware of an immense shift in my perception, a tug on my awareness. I was unsure where I was but felt I might be back in the land of the living once again. The feeling of heaviness gave it away. The ability to have a thought and move my body.

I heard a deep, soothing voice. Could it be Richard's? It had been so many years since I heard his voice. Unsure of whom the voice belonged to, I made my way toward it.

Chapter 37

Brooke

March 7, 2018

I was in the waiting room of Harbourview University's Human Rights office. I watched rain hit fern fronds outside the glass windows as I sat on a leather chair, awaiting my appointment. My letter must have had some effect, because earlier that week, I received an email inviting me to a meeting. This was my last chance. If nothing came of this, I would not graduate.

If I failed, I wasn't sure what I would do. If I succeeded, freedom awaited me. I would be a graduate and look for work. The outcome was unknown, but one thing was certain: I wanted to graduate. I hadn't wanted anything more in my life.

I bounced my knee up and down. I was on edge. I dreaded explaining everything another time. I wasn't just challenging Beverly anymore; I was challenging the dean of my program. I knew I was innocent, but would they believe me? I had my laptop with me, hoping they could see the timestamp on my computer document. Beverly would have nothing showing the proof of the assignment. If the Human Rights people didn't believe me, at least I could say I tried. Failure was a possibility. I watched raindrops hitting the fern fronds again; I tried to ground myself in the moment rather than think too far ahead.

"Brooke, come on in." My grounding was interrupted by a woman with short grey hair speaking to me.

I followed her down the hallway toward her office. I felt like my new hobby was touring the offices of Harbourview University. This one was minimalist, decorated in a simple way.

"Hi, Brooke, I'm Lucy. I see you're fighting the decision of the dean of Humanities made to reject your appeal."

"Yes, I am." I tried not to stammer. I tried not to break down in tears. I tried to remind myself to stick to the facts.

The woman had a paper in her hand—I assumed it was the letter I had given her—and her eyes scanned it.

"Can you tell me a bit about yourself?" she then asked. She placed down the paper, leaned back in her chair, and gave me her undivided attention.

I wasn't expecting this question. I had rehearsed my answer for a host of other questions, but not this one. I could have answered any variation on a question about the nature of my relationship with Beverly. I could have rattled on about my story and the assignment—anything about the character, the plot, or the outlining process. I could have told her in facts and devoid of emotion about any of the incidents of Beverly's interactions with me over the past school year. But this question about myself took me by surprise.

"Ah, well I was born and grew up in Doveport. I grew up in the foster care system and bounced around a lot when I was young. I've loved reading and writing since I was little. Books were always my escape." I smiled. She looked at me with an expression I couldn't place. She didn't say anything, so I kept going.

"In early high school, I got placed with two amazing Dads, and they helped me focus on school and become more confident. The two of them, along with my high school counsellor, are the reason I applied to university at all. I'm part of the Tuition Waiver Program. It runs out this year, so if I don't pass this upper-level English class, I'll have to take next year off and work. Hopefully, I'll come back the following year to finish my last class and graduate."

I hoped my story was clear enough and to the point. I was conscious of not making my explanation a sob story.

"So, the other student's insults and harassments about you being in the foster care system must have been really hurtful?"

Of all I said, I was surprised she tweezed this point out.

"Yes, they were. I tried my best to not let them get to me, but it's been impossible not to let it affect me a bit. Growing up, I got pretty used to people making fun of me for that. Kids are cruel, and they'll go after whatever perceived weakness or difference they can pick out, you know?" I asked her, not wanting to ramble on.

"Yes, I actually do know what you mean," she said shortly. "And what have you done to confront the other student about it?"

I was ready for this question, but I wasn't looking forward to it. I realized I hadn't done enough. When I was at home carefully planning my answers and my approach to it, I decided my only option was to tell her the truth and hope I had done enough.

"I tried to resolve it in person with her back in September. She didn't let it go and things got progressively worse, so I moved houses. When she didn't let it go even then, I wrote her an email. But things continued. After that, I sort of just ignored it and tried to focus on graduating, hoping it would stop. But it hasn't stopped. I should have done more, but I didn't know who to go to. I don't want her to get into any trouble; I just want to graduate." I exhaled, realizing I was nervous and talking very quickly.

"What are your plans after university if you graduate?"

This was beginning to feel more like a job interview than an appeal process. I was nervous with my answers. It felt like a disastrous job interview where I had answers to unasked questions and no answers to asked ones. I would be as authentic and straightforward as possible and hope for the best.

"Working in a library would be my dream job," I said. "Or something else to do with books."

She nodded. "Did you take her assignment?" she then asked.

"No, I didn't take it. I wrote the paper myself. It was my own take on a Brothers Grimm fairy tale. I outlined it and spent hours on it—probably twenty hours in total if I added them up. I was so proud of it, and I was devastated when I realized it had been stolen. I have all my notes from the outline and planning for it here. I also have my laptop that shows the date I last edited it." I reached my hand out, offering the folder bursting with papers to her.

She shook her head. "No need for those," she said and scribbled some notes on the back of my appeal letter.

I had no idea if her refusal of my notes was a good sign or a bad one. It was clear she had made up her mind about my case. But I was unable to tell what her decision was.

All I could do was hope.

≈

Two weeks after the meeting in the Human Rights office, I basked in morning sunshine in my yard. Spring had brought carefree, puffy clouds, delicate crocuses, and the smell of freshly cut grass. I was editing my cover letter and resume for the Doveport Public Library position. I had decided to apply for it after all; I had nothing to lose.

I wished my internal landscape was as carefree as the outer one. I sat uncomfortably with the uncertainty of my university graduation. I tried writing down my gratitude. The house air wasn't frigid, and I didn't have to layer in double sweaters. Tea retained its heat for more than two minutes. The sun showed itself, offering warmth. It had taken rain's place in the changing of the Doveport weather guards.

I tried embracing uncertainty and enjoying the sun. Watching the eagle take off with a healed bullet wound had inspired me to apply for the job regardless of the unknown outcome. I decided to apply despite not thinking I would get it. I was working through uncertainty with my counsellor. I was supposed to practise sitting with it. *"Inviting it in,"* she had said.

I pressed the send button in my email. I felt panic and relief at the same time. There was nothing to do but wait now. The outcome was safely out of my hands. I tried inviting in the uncertainty, but part of me still wanted to push it away and make up an outcome in my head—even if it was an unfavourable one—just to have some certainty. *Invite it in,* I told myself.

My phone buzzed beside me, interrupting my focus. I picked it up and answered.

"Hi, Brooke, it's Lucy from the Harbourview University Human Rights."

"Oh, hi," I said. This was it. This is where I would find out if I would graduate or not—if standing up for myself had been worth it. I took a deep breath and waited for her to announce my academic fate.

"I'm hoping you can make it to a meeting tomorrow afternoon at two o'clock. I realize it's short notice, but I saw you have no classes tomorrow and Beverly can make tomorrow afternoon. The meeting would be in my office."

My heart sank. Beverly. I couldn't face her. I had been expecting an answer, but instead, I got this horrible invitation.

"Ugh, I don't know if I want to see Beverly," I said. "She's probably very angry that I appealed the plagiarism claim. She doesn't like when people stand up to her." I was truly scared to see her.

"I can't tell you the outcome, but I need you to come in. I hope you can trust me as a mediator in any discussions between you two."

I didn't want to go. I didn't want to face Beverly. I nearly declined the invitation right there and then. But then I remembered the hours I had spent on assignments since starting university. I remembered the forms I had filled to be admitted, right at the start of this crazy journey. And I remembered the hours I took writing the appeal letter. An image of the eagle lifting off the ground with one wing slightly lower than the other came into my mind. I had come too far to turn back now.

"All right, I'll be there tomorrow at two."

Chapter 38

Brooke

March 22, 2018

I waited in the same seat I had waited in a few weeks before. Today, sun reflected off the shiny green fern leaves instead of raindrops.

Beverly was nowhere to be seen, but fear settled in my stomach. I dreaded seeing her. She would be livid. Had I known I would have to face her in person, I might not have started the appeal process. Flashes of the truck coming toward me played in my mind. I tried to remember that Lucy would be there, but even those thoughts didn't convince myself of safety.

I got through a few pages of my book until Lucy greeted me.

"Brook, we're ready for you."

I closed my book and followed her.

This time, she took me to a conference room rather than her minimalist office. I wished it were her office we were going to. The thought of the minimalist design and the window looking out to shade and ferns calmed me. But instead, she brought me into a room with a round table and Beverly sitting on the far side of it.

She sat with her elbows on the table, her hands one on top of the other. It gave the impression of her being closed off and in control. Her blonde hair was curled and hung at her side. She wore an overall dress that looked strange and designer.

As we entered the room, Lucy sat between us and motioned for me to take the seat near the door. It felt like Beverly and I were elementary school students and Lucy was the school principal.

"I've brought you both here because there were some issues between you," she started with.

I sat still and was too scared to nod. Beverly's eyes assessed me coldly. Her lips were closed. This was the first time I had seen her without control over her setting and situation.

"And because some of the things you said go against the university harassment policy. Beverly, as we had a discussion this morning, I think you have some things that you want to say to Brooke."

"I didn't take that assignment, Brooke. You're lying about that. I wrote it myself, and you took that from me. I can't believe you stole it from me and submitted it as your own."

So she wasn't backing down on it, I thought. I panicked a bit. Maybe they did believe her, but her words had said otherwise.

Then she continued, "But despite you stealing my work, they're making me apologize for the other stuff. So, I'll say sorry for the online things that they have proof of. I can't believe you ratted me out after all that I did for you in the first few years of university. I see that you aren't grateful for any of it."

Of course, she had made her apology manipulative and oozing with guilt-inducing words. It worked. Guilt flooded over me. I remembered her bringing me into the group, writing me notes she'd leave on my laptop, and inviting me to more social events than I had ever been invited to. I suddenly felt horrible for telling on her.

But then my rational brain kicked in. I was being manipulated. She wanted me to feel bad so I backed down and admitted to stealing her assignment—something that I hadn't done. I suddenly felt angry and I realized that I wielded as much control as she did in this moment. I too had a chance to talk.

The truck incident had scared me the most. But since there was no concrete proof of that, it wouldn't be included in her apology.

I took a breath and did something I had never done—stood up to someone who pushed me around. "Beverly, I wrote that assignment. I submitted that assignment. It's mine. I have all the notes, the outline, and timestamps on my computer document to prove it. Yes, we used to be friends and I'm sad with how it turned out. But I'm not going to lie about something that I submitted, and the other things you did were hurtful and uncalled for."

I almost didn't believe the words were mine.

"Those are good lies, Brooke. I was nothing but a good friend to you. I did so much for you. It's no wonder the friend group wants nothing to do with you after all of this."

This had gotten nasty quickly. Lucy intervened.

"We're not here today to discuss the plagiarism issue. The purpose of this meeting was for Beverly to apologize to Brooke for the social media harassment, which you have, Beverly. I thank you for that. You're free to go now."

Beverly cheeks were red, her lips were closed firmly, and her eyebrows angled downward. Her foundation had rubbed off in one spot, giving her skin a blotched appearance. She shook her head at me. Then she stood up, picked up a large pair of turtle shell sunglasses off the table, and swung a big brown leather purse over her shoulder. She shot me a death glare as Lucy looked down and scribbled something in her notebook. Beverly then strode out of the conference room.

She will not admit defeat, I thought. I worried what would be said next, and I hoped that I wasn't released to go straight after her. I wished for some physical distance between us to ensure we didn't meet in a corridor, or even outside the building. I still wasn't completely sure what was going on. I hoped it would soon be clear because my stomach was beginning to ache. *Invite in the uncertainty,* I told myself. But all I wanted was answers.

Lucy walked to the door, closed it, and then addressed me.

"Brooke, what happened to you was wrong, and it goes against everything Harbourview University stands for. We've taken a close look at the evidence and believe that it was Beverly who took your assignment and submitted it as her own."

I breathed out and couldn't believe what I heard.

They believed me—despite Beverly not backing down, despite the dean and his relationship with Beverly's dad, and despite Beverly's parents' obvious involvement.

"We couldn't prove all the allegations you put against her, but with the social media ones that you took screen shots of, we were able to put a case together for you. If you submit and pass the other assignments for ENGL 425, you will be granted credit for that class. That means you'll be eligible for graduation this spring. Congratulations on your work over the past four years."

"Thank you," was all I could manage. I couldn't believe my actions had made a difference, that fighting and advocating for myself had resulted in me passing the class. I felt bigger. I straightened my back with the news.

"And on a more personal note, I also went through the foster care system. For someone to harass you on that basis is completely unacceptable. You've done an outstanding job given your setbacks. I can see you've worked hard over the years. There are many people with much more family support who haven't done what you have, and in my personal experience, there are few people who understand the challenges of being a child in care. I did my best to bring you justice, but if you want to take legal action, that's at your discretion. I was glad to read in your email that you're continuing to see a counsellor. Mostly though, congratulations on your upcoming university graduation."

"That means a lot to me, "I said, feeling a warmth and immediate comradery of sorts with this person I barely knew. It was utterly unusual to see someone in a skirt suit and big leather chair with a fancy position admit something personal about themselves and show vulnerability. It made me well up with joy. I wanted to hug her but spoke instead.

"I agree. Not many people have first had experience with the foster care system. I'm thrilled to be graduating, and thank you for your help with this. I'm grateful for this outcome."

We shook hands, and I left the conference room through the same door Beverly had exited minutes before.

≈

Later that day, I was in the backyard of the yellow house when I got a phone call. I would always remember exactly where I was when I got that call. I was sitting underneath the wisteria tree, which now had bunches of purple blooms.

"Hello, Brooke speaking."

"Hi, Brooke, it's Sheryl from the Doveport Public Library."

My heart started racing as I remembered my interview the week before. I thought it had gone well, but it was hard to be sure. I was about to find out how well it truly had gone.

Strange as it was, the biggest result of the séance was how some of Tanner's words had spoken to me and moved me from my habits of avoidance and patterns of fear. That, and my weekly counselling sessions were helping me untangle and break apart the past year and the bullying. I hadn't realized how bad it was until I began untangling and until I had someone to support me.

"Yes, hi. Thank you for the interview last week."

"That's actually what I'm calling about."

The suspense built in me. I stared at the back door of the yellow house as I waited with trepidation for her next words.

"There was a lot of interested in the position, and many candidates had a wealth of experience and passion for books that would bring a lot to our team."

My heart sank. I should have known there would be people smarter and with more experience than me, people more outgoing and likeable than me.

"But your answers were unique and thorough, and we liked your personality the best. We would like to offer you the position if you are still interested."

My eyes played over the yellow siding and white trim on the house as the world slowed down. My dream job—I was being offered a job at a library. My first thought was to turn it down and say that I had to stay where I was. What would Edgard do? But it would be silly to turn down my dream job. Besides, maybe I was deserving of it after all. My counsellor was helping me challenge these thoughts of unworthiness and start accepting things offered to me, instead of pushing them away because I felt unworthy.

After what seemed like an eternity, I managed to speak.

"I would be delighted to take the job. Thank you for the opportunity and I'm completely thrilled."

It seemed too perfect to be real. Twice in one day, taking a risk and pushing through fear had proved favourable for me. I smiled and lay back onto the soft, sun-warmed blanket.

Chapter 39

Brooke

April 13, 2018

The person in front of me had just begun walking across the stage. In a few moments, it would be my turn. The sound of clapping reverberated through the theatre. It was an ongoing noise with just a short pause when the graduate's name came over the microphone. My heart pounded, and I was nervous for my turn. Don't get me wrong, I was thrilled to graduate, but being the focus of attention in a room of hundreds of people was a lot for me. I tried taking deep breaths and telling myself it would be over in a few minutes. *You can do it,* I told myself. *You've gotten through the rest of the year. You can do this.*

I felt better when I framed things this way in my mind. The worst of this year was behind me. If I had got through these past months, I could walk this stage. I was still in disbelief it had worked out. I was going to graduate.

"Brooke Daniels," the voice from the speaker said. I stood up and walked up onto the stage toward the person with the diplomas. I tried not to think about all the people watching me.

Applause rang out through the crowd. I tried not to look at them, like when you're walking over some high height and you know you'll be steadier if you don't look down—it was best not to look. But when I was halfway across, I couldn't resist. I glanced briefly below the stage and the flash of a camera caught my eye. The person behind the camera was Derek. He beamed with dad-like pride. David stood beside him, holding his phone up to take a photo. Seeing them gave me a boost of energy to keep walking.

Also in the aisle taking a photo with their phone was someone I hadn't seen in several years: Ms. Ellis, my high school counsellor. I almost didn't recognize her under bigger and very rosy cheeks and a large pregnant belly. Her floral dress flowed around her gave her identity away. Our eyes met and a grin came over my face. She put the phone down and winked at me.

I arrived at the man with the diplomas. The next few minutes were a blur of taking my diploma, shaking his hand, turning and smiling for the camera, and walking on past him. I walked off the stage. It was over. I was herded back to my seat to await the rest of the alphabet to be called. I pulled my gown under me and sat back into my seat, then wiped my brow with my hat and smiled at the tassel that was now on the left after being on the right when I was last at my seat. I had done it. I had graduated from university.

≈

Later that night, I sat at the yellow house's window seat. In a few minutes, I had to leave to meet Jade. We were meeting at Hawthorne's to celebrate our university graduation over pints of beer and games of pool. I looked around the house. First house on my own. I ran my hands over the lace curtains and looked fondly at a stack of books on my coffee table.

In my mind, I ran through the places I had lived in university. I thought back to the first day of my first year, when Derek and David dropped me off at residence and helped me carry boxes up the stairs and drop them in my new room, and of the trepidation of knowing I would be sleeping in that room every night for the next months with someone I had not yet met. Then I thought of the next two years, when I had lived in the three-bedroom family home that Beverly's parents had bought her and that she rented to her friends.

I remembered the first time I saw the yellow house. I was charmed by its canary yellow siding and intricate gable latticework. I thought of my fear with the strange sounds and happenings, the first time I heard something, and then how things with Beverly increasingly fell apart over the past months. I recalled when I had only left the house for work. I felt exhausted just thinking about the past few months. I was glad they were over.

I felt a fondness toward this house. Something about it was alluring—in a strange and frightening way. It was hard to put my finger on. It went beyond the character of its physical walls. My eyes went over its fireplace that held a few neat stacks of books. I scanned the scuffed wooden floors and the half circle window by the kitchen table where I had spent hours forming and organizing thousands of words.

The house was silent.

Since the séance, it had been quiet. No more light flickering, no more smells of sandalwood, and no more strange sounds. No more eerie feelings of not being alone. The lack of sounds, smells, and strange events was strangely off-putting. I had become so used to things happening that I had almost become accustomed to them. Maybe Tanner was right and the spirit had moved on to its next realm, its next life, or wherever it was that spirits went. Was it crazy that I almost missed the spirit in the house or, at the very least, worried for it?

I hoped whatever spirit we released was truly free and at peace now, free to move forward.

I looked at my phone. Time to leave. I put on shoes, closed the door, and locked it.

On the walk, my mind searched for something to fret over or analyze and then worry about. When it found nothing, I tried to look around and enjoy the evening light. I felt a strange freedom—a freedom of having nothing urgent in that moment that required my attention, but also a freeing feeling of reaching a goal that involved many setbacks. At times, I thought I wouldn't graduate. I had given up for a while. But like a warrior, I came out the other side.

The full moon reflected off the black body of water of the ocean. It cast soft light on the trees. I thought I saw movement in my periphery, but when I turned my head, there was nothing. I concentrated on putting one foot in front of the other. *I should start walking again,* I thought. I used to walk all the time; it had been a coping strategy for a long time, but I had gotten out of it with the events of the past year. Walking had been a great antidote to worry. It was ideal for staying in the present moment. I made a mental note to work walking back into my days.

I was nearly off Winfield Crescent when something in a house's window made me stop.

A family was seated around a table eating dinner. The man had dark hair and was laughing with his head back. Three children sat around the table—two older boys and a younger girl. But when I saw the woman, a shiver rain down my spine. She stood at the other head of the table opposite to the man with the dark hair. This woman, with her curly hair and strong chin, was the same woman in the old timey dress I saw in the kitchen. I was sure it was the same woman. But that was impossible. I observed them for a few moments as she served something out of a bowl. Then watched her laugh with her head held back. She then turned her head and gazed out the window. Our eyes locked; she smiled. Another shiver ran down my spine. I smiled back and kept walking. So many things were mysterious in this world; I tried to think of it as exciting and not scary.

I mused about uncertainty the rest of the walk. I thought about the hardships that had built up. The way I didn't know the outcome of what would happen when I decided to act and take matters with Beverly and happenings in the house into my own hands. I thought about the unknown, how I hated it so much. But I was starting to slowly accept a fact of life: there would always be the unknown, things that couldn't be neatly explained or rationalized. I was working on not fearing them and confronting things instead. I tried to stop using avoidance as a coping strategy. I had come a long way, but still had work to do. I supposed there would always be work to do.

I could see the faded sign saying "Hawthorne's" as I opened the door and stepped into the familiar sounds of pool balls knocking against each other.

≈

The soft light from a hanging light illuminated Jade's smiling face.

"We're finally graduates," she said.

"Indeed. What a year."

"We did it. That was a crazy four years."

We began a game of pool, and I mused over the last four years. When I started university, I thought life would get simpler after finishing, but now, I thought it would always be somewhat complicated and the best we could do was enjoy each moment and try to spend our time doing the things we loved. Jade and I reminisced about the past four years until the conversation landed in the present.

"So, are you going to move houses?" Jade asked.

"I don't think so. There have been no strange happenings since the séance."

"So the séance worked?" Jade said, sinking a solid red ball into the corner pocket.

"It must have worked. We must have set it free, whatever was in the house. Hopefully, it's at peace wherever it went."

"Hopefully."

"When do you start at the library?"

"In three weeks. I'll miss Passages, but it's time to use my degree. When do you start at fisheries?"

"Early September. I'll stay at the recreation centre for just the summer. I'll miss some parts of it, but time to move forward, too."

I sank the black ball, ending the game.

"Nice game," she said.

"To new beginnings," Jade said, smiling.

"Yes, new things and less fear." We held our glasses up and tipped them close until the clinking of glass on glass rang through the pub. We each took a sip and locked eyes.

The moment our eyes met, the light that hung above us popped, flickered, and went out.

Acknowledgements

Writing *Immortal Grit* has been a grand adventure. I'm grateful to all those who supported me on the journey. Thank you to my mom, Cathy Kuntz, who was my first draft beta reader and who offered immense support, writerly advice, and positive encouragement the entire way. Thank you to my dad, Michael Kuntz, for all the support with this project and for teaching me the meaning of grit. Thank you to my sisters, Carmen Kuntz and Alison Martin, for the encouragement and rich relationship of sisterhood, to my extended family, and to my grandfather Clair Kuntz for the support and inspiration. Thank you to the Healey family, who I'm grateful to be part of.

Thank you to editor Katie Heffring, whose insight, careful attention to detail, and talented editing made this book infinitely better.

For help with the printing process, thank you to Craig Shemilt and everyone at Island Blue Book Printing. To my female friends, thank you for the friendship, encouragement, and adventures.

I'm ever grateful to BC booksellers for their commitment to promoting and selling books. Special thanks to Best Choice Quality Used Books & Coffee to Go, Hilary Eastmure at Well Read Books, and Andree Bizier at Windowseat Books. To the readers of my first two books, many thank-yous and I hope you enjoy this one.

Lastly, thank you to Steven Healey for all the cups of tea, and for the unwavering commitment, support, and encouragement with this project and with everything.

About the Author

Haley Healey is the author of *On Their Own Terms: True Stories of Trailblazing Women of Vancouver Island* and *Flourishing and Free: More Stories of Trailblazing Women of Vancouver Island*. She is a high school counsellor in Nanaimo and enjoys exploring Vancouver Island's trails, waters, and wilderness. Find out more at www.haleyhealey.com.

Recommend *Immortal Grit* for your next book club!

Reading Group guide available at

www.haleyhealey.com